I remember something Lola said to me once: "There are all kinds of drag. Sometimes it looks like wigs and makeup; sometimes it's just a face someone shows you when they're afraid to show you their real one."

I didn't know what he meant at the time. Now I get it. You can't know who someone is just by looking at her. And maybe you can never really know. Maybe people always have secrets that they don't tell a single other person. Which of course makes me think about Tom Swift. He has a pretty big secret. And I know what it is. But maybe he has other, even bigger ones that he hasn't shared, and never will.

When I think about what I want *my* life to look like, I think about having someone who does know everything about me. Someone I'm not afraid to tell everything to. Someone who knows what I look like underneath all the drag I put on for the rest of the world. And I wonder if that even exists.

ALSO BY
MICHAEL THOMAS FORD

Suicide Notes

LOVE

& OTHER

CURSES

MICHAEL THOMAS FORD

An Imprint of HarperCollinsPublishers

Library of Congress Cataloging-in-Publication Data

Names: Ford, Michael Thomas, author.

Title: Love & other curses / Michael Thomas Ford.

Other titles: Love and other curses

Description: First edition. | New York, NY : HarperTeen, an imprint of
  HarperCollinsPublishers, [2018] | Summary: Sam, sixteen, spends his
  summer in small-town New York falling in love with a trans boy, spending
  time with his drag queen friends, and dealing with family issues.

Identifiers: LCCN 2018025431 | ISBN 978-0-06-279121-4

Subjects: | CYAC: Female impersonators--Fiction. | Gays--Fiction. |
  Transgender people--Fiction. | Love--Fiction. | Family problems--Fiction.

Classification: LCC PZ7.F7532119 Lo 2019 | DDC [Fic]--dc23 LC record
  available at https://lccn.loc.gov/2018025431

Typography by Jenna Stempel-Lobell

20 21 22 23 24   PC/LSCH   10 9 8 7 6 5 4 3 2 1

❖

First paperback edition, 2020

For Tara
who said yes

One

When Lola asks me to help him with his tits, I know it's going to be one of those nights.

"Come on, Sammy," he says, fluttering his long, fake lashes and puckering his red-lipsticked mouth. "I need the girls to look fabulous. I'm doing the Dolly Parton number."

The Dolly Parton number is "9 to 5," a song popular more than twenty years before I was even born. Don't get me wrong. It's a fun song, and I like it. But Lola is, well, not exactly the age Dolly Parton was when she took it to number one on the charts.

"I know what you're thinking," he says, jabbing the air with a finger tipped by a long acrylic nail painted bright pink. "But Dolly and I are the exact same age, and if she can still do the song in her shows, so can I."

I don't argue with him. There's no point. He owns the bar, so he can do whatever he wants to. Besides, getting onstage is the only thing that makes him happy. Well, that and the mai tais he drinks one after the other starting at around three in the afternoon. He's sipping one now as he plops into the chair in

1

front of the dressing room mirror and waits for me to put the fake breasts on him.

Most of the other queens create the illusion of cleavage using makeup, but Lola insists on these giant silicone boobs that he's had forever. He tells everyone that his fairy godmother gave them to him for his sixteenth birthday, and they look it. They're pretty beat-up, but he covers them with powder and pancake makeup and says he can get another couple of years out of them.

"How's Starletta?" he asks me as I fasten the strap around his neck.

"She's fine," I tell him. I know where this is going, and I'd like to avoid it. But Lola is determined.

"You know I took her out a couple of times back when we were kids," he says. "Nothing big. A church picnic. Maybe to the county fair. But if things had worked out differently, I could have been your grandfather."

"Great-grandfather," I correct him. "Hank is my grandmother. Starletta is my great-grandmother."

Lola laughs. "That's right," he says. "Sometimes I forget. Starletta had Hank young. What was she, sixteen?"

"Almost seventeen," I say. "Do you want the diamonds or the sapphires tonight?" I hold up both necklaces, hoping this will distract him from the conversation.

"Diamonds," he says. "I'm wearing the white jumpsuit, and the sapphires would be too much. Say, you're going to be seventeen yourself soon, right?"

"In August," I answer.

Lola shakes his head. "I don't know why I let you hang around here," he says. "Cops find out and I'd lose my license."

"That's why I stay back here," I remind him. "Besides, you know nobody cares about this place."

This is true. You'd think that in this part of the world, aka small-town central New York, aka the geographic center of nowhere, we wouldn't even have something like a gay bar. After all, the entire population of the town could take one of those Carnival cruises at the same time and still not fill up the ship. But since the nearest big-city bar is over an hour away, the Shangri-La attracts guys from all the other small towns around. It's not particularly busy on weeknights, but on the weekends it gets crowded.

You'd think people around here would be freaked out by a gay bar. And maybe they were at first. But now nobody thinks twice about it. Or if they do, they don't tell anybody that they think about it. That's one of the rules. Another rule is that if you see somebody at the Shangri-La one night and then the next day you run into him shopping at the Price Chopper with his wife and kids, you especially don't say anything. And that happens more than you might think.

Even so, I don't tell anybody that I come here. Especially not my family. Not that they'd care about the gay thing. We've already been through that, two years ago, and now it's just the way things are. But there are other things I'm not ready for them to know about just yet.

"Seventeen," Lola says, looking at me in the mirror. "That's a big year."

It is. Especially in my family. Because of the curse. But that's something else I don't want to talk about. Not that Lola would. Despite what he said about my great-grandmother, I don't think he knows about it. But my family talks about it all the time. Especially now that my birthday is getting closer.

"We should have a party for you," Lola says. "Get Paloma to make you one of her *tres leches* cakes. That would be fun."

It would be fun. If there's one thing drag queens know how to do well, it's throw a party. And the queens at the Shangri-La are my best friends. My second family. Not that there's anything wrong with my actual family. I love them too. But sometimes being a Weyward is a challenge, and when I'm at the Shangri-La I can be someone else. Even if I haven't quite decided who that someone is yet. But I'm working on it.

The door to the dressing room opens and Farrah bursts in, all drama and attitude. He tosses a handful of damp dollar bills on the table and pulls his wig off.

"Cheap mothercrackers," he says.

Lola looks at me in the mirror and we both try not to laugh. Farrah's temper is legendary, and we don't want to make him any madder than he already is.

"Did you do the Beyoncé number?" Lola asks. "Or the Tina Turner?"

"Beyoncé," Farrah mutters. "'Crazy in Love.' I danced so hard my feet just about fell off."

"Just like Moira Shearer in *The Red Shoes*," Lola says, sighing happily. "So tragic."

"That another one of your movies?" Farrah asks. "You know I don't watch that old shit."

Lola gasps. "Watch your language!" he scolds. "*The Red Shoes* is one of the most heartbreaking stories ever told."

"They're *all* heartbreaking," says Farrah, looking at me and rolling his eyes.

"Yes, well, the best stories are," Lola says. "Because *life* is heartbreaking."

"We can agree on *that*," Farrah says. "So why would I want to watch movies that are sad too? That's just stupid."

Lola asks me to get him his Dolly Parton wig.

"Do you know why I named this place Shangri-La?" he asks as he pulls a wig cap over his head.

"Yes," Farrah and I say in unison, hoping this will stop him. It doesn't.

"When I was eleven years old, I saw *Lost Horizon* on the television at my grandmother's house," Lola begins. Because he loves this story, and because he's had so many mai tais, there's no distracting him.

I tune him out, concentrating on teasing the Dolly Parton wig to life. I've heard the story so many times, I can recite it by heart. Besides, Lola made me watch the movie. It's actually pretty good. It's about these people whose plane crashes in the Himalayan mountains. They're rescued by a group of men who take them to a valley called Shangri-La, where it's always summer and everyone is really beautiful and happy. Only something seems kind of weird about the whole thing, and when some of the people try to leave and go back to their old lives, they find out what it is: As long as you stay in Shangri-La, you stay young and healthy. But once you leave, the spell wears off and you die.

"So I decided that when I grew up I would build my own Shangri-La," Lola says as I put the wig on his head and pull it down. "Where people could be happy and beautiful."

"As long as they never leave," I say.

"You're too young to be so bitter," Lola tells me, teasing the wig.

"I'm not bitter," I say. "That's just how it worked. Everyone was happy as long as they stayed in Shangri-La. But when they left, they weren't."

"Poor Maria," Lola says. "That scene where they turn her body over and see that she's become a dried-up old thing is so sad."

"Speaking of dried-up old things, you'd better hurry," Farrah remarks. "They just started playing Paloma's Madonna number, which means you've got about five minutes until you're on."

"Jumpsuit," Lola barks, and I run off to the wardrobe closet.

The next few minutes are crazy as we stuff Lola into his costume, make sure his wig is straight, and do touch-ups to his makeup. I'm just strapping the rhinestone-covered sandals to his feet when Paloma sticks his head in and says, "Time to work, gurl."

Lola leaves, following Paloma down the hallway to the main room and the tiny stage. I can hear people hooting and calling out Lola's name. The energy from the bar pulses down the hallway, and I wish I could go out there. Then Farrah shuts the door and all I hear is the muted thump of the song as Lola starts to do his number.

"You're right about Shangri-La," Farrah says as I sit down in the chair in front of the mirror and pick up a makeup brush.

"What do you mean?"

"You're only happy as long as you never leave," he says. "And you know what that makes it—a trap. Just like this place."

I turn and look at him. "You don't like it here?"

He waves a hand at me. "I like it just fine," he says. "I'm just saying, the only way to keep the illusion alive is to never let it wear off. And that's a lot of work."

I look at the color I've added to my cheeks. My skin is already pretty pale, and the pink blush makes me look almost doll-like. I switch to eye shadow and apply some blue to the crease of my eyelid, the way Paloma has been teaching me to.

"You look like one of those anime girls," Farrah teases. He comes over to the mirror, takes the brush from me, and puts some more shadow on my eye. "Now blend it with your fingertip," he says, doing part of it for me and then watching as I repeat what he did on the other eye. "That's good. You decide on a name yet?"

I shake my head. My drag name is an ongoing topic of conversation at the Shangri-La. Everybody has an opinion. But I don't know who I am yet. Besides, it will be another year before I can even legally perform here. By then I might be an entirely different person.

Farrah finds a wig and brings it over to me. It's red, the color of a campfire after the flames have burned down and only glowing embers remain. When Farrah puts it on me, the long curls fall around my shoulders. I stare at the glass and wonder who this girl is looking back at me.

Then I notice the time. It's 11:35. "Shit," I say, snatching up a washcloth and some cold cream. "I'm going to be late."

I told my dad I would be home by midnight. Even though it's summer, and I don't have to be at school in the morning, he doesn't want me running around all night. Besides, I'm supposed to help out at the Eezy-Freezy tomorrow.

I get the makeup off in record time, give Farrah a kiss on the cheek, and start to leave. Then I remember the wig. I pull it off and toss it to Farrah, who catches it in one hand like it's a fly ball.

"I'll see you on Saturday night," I say, and go out the back door to the parking lot.

Thankfully, my old truck starts up with no problem. It's a 1965 Ford F100 stepside pickup, cherry red, that belonged to my great-grandfather, whose name was also Sam. He bought it when he was eighteen. It cost $1,900 new, which he earned washing bottles at the Adirondack Ale brewery for $1.25 an hour. I figured out he had to work 1,520 hours for this truck. Plus, he was married to Starletta and they had my grandma, Hank, to take care of, so really he worked a lot more hours than that.

He didn't get to enjoy the truck for long. He died when he was nineteen. Blew up on the Fourth of July when a sparkler he was holding burned his fingers. He dropped it, and it landed in a case of Roman candles he was supposed to be taking over to the firehouse for the annual fireworks display. Starletta was sad, of course, but she'd kind of expected it because of the curse and all.

I'm told I look like my great-grandfather. There's only one picture of him, taken the day he bought the Ford. He's sitting in the cab, leaning out the window and grinning like a fool. Like me, he's skinny and has light brown hair. And even though he's smiling, his eyes look sad. I think it's because part of him knew he wouldn't be that happy ever again, but Starletta says his eyes were always like that. She says I have those same eyes, although I'm not really sad. I just think about things a lot.

The truck is still in great shape, because someone in every generation learns how to keep it running. It's kind of a tradition. As soon as I was old enough, my dad started teaching me how to change the oil. Then he showed me how the engine worked, and how to replace the spark plugs and belts, before we moved on to the harder stuff like the brakes and the engine. I'm pretty sure I'm the only guy in my school who can replace a faulty kickdown switch and also create the perfect smoky eye.

I drive with the windows open, and the warm air blows through the cab of the truck. It smells like grass and tar from the recently repaved road. Reaching into the glove box, I take out a packet of cigarettes. Camels. The same brand Great-Grandfather Sam smoked. I remove one and light it with the dashboard lighter. I take a drag and let the smoke fill my lungs, then blow it out.

I don't really smoke. Only once in a while when I'm driving late at night like this. Then I imagine that the swirling smoke exhaled from my mouth forms a ghostly shape and that the other Sam—the one I never met but whose name and eyes I have—is sitting in the cab with me, his arm on the edge of the door as we travel down the road.

I finish the cigarette right before I get home. Sam's ghost swirls away in the wind, and when I pull the truck up in front of the house, I'm alone again. I walk to the back door, which leads directly into the kitchen. Inside, my grandmother, great-grandmother, and great-great-grandmother are seated around the table. Each one has a tall glass of strawberry Nehi in front of her, and they're playing cards.

"It's too hot to live," says Hank.

"There's peach pie on the counter," Starletta informs me.

"Gin!" crows Clodine, throwing down her cards. Millard Fillmore, her ancient brown Chihuahua, is sitting in her lap. He opens one eye, sees that no one is offering him anything to eat, and goes back to sleep.

"Where's Dad?" I ask, considering the pie.

"In the trailer," Hank answers. "You lucked out."

"I'm not that late," I say, taking a plate from the cupboard and spooning a piece of pie on it. "It's just past midnight."

I'd ask them what they're doing up, but I already know the answer. They almost never sleep, not for more than a couple of hours a night anyway. They'll probably be in this same spot when I get up in the morning, only they'll have swapped the sodas for cups of coffee, and the pie for donuts covered in powdered sugar.

I pick up the pie, kiss each of them on the cheek, and go

upstairs. My room is on the third floor, which is actually the attic, and which I have to myself. My father mostly lives in an old Airstream trailer parked behind the house. He comes inside to eat, but he says sleeping in a house with too many people makes him dream their dreams, so he prefers to be in the trailer.

I go inside, shut the door, and set the pie on top of the stack of books on my bedside table. I get undressed and sit on the edge of the bed, eating the pie. It's super sweet, and I wonder if I'll regret having so much sugar before I try to sleep, but it's so good that I actually think about going downstairs for another piece.

Instead, I lie on my bed. On the floor beside it is a telephone, the old-fashioned kind with an actual dial. I pick it up and place it on my stomach, then turn off the light so that the room is dark except for the little bit of moonlight that comes in through the window.

I run my fingers over the dial until one of the holes feels right, then I turn it. I do this nine more times, press the receiver to my ear, and wait. When the ringing starts, I hold my breath. After four rings, a man's voice says, "Hello?"

"Tell me a story," I say.

"Who is this?"

"Tell me a story."

There's a pause, then the man says, "Asshole," and the line goes dead.

I put the receiver back in the cradle and set the phone on the floor. I'm disappointed, but not surprised. Most people don't respond. I guess they don't have stories to tell.

Two

"How many toads in Millard Fillmore's water dish today?" Starletta asks.

I open the kitchen door and glance at the bowl sitting in the grass beside the steps.

"Five," I report.

Starletta looks at Clodine, who is pulling the chocolate sprinkles off of a cruller. "What's five mean, Ma?" she asks.

Clodine shrugs. "Hank is better at prognostication," she says, pinching the sprinkles between her thumb and forefinger and dropping them into her coffee mug. "I always forget what the numbers signify."

"Five is good," Hank says. "Six would mean a lot of money coming in, but five means something interesting will happen. Four would mean rain."

"Something interesting," Clodine repeats. "That's right. I remember now. And what would seven mean?"

"That we have a toad problem," says Hank.

"Sometimes I think you all just make this stuff up," I say as I open the refrigerator door and take out the milk.

"And why would we do that?" asks my grandmother.

"I don't know," I admit. "But honestly, do you think the number of toads sitting in the dog bowl really means anything?"

"We'll see," Clodine says. "Something interesting happens today, then it does."

"And what does *interesting* mean, anyway?" I ask. "To some people, that could be finding a penny on the sidewalk."

"What's gotten into you?" Starletta says, fixing me with a stare. She makes me nervous, and I spill Froot Loops on the counter.

"Nothing," I mutter, sweeping the cereal into a bowl and sloshing milk over it.

Reluctantly, I sit down at the kitchen table. I can feel the three of them watching me, so I concentrate on the calendar that hangs on the wall beside the door. At the top of the page is printed COMPLIMENTS OF TOONEY'S FEED & FARM. WE APPRECIATE YOUR BUSINESS! Below that is a painting of a tractor moving through a field of corn. The farmer driving it is waving and smiling, as if harvesting corn is the most exciting thing anyone could ever do. The month is August. The date of the seventeenth is circled in red, and in the box is written: ILONA'S BABY.

Ilona is my mother. The baby is me. The calendar hung on the wall the summer she was pregnant with me. And the reason the calendar is still on the wall is because of the curse. I was born on a Monday, and seventeen years later the seventeenth of August also falls on a Monday. So the calendar not only marks my birthday, it marks the day I have to make it to without the curse coming true. We've done this for every baby born into the family since we became unlucky, starting with my great-great-grandmother Clodine back in 1930. The idea is that the calendar acts as a kind of good luck charm. Or maybe a warning. When you see it every single day of your life, it's hard not to pay attention.

So far, though, it hasn't worked.

Nine more weeks. If I can make it nine more weeks, I'll be the first to escape. It sounds easy enough. But we've come close in the past. Hank made it to three days. Clodine and Starletta were so sure she was going to do it that they planned a big celebration for her birthday, which is on January 3. But then she went to Ruby Ginnison's New Year's Eve party and got caught unawares. Starletta says it's because they got too cocky, so now we don't celebrate birthdays at all. Not until number eighteen.

I can practically feel the three of them doing the math in their heads, so I finish my cereal and get up. "I'm going to be late," I say. I rinse my bowl in the sink, then head out before anyone can say anything else.

The Eezy-Freezy is a ten-minute drive from the house, but I drive extra slowly so it takes almost twice that long. My father has probably been there for a couple of hours already. Even though we don't open until eleven, there's a lot to do to get ready. Also, he just likes being there.

This is my sixth summer working with him. He opens on Memorial Day and closes the day after Labor Day. In the fall and winter, there aren't enough people wanting hot dogs and soft-serve ice cream cones to make it worth staying open. Those months, he works at the garage in town as a mechanic. He's not as happy then.

If we just counted on the people who live around here for business, we wouldn't be open at all. But in the summer we get tons of people who have camps on the lake. The Eezy-Freezy is right on the road to the cabins, so every car passes by it coming and going. It's kind of a tradition for a lot of people to stop there, especially if they have kids. My father painted a sign that says SCREAM UNTIL DADDY STOPS THE CAR and put it on the side of the road, and sometimes when I'm working the order window I can see and hear them do exactly that. It's pretty funny, actually, even though I've seen it a million times.

When I pull into the crushed-gravel parking lot, my father's black 1970 Chevy Chevelle SS 454 is the only other car there. I can tell he's already been here awhile because all the trash is picked up and the eating area looks great. We repainted the seven wooden picnic tables just a few weeks ago. We choose a different color every year. Starletta says the color affects how well we do. My father wanted to prove her wrong, so last year he painted them yellow, even though she said that was a bad choice. Business was slow, so this year they're red, which according to Starletta is lucky. We'll see.

The Closed sign is hanging in the order window, but the window itself is open. Through it I can hear the radio playing and my dad singing along. "Here I am!" he shouts. "Rock you like a hurricane!"

The Scorpions. One of his favorites. My father likes hair

metal bands from the '80s. I do too, probably because he's been singing those songs around me since I was a baby. I don't even mind that he can't really sing.

"Rock on!" I shout through the window. My father turns around and flashes me the sign of the horns, sticking his tongue out and thrashing his head. This was more effective when he had long hair, but he cut it when he turned thirty a few years ago and decided he had to start acting more like a responsible adult, and it's not quite the same now.

"Sammy!" he says when I enter the kitchen through the screen door on the side of the building. "Nice of you to show up."

"Well, it was this or watch game shows with the Grands," I joke, using our name for Hank, Starletta, and Clodine. "What's going on here?"

"I got the frozen yogurt machine working again," he says. "But we're just about out of pistachio ice cream and won't get a delivery until Tuesday, so push the other flavors. Especially the candy cane. I overestimated how popular that would be, and we have a bunch of it."

"Got it," I say as I put on an apron and get ready for a day of scooping, frying, and sundae making.

The first customers show up about an hour later, just as I'm turning the sign to Open. It's a family of five. I've never seen them before, but they look like most of the people who come here early in the season—happy, relaxed, like they have all the time in the world. They haven't gotten bored with swimming, aren't covered in mosquito bites or poison ivy, and haven't yet had their first fight after spending four straight rainy days together in a small cabin with no Wi-Fi. That will happen soon enough, but for now they're in love with summer.

I get busy making their fries while my dad makes their hamburgers. He likes to stay at the stove most of the time, singing along to the radio and cooking burgers and hot dogs to order. His favorite thing to make is chili burgers, and he's thrilled that this family has ordered two for their little boys. As he grills the hamburger patties and stirs the big pot of chili, he sings along to Twisted Sister. "We're not gonna take it!" he informs the spatula.

The family of five is just the beginning. We're busy all day, and I barely have time to wolf down a plate of cheese fries for lunch because so many people are stopping by. From time to time I steal a glance at the tip jar that sits on the counter just outside the order window, and I see that it's filling up. Most people just put whatever change I hand them into it, so usually it ends up filled with sticky dimes and nickels, but a couple of people have stuffed dollar bills in there.

My dad lets me keep all the money from the tip jar, even though he does just as much work as I do. The only rule is that I have to save at least half of it. That's fine with me, as the only thing I really spend money on is my truck. Oh, and wigs and makeup, although no one knows about those because I keep it all at the Shangri-La. And it's not like I have a lot of that stuff anyway. Mostly I borrow from the other queens for now, until I figure out what my style is.

I'm thinking about this whole style thing during a break in customers later in the afternoon when I hear someone say, "What exactly is a Roadkill Skunkcicle?"

I look up and see a guy leaning on the counter, his head poking through the window. He seems to be about my age, with blond hair that falls over one eye. The eye that I can see is blue. He's wearing a black T-shirt with Finn and Jake from *Adventure Time* on it.

I groan, as I do every time someone asks this question. "It's a chocolate-and-vanilla-twist soft serve dipped in cherry coating," I tell him. "My dad came up with the name. It's supposed to remind you of a squashed skunk."

He laughs. "That's great," he says. "I'll take one of those."

As I make the cone, he keeps talking to me. "So, what's there to do around here?"

"That depends on what you like," I tell him. "Are you staying at the lake?"

He nods. "With my grandparents," he says in a way that makes it sound as if this is a tragedy of epic proportions.

"Well, then there's always swimming and kayaking," I say. "Hiking. There's mini golf over in Midgeville, and on Wednesday nights they show old movies on the side of the VFW hall here in town."

"Right on the building?"

"Yep." I hand him his cone. "It's painted white, so it works just like a big screen. People bring lawn chairs and blankets and sit on the grass. I think this week they're showing *Jaws*."

"Sounds fun," he says. "You going?"

"Probably not," I answer. "By the time we close up here, I'm pretty tired."

"You don't get days off?"

"Sometimes."

"And what do *you* do for fun?" he asks, handing me a dollar and change. "When you're not here, I mean. Because this totally looks like fun."

"If it's really hot, I like to go tubing," I tell him, not sure if he's teasing me or not.

"Explain," he says, licking the edge of his cone.

"On the creek. You take a big inner tube and float on it. It's best if you start up by the falls, because when they open the dam the water moves faster and there are some small rapids. Nothing dangerous. Then you just float the rest of the way. You can get out at the bridge just outside of town. Takes a couple of hours."

"Now that does sound like fun," he says. "Know where I can get an inner tube?"

"My father works at a garage," I tell him. "When he's not working here. So we get them there."

"The garage," he repeats. "I guess I could ask there." He smiles, and I see that his teeth are a little bit crooked.

"Or you could just use one of ours," I hear myself say. I shut my mouth tight, as if someone else has somehow taken over my body and spoken through me. I don't know why, but suddenly I'm afraid of looking like an idiot.

"You mean we could go together?" he asks. "Cool," he adds before I can answer. "I guess I should get your number, then. So I can call you."

"Good idea," I say. "Here." I take a napkin and write my

name and number on it, although I have to concentrate really hard to remember what it is. I hand it to him.

"Sam," he says, reading what I wrote. "Hey, Sam. I'm Tom. Tom Swift."

"Hi, Tom Swift," I say. "It's good to know you."

"We'll see," Tom says. He writes his name and number on another napkin and slides it to me. Then he reaches into his pocket and pulls out a dollar, which he stuffs into the tip jar. "Maybe this summer won't be so bad after all," he says.

"Jennifer, are you finished? Your grandfather is waiting."

Tom stiffens. Behind him, an older woman is standing with her arms crossed over her chest.

"I'll talk to you later," Tom says to me, but his voice is tight. He turns and walks past the woman. As he passes the garbage can beside the picnic tables, he drops his unfinished cone into it.

Three

In the darkness of my room the fireflies hover like small green spaceships. I've put the screen on the window up so that they can come in. I like watching them float through the air, blinking their messages to one another. Occasionally one of them settles on something—the dresser, a lamp, the footboard of my bed—and winks on and off for a moment before taking flight again.

It's keep-awake hot, even at a few minutes past midnight, and I'm lying on top of the quilt with just my boxer shorts on. Even so, I'm still slightly sweaty, and the occasional breeze that blows across my skin is not quite enough to cool me off. It's like the house is holding its breath.

I have headphones on, the big, puffy kind that cover your whole ear and block out everything but the music. They're plugged into the receiver beside my bed. On top of that is an old record player, on which is spinning an original vinyl pressing of Wanda Jackson's 1961 album *There's a Party Goin' On.* The fifth song of side 1 is playing.

"I got the feelin' I'm a fallin,' like a star up in the blue,"

Wanda sings in her raw, gritty voice. "Like I was fallin' off Niagara, in a paddle-boat canoe."

This is my favorite song on the album. I love the way Wanda yips at the end of some of the lines. I love the rockabilly guitars. I love the occasional pop and hiss in the sound as the needle travels around the groove. It sounds *real*.

There's a Party Goin' On is number two on the list of the 21 Most Perfect Albums of All Time, at least as compiled by my mother, Ilona Weyward. (Actually, she's not a Weyward, as she didn't take the name. But last names are a whole other story in my family, and I don't know hers.) It's what she left me when she, well, left me. A cardboard box with twenty-one albums in it. Plus her record player.

The albums were arranged in chronological order in the box, and that's how I first listened to them. It's how I still listen to them. I work through them from one to twenty-one, then start over. Sister Rosetta Tharpe's *Gospel Train*, from 1956, is the first one. Lucinda Williams's *Car Wheels on a Gravel Road* is the last one.

Inside each album is a note. Some of them are written right on the liner sleeves, some are on slips of paper when there's no clear space on the sleeve. Mostly they explain why my mother thinks the album is perfect, or almost perfect. Sometimes they say other things.

The note inside the Wanda Jackson album, written in my mother's sloppy handwriting, says:

Some people call Wanda Jackson the "female Elvis," or say that she was the first woman to sing rock and roll. This isn't true. Sister Rosetta Tharpe was probably the first. But Wanda did it better than almost anybody. Her best song is "Funnel of Love," but that wasn't on any of her albums, so you'll have to find that and listen to it somewhere else. But this is her best album. It's only 29 minutes long, and every second of it is great.

She's right. There's not a bad song on the album. When "Hard Headed Woman" ends, I lift the needle, flip the record over, and start side 2.

I've played the twenty-one albums so often that I know every note and every word. Some of them I can even play on the guitar my father got me for Christmas a few years ago. But mostly I just listen to them, looking for whatever it is that made my mother fall in love with them. I figure that if I can understand what she liked, I can understand her, and maybe what she did.

Wanda sings about falling in and out of love. As the first notes of "Tweedle Dee" begin, I find myself thinking about Tom Swift and what happened this afternoon. I can't forget the look on his face as he turned away, like someone had just told his biggest secret to the world. Which I suspect is exactly what happened.

I think about calling him. But it's late, so instead I listen to the rest of *There's a Party Goin' On*. Then I turn the stereo off and pick up the telephone. My fingers search out ten numbers at random. After seven rings, someone answers.

"Hello?"

It's a girl's voice.

"Tell me a story."

There's a long pause, and at first I think she's hung up on me. But then there's a sigh, and I know she's still there. One of the rules is that I don't talk again until they do, so I don't say anything.

"Once upon a time, there was a girl," she says after a minute. "She had brown hair and brown eyes. She was the average height and weight for her age. She looked like a million other girls. She had the same name as a million other girls, and listened to the same music that they did, and read the same books that they did, and ate the same food that they did. And when she slept, she had the same dreams that a million other girls had. She was perfectly ordinary.

"But she didn't want to be ordinary. She wanted to be special. She hoped that one day a fairy godmother would show up and tell her that she was really the daughter of the king and queen of Elfland, or that on her thirteenth birthday she would discover that she had magic powers. Sometimes she wished on falling stars, and didn't tell anyone that what she wished was that one day everyone would see how different she really was from the million other girls who had her name.

"On the day of her thirteenth birthday, as she was walking home from school, an old woman suddenly appeared in front of her. The old woman was dressed all in black, and the girl knew right away that the woman was a witch, because her hair was tangled and she was wearing a button that said 'My Other Ride Is a Broom.' To be sure, though, she asked her, 'Are you a witch?'

"'Of course I am,' the witch said.

"'Have you come to tell me that I'm a witch too?' the girl asked her.

"The witch rolled her eyes and said, 'No. I'm just on my way to the store for some milk, and you happen to be in my way.'

"'So I'm not a witch?' the girl said.

"The witch shrugged. 'Probably not,' she said. 'You seem perfectly ordinary to me. But give it a try if you want to. It can't hurt.' Then she walked away.

"So the girl went home and tried to be a witch. But none of her spells worked, the black dress she put on looked ridiculous, and it turned out she was allergic to cats. So she gave up and went back to being perfectly ordinary, because in the end she really was just like the million other girls with the same name.

"The end."

"What was the girl's name?" I ask her.

"Linda," she tells me. "Plain old Linda with an 'i.' No 'y' or anything like that. Just Linda."

"It's not a very happy story," I say.

"You didn't ask for a happy one," the girl says. "Besides, it's better than a happy one, because it tells the truth."

"But most people would probably want the girl to find out she really is special," I tell her.

"Of course they would," she says. "Because *they* want to be special. But that's not the truth, is it? I mean, not usually. Most people really are ordinary. They might not want to be, but they are. I hate those stories where someone finds out she's the Chosen One or whatever. That's false hope."

"So there should only be stories about people being like everyone else?" I ask.

"More or less," she says.

"That wouldn't be much fun," I argue.

"Life isn't much fun," she counters. "Not most of the time anyway. Mostly we're all just a bunch of Lindas."

"Are you?" I ask.

"Sure," she says. "I'm perfectly ordinary. Nothing special about me."

"I don't know," I say. "I don't think most people could come up with a story like that. Especially not when a total stranger asks them to do it."

"Maybe this is my one shining moment," the girl says. "It will never get any better than it is right now. I should probably hang up so that I can enjoy the thrill before it's gone."

And then she does. At first I think she's just being funny. But she's really not there. And for some reason, it makes me sad. I don't know why, because really her story kind of sucked. But she was right about one thing—it was the truth. I guess I like that.

I consider calling her again. I've never wanted to do that with any of the storytellers before. But I don't even know what number I dialed. That's part of what makes the game interesting. Besides, I think, what else would we have to say to each other? She was probably right to hang up. But I still would have liked to at least thank her for her story.

I put the phone down. Then I realize that my room is filled with fireflies. Dozens and dozens of them. Their blinking lights twinkle as they form constellations over my desk and swoop like meteors through the dark. There's something magical about the way they're behaving, as if this is all some kind of choreographed ballet.

This goes on for a long time. Then the fireflies start leaving through the open window, back out into the yard, until eventually there's only one left. This one lands on the needle of the record player. It sits there and blinks steadily on and off, like a beacon.

Because I have lived with Hank, Starletta, and Clodine for my whole life, I believe in magic. Despite what I said about the toads at breakfast. And something about this feels like magic.

"What?" I say to the firefly. "Am I supposed to do something? Was I supposed to count how many of you there were so that Hank can tell me what it means?"

The firefly puts its light on and flies away, drifting lazily toward the window. I half expect to look up and see a bunch of them spelling out a word or forming a symbol of some kind. But there's just the one, and pretty soon it's gone as well.

I lie down again and stare at the ceiling. I think about the girl on the phone, and wonder where she is. Is she also lying in a bed in a dark room, unable to sleep because it's so hot? Is she thinking about the strange boy who called her up, and wondering who he is? Maybe she's telling someone else about it. (*Hey, listen to this weird thing that just happened.*) Or maybe she's already forgotten about it.

The sound of laughter floats up from downstairs. The Grands are still up, of course, talking about who-knows-what. I consider going down and asking them about fireflies. I'm sure they have an opinion about them; they have opinions about everything. Maybe I'll tell them about Tom Swift, or the girl on the phone. (It occurs to me that either one could be the interesting thing the toads predicted.) Or maybe I'll ask them to tell me about my mother. Or the curse. All of a sudden, I have a lot of things on my mind.

Instead, I go to the cardboard box and take out album number three. *Revolver.* The Beatles. 1966. I slip the headphones over my ears, set the record on the turntable, and gently put the needle down. The countdown that begins "Taxman" starts, and I mouth the words.

The note my mother included with this album is one of the shortest.

a lot of people think the Beatles are the
greatest band that ever existed. Maybe
they are. I think what they really did was

show the world what music could be, and other bands took it from there. This album is all about ideas.

I didn't understand what she meant by that when I first read her note. And I didn't like *Revolver* for a long time, even though there are songs on it that pretty much everyone knows, like "Eleanor Rigby" and "Yellow Submarine." But the more I listened to it, the more I started to hear the ideas she was talking about. Sometimes it would be just a couple of words, or a few particular notes. They would stay in my head after the album was done playing, or pop up when I was thinking about something completely different. But little by little, these bits and pieces grew into bigger ideas, and the songs started to mean something to me.

I think that's what she meant, that listening to what the Beatles have to say in the songs on *Revolver* makes me think about other things in different ways. Like the music turns on another part of my brain or something. It's hard to explain.

Suddenly, I'm very tired. I close my eyes and listen as Eleanor Rigby wears the face that she keeps in a jar by the door. I make it through "I'm Only Sleeping" and "Love You To." But by the second chorus of "Here, There and Everywhere" I'm drifting off.

I dream of fireflies. They come into the room through the window, a large group of them. They swirl over the bed. And then they start to sing.

sleep and dream your heart's desire
sleep and dream the face of love
when you need me, call my name
i'll come to you and keep you safe

The voice is a woman's. It comes from each of the fireflies, but really it's just one voice being shared among them. It sounds familiar, but I can't place it.

in my arms find rest and comfort
in your bed sleep warm and dream
night will pass in hours untroubled
till you wake at morning's gleam

The words are barely a whisper now. I know I've heard this song before. I search my mind, trying to remember where, trying to hold on to the melody and replay it over and over until a memory forms. But it slips away, becomes something else, an indistinct murmur that clouds my thoughts and lulls me to sleep. I try to sing the words to myself, to keep them alive, but they're gone now, nothing more than the gentle thrumming of firefly light. I let it surround me, a luminescent cocoon of gold and green, and I sleep.

Four

I call Tom Swift on Wednesday morning. This year my father has hired Becky Roth to help out at the Eezy-Freezy a couple of days a week, and she's there today, so I'm off. I'm supposed to be painting the front porch floor, but Hank, Starletta, and Clodine are camped out there in rocking chairs because it's too hot in the kitchen, even for them. They're drinking iced tea and discussing what it means that the hydrangeas have come out a particularly bright shade of blue this year.

I hope that Tom answers the phone, but it's an older man. I hesitate for a moment before asking, "Is Jennifer available?"

"Just a minute," the man answers. Then I hear him say, "It's for you."

Then Tom is on the line. "Hello?" he says, sounding suspicious, like maybe I'm somebody calling to try to sell him car insurance.

"Hi," I say. "This is Sam."

He doesn't say anything.

"From the Eezy-Freezy," I add.

"I remember," he says finally, still sounding unsure. Then nothing.

"I was wondering if you wanted to go tubing today," I tell him. "They usually open the dam around noon, and that raises the water level downstream and makes the rapids a little faster."

There's a long pause before Tom says anything. Then all he says is, "Okay."

"Great," I say. "How about I pick you up at eleven thirty? We can leave my truck at the falls and Hank can pick us up at the bridge and drive us back."

"Hank?"

"My grandmother," I explain.

"Okay," Tom says again. Then he tells me his address, and I hang up.

An hour later, I pull my truck up to a cabin not too far from the Eezy-Freezy. It looks like most of the cabins that encircle the lake, except that someone has put a concrete garden gnome beside the front porch. It holds a sign that says *The McCrackens*.

Before I can get out of the truck, the front door opens and Tom comes out. I see the same old woman from the other day standing inside, peering out at me. She doesn't look happy.

Tom opens the passenger side door and gets in.

"Hey, Tom Swift," I say.

"Hey," he says. "Do you mind if we just go?"

I pull away from the cabin. As we drive away from the lake, I can feel the worry coming off Tom like heat from a sunbaked road. He still isn't looking at me. Instead, he's staring out the window.

I try to decide if we're going to have to talk about this. On the one hand, it's none of my business. On the other, I don't want to spend the afternoon floating down the creek with all kinds of weird tension going on. And I would like to be his friend. I decide that we do have to talk about it.

"When I told the Grands that I'm gay, Clodine wanted to know if it meant I was going to be a hairdresser," I say. "She was all excited because she thought she could stop paying Pearleen Hepworth to do her permanents."

"I'm not gay," Tom mutters.

"Oh," I say, because I'm not really sure what's happening here.

"I'm trans," he tells me.

"Oh," I say again, but in a totally different way, because now I understand. "Okay, then."

He turns and looks at me. "Are you being a dick right now?" he asks.

"What?" I say. "No. I mean it. It's okay."

"Do you even know what being trans means?" he says.

I nod. "It means your inside doesn't match your outside," I say. "Well, that's how Farrah describes it. I know it's more than that, but that's a pretty good definition, right?"

"Who's Farrah?" Tom asks me.

"One of the queens," I explain. "At the Shangri-La."

"The what?"

I realize that this is going to be a much longer conversation, so I say, "I'll explain while we're tubing."

We arrive at the falls, and I park the truck. It's a little before noon, and there are a couple of other people there waiting for the dam to be opened. I nod at the ones I know, and can't help but notice some of the girls looking at Tom and smiling. One of them, Anna-Lynn Burling, comes over to us.

"Hey, Sam," she says, flipping her long blond hair out of her eyes. "Who's your friend?"

"This is Tom Swift," I tell her. "He's a summer person. Tom, this is Anna-Lynn. We're in the same class at school."

Anna-Lynn beams at Tom. "A summer boy," she says. "Nice to meet you, Tom."

"You too," Tom says, but he doesn't sound all that happy about it.

A horn blasts, interrupting the introductions. "Five-minute warning!" Anna-Lynn screams. "Everybody in the water."

People rush toward the edge of the rocks. The dam is about two hundred feet upstream. It's a small dam, nothing impressive or anything. It just lets out water from the reservoir. But it's enough to make the creek rise and make rapids over the smaller rocks. Everybody wants to be in the water when it opens, to get that first rush.

I take the two inner tubes that I've brought in the back of the Ford and hand one to Tom. We're both already dressed in swim trunks and sneakers. I take off my T-shirt and toss it in the truck, but Tom keeps his on. Then we walk to the creek and he watches me sit down in my tube. A moment later, he's beside me.

The horn blasts again. The one-minute warning. "Ready?" I say, grinning at Tom.

He nods. Anna-Lynn, who is a little downstream from us,

calls out, "Race you to the bridge, boys! Last one there buys Cokes for everyone!"

"You're on!" I shout back. I wink at Tom. "I think she likes you."

He frowns, but doesn't say anything. I wonder if I've made a mistake, joking with him like this, but before I can apologize, the little gate in the dam opens and water comes streaming out.

It hits us about thirty seconds later, lifting our inner tubes up and sending us into the middle of the creek. The water is funneled between two rows of large rocks, and one by one the tubes and their riders shoot down the rapids. The water is freezing cold, but the thrill of being carried downstream makes it so you don't notice.

My inner tube twirls around as I bounce off a boulder, and I see Tom behind me. At first he looks a little bit scared, so I wave at him and let out a happy whoop. He can't help but laugh, and when his tube bumps up against mine, he's got a big smile on his face.

"I told you it would be fun," I say.

We ride the rapids for a while, until the creek has risen as much as it's going to and the water calms down, flattening out into a wide ribbon. Now we're floating more slowly, passing beneath overhanging tree branches as the creek turns in a series of curves that carry us into the woods. Anna-Lynn and her friends are still ahead of us, and although we sometimes see them on the long, straight stretches, when they disappear around a bend, Tom and I are all by ourselves.

"Sorry about what I said earlier," I tell him as I lie back on my tube, staring up at the bright blue sky. "You know, about Anna-Lynn. I was just joking. Although I do think she thinks you're hot."

"It's okay," he says. "It's just that . . ." His voice trails off.

I sit up and look at him. "You don't have to explain anything," I tell him. "Really."

"I guess she is kind of pretty," he says after a while.

"She has an identical twin sister," I tell him. "Lynn-Anna."

"She does not," Tom says.

"It's true," I tell him. "The only way you can tell them apart is that Anna-Lynn is left-handed and Lynn-Anna is right-handed. So if you ask Anna-Lynn out, be sure to toss a baseball at her and see which hand she catches it with. Otherwise, you might be smooching her sister."

Tom splashes water at me. I splash back. Something has changed. I can feel it. He seems lighter. Happier. Secrets are heavy, and he's carrying a lot of them.

"So," I say when we're done with our water war. "Want to talk about it?"

Tom sighs. "No," he says. "And yes. Not right now. It's been a rough couple of months. I'd like to just have fun. But how about this? You can ask me one question. Anything."

I know immediately what to ask. "How'd you come up with Tom Swift?" I'm curious about his name, particularly because I'm having trouble coming up with my own for the other me.

"Really?" he says. "That's what you want to know?"

I nod. "Yep."

Tom dips his head back until it touches the water. "When I was little, we used to go visit my grandparents a lot. Not the ones here. These are my father's parents. I mean my mom's parents. They lived in Maine, right on the ocean. Their house was big and old and I loved it. I had my own bedroom there, and it had a bookcase in it filled with books my grandfather had read when he was little. There was a series about a boy named Tom Swift. He was an inventor, and he had adventures. The books were called things like *Tom Swift and His Giant Robot* and *Tom Swift in the Race to the Moon*. I used to curl up in bed and read them. I wanted to have adventures too. I wanted to explore the ocean in a submarine, and study comets, and go into caves. And I did kind of do those things with my grandfather. He took me fishing, and hiking, and sailing, and he never told me I couldn't do something because I was a girl. Then he died. When I was eleven. My grandmother gave me all the Tom Swift books. So when I realized what was going on with me, it seemed to fit. I guess it's silly."

"It's not silly," I tell him. "It's cool. You wanted to be something, and now you are."

"Not really," Tom says. "It's just a name. And actually, you're the first person I've ever tried it out on. I was too scared to use it back home, where people know me. But I figure here nobody does. And then my grandmother had to go and fuck it up."

"It's all right," I tell him. "Nobody else heard her."

"Now can I ask you one question?" he says.

"Sure."

"Did you know?" he asks. "About me. Before my grand-mother said that?"

"No. I just thought you were a cute guy." I realize too late what I've just said.

"You think I'm cute?" Tom says.

"That's two questions," I say. "Sorry."

"Not fair!" Tom cries, and smacks the water.

"Rules are rules," I say, spinning my inner tube away from him.

But now that I've said it, I realize that it's true. I do think Tom Swift is cute. And since the rule about asking only one question doesn't apply to ones I ask myself, the next logical one is: Do I still think he's cute now that I know he's not exactly who I thought he was?

As an almost-seventeen-year-old guy, I've thought about sex. A lot. And I've had a lot of the one-handed type. But so far I haven't had any with another actual person. Not that there are a ton of options around here. At least not with guys my age. I've thought about maybe trying it out with one of the men who come to the Shangri-La. Believe me, I've thought about it *a lot*. But Lola says he'll disown me if I do. Lola says that a guy's first time should be special, and he doesn't want me hooking up with just anyone. So I haven't.

But when I think about doing it, it generally involves—how do I put this—something Tom Swift doesn't have. And what Tom does have is not something I've ever thought about. Not that I'm freaked out about girl parts or anything. I've just never considered what I would do with them.

Not that I think of Tom as a girl. I don't. He's Tom. I get that. I mean, I'm not new. I've read books. I know what trans is. And everything isn't about sex. But a lot of things *are,* and I can't help thinking about it. Which makes me feel guilty, like I've failed some kind of test for being an enlightened person.

"Hey," Tom calls out. "What's this? And that's not a personal question, so it doesn't count."

I look over at him. He's on his stomach on his tube, peering down into the water with his hands cupped on either side of his head.

"It looks like a pair of boots," he says. "Stuck on the bottom."

By accident he's discovered one of the secrets of Coldwater Creek.

"They are boots," I tell him. "Wading boots, actually. Fishermen wear them. Those are bronze ones, but they were cast from a pair that belonged to Ezra Browncow."

"Ezra Browncow," Tom repeats. "You're kidding, right?"

I shake my head. "That was his name," I say. "When he was nineteen he came here fishing for trout. It was his favorite place to be. He hooked one, and was trying to reel it in when the dam opened. He tried to get out of the creek, but his foot got wedged between a couple of rocks. The creek rose, his boots filled up with water, and he drowned. Everybody in town liked him, and they felt terrible, so they took up a collection and used the money to have those bronze boots made as a memorial. His ashes are mixed in with the metal, so basically he's buried here."

We're long past Ezra Browncow's boots now, but Tom keeps looking down into the water.

"I think that's the best story I've ever heard," Tom says. "When did it happen?"

"Nineteen eighty-three," I answer. "October third."

Tom looks over at me. "You remember the exact date?"

I nod. "I kind of have to," I explain. "He was my grandfather."

Five

According to Farrah and Paloma, you have two basic options when choosing a drag name: you can be funny, or you can be fabulous. A funny name is usually a play on words, like calling yourself Anita Mann, Sharon Needles, or Lois Common Denominator. A fabulous name is something that just sounds great.

"Like Paloma," Paloma says as he applies a glue stick to his eyebrows. "Paloma sounds exotic. People see Paloma and ask themselves, where does Paloma come from? What does Paloma do? Who does Paloma love? I'm a mystery. Like Cher, or Madonna. Or that place with all the stones. The ones the aliens made."

"Stonehenge?" I suggest.

Paloma points the glue stick at me. "That's it," he says. "I am a mystery like Stonehenge."

"You're a mystery all right," Farrah says. "The mystery is how the hell you manage to say things like that without laughing at your damn self."

I stifle a laugh. Paloma can be touchy about being teased.

When he's not Paloma, he's Ricky Escovedo. And Ricky Escovedo is not a very good-looking boy. He has bad skin, a wonky nose, and eyes that are a little too far apart. If you were to see him busing tables at the Mexican restaurant he works at during the day, you probably wouldn't pay any attention to him.

But Paloma is something else. Paloma is beautiful, and fierce, and everyone pays attention to her when she performs. Paloma has a comeback for everything, and she doesn't let anyone take advantage of her.

There's an old animated Christmas special about Frosty the Snowman, who is just a plain old snowman until a little girl places a magic top hat on his head and he comes to life. That's what it's like when Ricky turns into Paloma. As the makeup goes on, he comes to life, and when he takes it off again at the end of the night, it's like a flower wilting.

Farrah is different. Even as Brandon Thomas he's still funny and loud and doesn't care what anyone thinks. He's also really handsome. He has a couple of different boyfriends, and isn't shy about giving his number out to potential new ones either. I've actually seen men get into fistfights over him, both as Farrah and as Brandon. He even has another name for himself when these things happen: Mama Dramarama. "Mama Dramarama does not have time for this!" he'll shriek, laughing as he walks away from whatever trouble he's the center of.

Paloma rolls his eyes and looks at me. "She's just jealous because I have a new pair of Louboutins," he says, lifting one leg to show me a ridiculously high-heeled shoe.

"Louboutins?" says Farrah, slapping a tube of mascara on

the dressing table and putting his hands on his hips. "Bitch, I *know* you got those at the Payless for nine ninety-nine and just spray-painted the bottoms red." He reaches over, as if he's going to run his fingertip down the sole of Paloma's shoe to see if any of it rubs off.

Paloma pulls his foot away and wags a finger at Farrah. "Do not sit there in that Tina Turner fright wig that looks like some kind of mangy Pekingese sitting up on top of your head and criticize my footwear."

Farrah gasps. "I know you did not just drag Miss Anna Mae Bullock into this. You did *not*." He turns to me as he pretends to remove one of his rhinestone earrings. "Gurl, hold my clip-ons, because there is going to be a fight."

Now we do all laugh. This is what I like about drag queens. Everything is over the top. But it's usually all just in fun. Usually.

"Sammy, tell that bitch I apologize for pointing out that her heels are knockoffs," Farrah says primly as he picks up a lipstick and begins applying it.

I turn to Paloma. "Farrah would like you to know that he is . . ."

"Pronouns!" Farrah and Paloma say in unison.

"Sorry," I apologize. "That *she* is very sorry for insulting your Louboutins."

"More like Foolboutins," Farrah says under her breath.

"Shh!" I hiss.

"Thank you," Paloma says, powdering her nose. "And please tell my sister that I forgive her rudeness and am sorry about pointing out the tragedy of her wig. I did it out of love."

"Now back to you," Farrah says to me. "How many times do we have to tell you to say *she* and *her* when talking about a person's drag self?"

"I know," I say. "I know. But it's confusing. Like, do you only use *she* when someone is in full drag? What about while he's putting on his face but doesn't have his hair on?"

Drag has its own language, and I haven't mastered it yet. I've finally gotten the difference between *girl*, which just means a girl, and *gurl*, which means, well, different things depending on how you say it. Mostly it's something some gay guys call one another. And the only difference is that when you say *gurl*, you kind of draw the word out. But that difference is important.

"When in doubt, use *she*," Paloma instructs me. "Most guys won't be offended if you call them she, but call a queen a he and you're asking for a slap."

This conversation makes me think about Tom Swift. For some reason, I have no problem thinking of Tom as he. Even after his grandmother let his other name slip out, I've never once considered him a she. Maybe because Tom is who Tom is. Jennifer is who he *was,* but isn't anymore. But Paloma is usually Ricky, and Farrah is usually Brandon. They're only Paloma and Farrah a couple of times a week.

Which brings us back to what we were talking about earlier. Who *I* am.

"Funny names are kind of old-school," Farrah says, picking up the conversation as if we'd never left it. "Usually girls with funny names are comedy queens."

"Clowns," Paloma adds.

"Kind of," Farrah agrees. "But really fucking funny ones. Not the creepy-ass kind like they have at the circus. But finding a name no one has used already is a bitch."

"Where did you get yours?" I ask Farrah.

He—she—points to a poster taped to the wall beside the mirror. It shows a gorgeous blond woman wearing a red one-piece swimsuit.

"Miss Farrah Fawcett," Farrah says. "The star of *Charlie's Angels*."

"One of the stars," says Lola, who has walked into the middle of the conversation, and who now sits down in an armchair to watch the other queens get ready. He's still dressed in his regular clothes, so I think of him as, well, him. He's holding a drink in one hand.

"*The* star," Farrah insists. "Child, just look at that hair. In 1976, every man and boy in America had that poster on their walls. Even the gay ones. Everybody loved Farrah Fawcett. *Everybody*."

"You weren't even alive then," Lola says.

"That's true," Farrah agrees. "As you know, I am only twenty-one years of age."

Paloma and Lola snort. Farrah flips her middle finger at them. "Anyway, I saw the show in reruns, and I thought Miss Farrah was the prettiest thing I had ever seen. So when it came time for my naming, she's the first thing that came to mind. And my last name, Monroe, is a play on Farrah's character's name in *Charlie's Angels*. Hers was Jill Munroe, with a 'u.' Mine is Monroe, with an 'o,' because it's also an homage to Miss Marilyn. Farrah Monroe. And there you are."

"Kind of ironic, a little black boy wanting to be a pretty white girl, isn't it?" Lola says.

Farrah doesn't respond, and I can tell Lola has said something that hurts her. But a moment later she snaps out of it and says, "Better than naming myself after a demon, old man."

"A demon?" I say.

Lola takes a sip of his drink. "Lola is a character from the musical *Damn Yankees*," he explains. "She's a kind of demon who works for the devil and tries to seduce the show's main character, Joe Hardy. When I was eleven, I visited my uncle in New York City. He was a homosexual, although back then everyone just called him a confirmed bachelor. He took me to the show. I'd never seen anything like it. The whole rest of the week I went around singing 'Whatever Lola Wants,' which was Lola's big number from the show, and his friends all thought I was adorable. But when it came time to put me on the train to come home, my uncle told me not to sing it around my parents. I didn't understand why, but I told him I wouldn't. But whenever I was alone in my room, I'd sing it and remember how it felt to have all those people clapping for me."

He starts singing, and I recognize the song as a tune I've often heard him humming. But I didn't know it had words. I wonder why he doesn't do it in his act, but before I can ask him he gets up and leaves without saying anything else.

"Now you've done it," Paloma says to Farrah. "She'll be drunk before we even open the doors."

"She's already drunk," Farrah says.

"Why?" I ask. "What's wrong?"

"That uncle she talked about?" Paloma says. "He killed himself."

"Why?"

"He was a schoolteacher," Paloma explains. "Taught English to eighth graders. Someone found out about him and reported him. Back then, you couldn't be gay and teach kids. They fired him. He was afraid everyone would find out, so he killed himself. Family told everyone he'd had a heart attack, but Lola found out the truth when a letter came from him for her a week after he died. That letter also had a check in it. A big one. He left her the money that she used to open this place."

"That's horrible," I say, feeling bad that I asked Lola about his name.

"You scratch anybody and you'll find some tragedy just below the surface," Farrah says. "It's called life."

That makes me think about the curse, which is something I really don't want to think about right now. So I ask Paloma, "Is there a story behind your name?"

"Paloma means 'dove' in Spanish," she says. "It's what my *abuelita* Marisol always called me."

"I didn't know that," Farrah says. "That's sweet. I thought you named yourself after Paloma Picasso."

"Who?" says Paloma.

47

Farrah lowers her eyelids. "Really? And you call yourself a fashion queen? Look it up."

"Has anyone in your families ever seen you perform?" I ask them both, trying to head off another squabble.

Paloma shakes her head. "My brothers think I work a night shift washing dishes," she says. "My parents are still in Mexico."

"Mine know, but we don't talk about it," says Farrah. "As long as I show up to sing in the choir come Sunday, we don't have a problem."

I try to picture Hank, Starletta, and Clodine standing in front of the stage at the Shangri-La, watching me perform. Oddly enough, I don't have any trouble imagining it. I think they'd actually probably enjoy themselves. But I'm not ready to tell them about this part of myself. Not yet.

I stick around while Paloma and Farrah finish getting ready. But I leave earlier than usual. I haven't talked to Tom Swift since our tubing adventure, and I want to call him. It would be easier if he had a cell phone, but his parents took it away when they sent him here for the summer. He says it's so his grandparents can monitor who he talks to.

When I get home, I talk to the Grands for a few minutes before heading up to my room. I dial Tom Swift's number, but it just rings and rings, with no answer. It's not that late, but I worry that maybe his grandparents go to bed early. I don't want to wake them up and get him in trouble, so I decide to try him in the morning.

I lie there for a while, thinking about the stories I heard earlier at the Shangri-La. And I think about what Farrah said, about all of us having tragedy in our lives. My family certainly does. The Grands have all lost their husbands. My father has lost his wife. I've lost my mother.

Suddenly, I need to see my dad. I go downstairs and tell the Grands I'll be back in a little while. Then I get in my truck and drive to the Eezy-Freezy. It's really busy, and a bunch of people wave and talk to me. But I need to get inside. For some reason, I have this horrible feeling that when I open the door, my father won't be there.

But he is. He's standing in his usual spot by the stove. He's got six burgers going at once. Sweat is running down his forehead, and his apron is covered in grease. He's tapping the spatula against the grill, playing the drum part to Lita Ford's "Kiss Me Deadly," which blasts from the radio. He looks tired and totally happy.

"Hey," he says when he sees me watching him. "What's up? Everything okay at home?"

For a moment, I think I might start crying. I don't even know why. "Yeah," I say. "I just drove by and saw you were slammed, so I thought you and Becky might like some help."

He smiles. "That would be great," he says. "Want to work the window or help me put together burgers?"

I take an apron from the hook on the wall. "I think I'll stay back here with you," I tell him. "If that's okay."

"Of course it's okay," he says. He turns the radio up even louder. "You're just in time. The guitar solo is coming up."

Six

On Sunday, Tom Swift spends the night at my house.

I wasn't planning on asking him to come over, but when I call him earlier in the day, he tells me that his grandparents have friends coming to visit. He's not looking forward to it, so I suggest a sleepover. I think we're both surprised when his grandparents say yes, but they agree to bring him to the Eezy-Freezy that evening so that he can ride home with me.

I don't get to meet them. Tom is sitting at one of the picnic tables when I finish up and go outside. He has a backpack with him.

When we get to my house, I take a shower while Tom hangs out in my room. I put record number four on the stereo before I leave. It's Dusty Springfield's *Dusty in Memphis,* from 1969. The songs are short, and by the time I get back, side 1 is almost over.

"I've never heard anything like that," Tom tells me. "Her voice is really . . . I don't know how to describe it."

"I know," I say. "It's something else, isn't it?"

I haven't told him yet about my mother, who said that Dusty Springfield's voice sounds like what a heart feels like when it breaks. I take the note she left for me inside the album sleeve of *Dusty in Memphis,* but before I can start reading it, Tom says, "I'm going to the movie at the VFW with Anna-Lynn on Wednesday."

"Really?"

"Yeah. I went grocery shopping with my grandmother on Friday, and I ran into Anna-Lynn at the Bi-Rite. She works as a checker there."

"You're sure it wasn't Lynn-Anna?" I joke.

"Pretty sure," Tom replies. "I didn't have a baseball, but I kind of let an apple roll toward her, and she picked it up with her left hand. Besides, she was wearing a name tag."

We both laugh, but I have a question. "Did you ask her out in front of your grandmother?"

Tom snorts. "Are you nuts?" he says. "I pretended I'd forgotten to buy a pack of gum, and went back inside while she was getting in the car."

I have another question, a bigger one, but I don't know how to ask it, so I don't. Instead I say, "Good for you."

Tom shrugs. "I guess," he says. "I've never asked a girl out before."

"This is a big deal," I tell him. "Your first date. We should celebrate. Let's go get some Cokes."

We go downstairs to the kitchen. I'm surprised that the Grands aren't in there. Then I hear their voices coming from outside. I look out the screen door, and they're wandering around in the yard with flashlights.

"How many do you have?" Starletta calls out.

"Three," Hank answers.

"Six," says Clodine. "I'm going inside."

"Wait a minute," Starletta says. "Let me see those."

I see one of the flashlights cross the lawn. Then Starletta says, "Ma, that's a tomato from the garden. And that's a zucchini. Those aren't flowers."

"The fruit grows from the flower," Clodine argues. "I say they count."

"It won't work unless they're flowers," says Starletta. "You know that."

"What are they doing?" Tom asks me.

"I have no idea," I tell him. "Let's find out."

We go outside. "What's going on?"

Three flashlight beams blind me. I hold my hand up in front of my eyes, and the Grands lower their lights.

"Just a little midsummer magic," Hank tells me. "You gather six different kinds of flowers and put them under your pillow. Whatever you dream about comes true."

"What if you have a bad dream?" Tom says.

"That's the chance you take," Clodine tells him, marching back toward the house, the zucchini gripped in one hand like a wand.

"Vegetables don't count!" Starletta calls after her. But Clodine ignores her, going inside and letting the screen door slam behind her.

"Stubborn old woman," Starletta says, then goes off to another part of the yard, presumably in search of more flowers.

"Can we do it too?" Tom asks me.

I hesitate. The Grands' magic doesn't always work the way you—or they—think it will. But Tom seems excited by the idea, so I say, "Why not?"

I get two flashlights from the kitchen, and we start hunting for flowers. Pretty quickly I find an iris and a hydrangea right along the side of the house, and a tiger lily from the clump that grows beside the mailbox. In the field that grows wild behind the house there are daisies and black-eyed Susans. But I need one more.

Growing along one side of the old barn where we store the 1957 Rambler Six my father and I are going to restore together one of these days, I find some foxgloves. I pick one, then return to the front yard. Starletta and Hank are standing by the porch steps, where I join them. Tom arrives a moment later.

"I've got six," he says. "That wasn't so hard. And smell this rose. It's amazing."

I look at Starletta and Hank, who are looking at each other.

"Where did you find that?" I ask Tom, although I'm afraid I already know the answer.

"There's a bush on the other side of the house," he says. "Right under one of the windows. It's covered with flowers."

The window is the one to Clodine's bedroom. And the rose-bush marks the spot where my great-great-grandfather Wild Ruckus is buried. Well, the part of him the bear didn't eat, which was mostly his left hand. They identified it because of the wedding band, which he'd only worn for nine days. Also, the tattoo on the back, which was of a rose.

Wild Ruckus was the first victim of the curse. Clodine too, of course, but I think Wild Ruckus got the worst of it. Clodine, who was only sixteen, insisted on burying the hand beneath her window. She said it would keep his ghost near her so he could protect her and the baby she was carrying, who turned out to be Starletta. When the rosebush grew there, almost overnight, and the roses were the same color as the one Wild Ruckus had tattooed on his hand, she said it just proved that she was right.

Only Clodine is allowed to pick the Wild Ruckus roses. But now Tom Swift has one in his hand.

"Well, he can't put it back, and he can't throw it away. Ruckus wouldn't take to that," Starletta says. "So I guess he'll have to use it."

"This should be interesting," Hank adds.

"Interesting?" says Tom Swift, who doesn't know what we're talking about. "Interesting how?"

"Don't worry about it," Starletta tells him, putting her arm around him. "I'm sure it will be fine. You're not afraid of ghosts, are you?"

We enter the house. Clodine is sitting at the kitchen table with her flowers spread out in front of her. She looks at us, sees what Tom is carrying, and lifts one eyebrow. "Brave boy," she says. I'm just relieved she isn't angry.

Hank tells us we can put the flowers in bags so that they don't make a mess under our pillows. She gives me and Tom plastic grocery sacks from the Bi-Rite, and we stick our flowers inside. The bags remind me of Anna-Lynn, and I wonder if Tom is thinking about her too.

Once we're back in my room, Tom says, "What was all that about the rose? Did I do something wrong?"

"No," I assure him. Then I tell him about Clodine, Wild Ruckus, and the bear.

"What happened to the bear?" he asks when I'm finished.

"Some guys wanted to find it and kill it," I say. "But Clodine told them to leave it alone. She said any bear that could best a man who had killed seven Nazis with a pistol during World War II had to be pretty special."

Tom shakes his head. "Great-great-grandfather killed by a bear. Grandfather drowned fishing in a creek. Do I want to know what happened to your great-grandfather?"

I tell him about Sam and the fireworks.

"The men in your family don't seem to be too lucky," he says. "Is your father worried something might happen to him?"

"It already did," I say. What I don't add is that my father doesn't have to worry about being the one to die. The curse doesn't kill Weywards. Just the people we love.

"And what about you?" Tom says.

I could tell him that as long as I make it to seventeen without falling in love, I'll be okay. But the whole thing already seems completely ridiculous, so I just say, "I think my mother leaving is about as bad as it can get."

"I wondered about that," Tom says. "So your parents are divorced?"

"No," I say. "She just left. And they never actually married, because my father thought that if they didn't, it would break the—because they didn't believe in it. We don't even know where she is." This is not entirely true. There's another little piece of information about the situation that I don't share with him.

"Ouch," Tom says. "That's rough."

"It's hard to get too upset about it," I tell him. "She left when I was three days old. I never knew her."

"If it helps any, having both parents around isn't always the greeting-card experience people want you to think it is," Tom says.

"So I hear," I say. "I guess everybody has their hard stuff to deal with."

We talk for a little while longer, and then it's time to go to sleep. There's just the one bed in my room, and I offer it to Tom, but he says we can share. "If that doesn't freak you out or anything," he adds.

"It's a big bed," I tell him. "I think I can handle it."

I do take some precautions, though. I usually sleep in just my boxers, but I feel weird doing that, so I put on a pair of shorts. This has nothing to do with Tom, and everything to do with the fact that I frequently wake up with a boner, and I don't want to accidentally introduce him to it.

I expect Tom to want to change in the bathroom, but he surprises me by doing it right there. He takes a pair of sweat shorts and a T-shirt out of his backpack. He seems fine with changing in front of me, but I look away while he dresses. When I look back, I see that he's put on a T-shirt featuring Optimus Prime.

"Transformer," I say. "Nice one."

"Thanks," says Tom. "It's kind of my personal in-joke with myself."

Before we get into bed, we put the bags with the flowers in them under our pillows.

"So, whatever we dream comes true, right?" Tom says.

"Supposedly," I tell him as I slip under the quilt. Tom gets in on the other side. I can tell we're both trying not to touch each other, and I wonder if for him it's about being a straight guy sleeping in a bed with a gay guy, or just general awkwardness.

"In that case, sweet dreams," he says.

"You too," I tell him, and turn off the light.

In my dream, I'm walking down a street in a small town I'm certain I've never been in. I walk past a hardware store, then an antique store. I stop in front of a coffee shop called the Perk Me Up.

I push open the door and go inside. A waitress is wiping off a table. She glances up at me and says, "Sit anywhere. I'll be right with you."

I sit down and look at the menu on the table. I'm not hungry, so I don't know why I'm here. I think I've come to see someone. But who? There are four other customers in the shop. Two are old men sitting at the counter reading newspapers. The other two are a mother and a little boy. She's eating a piece of pie, and he's spooning ice cream out of a bowl and into his mouth, although a lot of it seems to be sticking to his face. I don't think any of them are who I'm looking for.

Then the waitress is standing next to me. I look up at her. She's probably sixty or so, with red hair that's going gray. Her name tag says *Rhonda*.

"What can I get for you?" Rhonda asks, and right then I know that it's her I've come to see.

Seven

As the Creature from the Black Lagoon swims along a few feet underneath the unsuspecting girl he's fallen in love with, I watch Tom Swift and Anna-Lynn. They're sitting together on a blanket not too far away from me. Tom has asked me to stay nearby for moral support on his first date. I'm sitting with Clodine, Starletta, and Hank, who decided at the last minute that they wanted to come. It's a double feature at VFW movie night: *Creature from the Black Lagoon* and *The Wolf Man*. Clodine loves classic monster movies. So, apparently, does everyone else in town. The lawn is packed.

Clodine hands me a jar of pickled green beans that she put up last summer. I take one and chew on it while I wait for Tom to make his move. He's been working up to it since the scientists arrived in the jungle. Finally, just as the Creature reaches up to touch Kay Lawrence's foot, he reaches over and puts his arm around Anna-Lynn. She leans into him, and for a second she rests her head on his shoulder.

I'm happy for Tom, but I'm also sad. I know this is a terrible thing to think, but I can't help being a little bit jealous that because he looks like a guy, and because he likes girls, it's easier for him to find someone. Not that being Tom Swift is easy. I know that. And who knows what Anna-Lynn will say if or when he tells her about himself. But for right now, the world looks at them and sees a guy with a girl, and that makes his sitting with his arm around Anna-Lynn okay.

If I had my arm around another guy, you can bet someone would say something.

The pickled green bean makes me thirsty, so I take a bottle of soda from the cooler. The Grands packed it, so of course it's full of Nehi. I don't look at what flavor it is, so it's a surprise when the cold blast of grapey goodness hits my tongue. I don't even mind that it mixes with the vinegar and garlic from the beans. It's so sugary that my teeth ache.

Tom and Anna-Lynn sit like that for the rest of the film. At intermission, Anna-Lynn disappears for a while, and Tom comes over to me.

"Looks like it's going well," I say, trying to sound like I'm happy for him. Which I am. Sort of.

He sits down beside me. "The funny thing is," he says, "this is what I dreamed about the other night. You know, when we did the thing with the flowers."

"Really?" I say. We haven't talked about our dreams, because Starletta said if we did, they wouldn't come true. I guess now that his has, it's okay. But I still don't tell him mine.

"Yeah," Tom says. "I dreamed I was here with Anna-Lynn."

"Is that all?" I ask.

Tom rubs his ear. "Not all," he says, and he sounds embarrassed. I know immediately what he's not saying. Then he scrambles to his feet, and I see Anna-Lynn coming back. "I'll see you later," Tom says.

I leave halfway through *The Wolf Man*. I've seen it before, and I don't want to be around when Larry Talbot is killed by his own father, who doesn't know that his son is under the wolf curse. Besides, the whole curse thing makes me kind of uneasy. I suspect it makes the Grands uneasy too, because it doesn't take much to convince them to come with me. Besides, Clodine has eaten the last of the pickled beans anyway.

I don't say goodbye to Tom Swift.

We don't talk on the way home, the four of us squeezed into the Ford's cab. I know we're all thinking about the curse. Or maybe not. Maybe just I am, and the Grands are thinking about other things. Whatever the reason, we drive in silence.

Back at home, I go to my room. I take out the fifth record from my mother's collection. Black Sabbath's self-titled album from 1970. I put it on the stereo, place the headphones over my ears, and listen to the sounds of a thunderstorm and church bells that starts the record off.

I hesitate a moment before taking out the note that my mother put inside this particular sleeve. Number five is always a tough one for me. Sometimes I'm tempted to skip it. But I never do. That would be cheating.

The note my mother put inside *Black Sabbath* says this:

Your father is going to tell you that I ran away. I know why he wants you to think this, but it's not true. I'm dead. I know this is hard to understand, and maybe you never will. But some people just can't live in this world. I'm one of them. This isn't your fault. It's nobody's fault. It's just the way things are. So please, don't wait for me to return. I can't.

The first time I read this note, I wanted to run to my father and show it to him. But I didn't, because I wanted to see if he would ever tell me the truth. He didn't. And then I started to wonder if he even knew. Maybe he really did think my mother had just run off and left us. Or maybe he was just trying to protect my feelings. And eventually I decided that it didn't matter. Either way, my mother was gone.

I've never told anybody about the note. I know that sounds weird. But the thing is, my mother left the records to me. Not to my father. Not to anyone else. And (as far as I know) he didn't look at them for thirteen years, until he gave the box of them to me on my birthday. And I really don't think he did look inside them, because I'm pretty sure he would have discussed at least this one with me.

So there's another one of my secrets: I'm the only one who knows that my mother killed herself.

I almost told Tom Swift about it during our sleepover. I

don't know why. I guess I wanted him to know that I have this huge thing I can't tell anyone either. But I'm not ready for it to not be my secret anymore.

Some people would probably think it was creepy that my mother left what is basically a suicide note inside a Black Sabbath album. I don't know. I mean, it's a great album. Yeah, it's dark. My favorite song on it, "N.I.B.," is a love song sung from the point of view of the devil asking someone to be his lover. But that's interesting. Who would the devil fall in love with? Is it a man or a woman? The lyrics don't say. All we know is that the devil has never been in love before, and that this person has changed all that. That's pretty cool when you think about it. I can see why this is one of Ilona's favorites. *Was* one of Ilona's favorites.

All of a sudden, I do want to tell someone my secret. But not anyone I actually know. I pick up the phone and do the dialing thing at random. When someone answers, I say, "I want to tell you a story."

"Oh," says a girl's voice. "It's you."

I hesitate. "Who do you think I am?" I ask, because what I think might be happening is pretty much impossible.

"The guy from the other night," she says. "You asked *me* to tell *you* a story. Remember?"

Of course I remember. But how have I managed to call her again? I have no idea what number I dialed that night. I have no idea what number I've dialed now. But I recognize her voice.

"This is weird," I say.

"You think?" the girl says.

"I didn't know I was calling you," I tell her. "Honest. I dialed at random. I never call the same number twice. I don't even know what number this is."

She doesn't say anything. But she doesn't hang up either.

"So, tell me a story," she finally says.

"My mother killed herself," I blurt out.

"That's it?" the girl says. "That's a crappy story."

"She killed herself, but everybody wants me to think she abandoned us," I clarify.

"That's better," she tells me. "But not much."

And so I tell her the whole story about my mother and the albums and the notes, and about how my father may or may not know the truth.

"Okay," she says when I'm done. "Now *that* is a good story."

And she doesn't even know about the curse part. I left that out because I thought it might be too much.

"Tell me another one," she says.

It felt good to tell her the first one, so now I tell her about Tom Swift and Anna-Lynn, and how I think I'm jealous of them. Most of it, anyway. I don't tell her about Tom Swift being born Jennifer, because I think that's his story to tell if he wants to, not mine.

When I'm done, the girl says, "I wrote a song kind of like that once."

"You write songs?" I say. "That's awesome."

"Is it?" she says, like it's never occurred to her. "I don't know. It's just something I used to do."

"Sing it for me," I say.

She laughs. "I can't," she says.

"I bet you can," I counter.

"Okay, I *won't*," she says.

"Come on," I argue. "You can't tell me you wrote a song that's like my story and then not sing it for me."

She sighs. "Okay. Fine. Whatever. But I can't play the guitar and hold the phone, so I have to set it down."

"That's okay," I assure her.

There's a clunk as she puts the phone down. Then I hear her strum a guitar. She makes some adjustments, tuning it, and then she starts to play. The music is soft and sad. Then she sings.

How Can You See Me (When You're Looking at Her)

it's almost half past midnight
and you call me on the phone
to say you're sad and lonely
scared you'll always be alone
i say i want you to be happy
and i know you'll find true love
that it's time your heart was healed
and i hope you won't give up

if you'd look at me you'd see
the face of love look back at you
and in my eyes you'd find your home
your comfort and refuge

but someone stands between us
the one who broke your heart
the one who said forever
and then left you in the dark

tell me, how can you hear me
when her voice is in your head?
tell me, how can you touch me
when she's with you in your bed?
you're fevered with a sickness
and I'd like to be the cure
but tell me, how can you see me
when you're looking at her?

she's gone but not forgotten
a ghost who haunts your halls
you gave her all the love you had
she gave you none at all
you know you should forget her
but her memory's like a bruise
she's a mystery that you'll never solve
but you still look for clues

tell me, how can you hear me
when she's calling you again?
tell me, how can you touch me
when she's underneath your skin?

i'm what you need, i'm what you want
the one you're looking for
but tell me, how can you see me
when you're looking at her?

the hour's late, i'm out of words
there's nothing left to say
so go to sleep and in your dreams
maybe this time she'll stay
hold her close, kiss her mouth
tell her that you're sure
and i hope that you see me
when you're looking at her

When she's done, she picks the phone up again. "Well?"

"I really like it," I tell her. "I get exactly what you're saying. But it's not really like my situation. I don't want Tom Swift to look at me instead of Anna-Lynn. I just want *someone* to."

"Are you sure you don't want him to?" she asks. "Because I kind of think you do."

I start to argue. But then I think, what if she's right? What if I'm not jealous that Tom Swift found someone to put his arm around, I'm jealous that the person isn't me?

"Oh, crap," I say.

"Sorry," the girl says. "I thought you knew."

"I guess I didn't," I admit. "I need to think about this."

"It's just a song," she says.

"It really is good," I tell her. "You should record yourself singing it. Put it on YouTube or something. Who knows, you could get discovered."

"I don't know what that is," she says. "But thanks. I should probably go now."

"Hey," I say. "Is your name really Linda?"

"No," she says. "Maybe. Does it matter?"

"I suppose it doesn't. I just wondered. I'm Sam."

I wonder if now that I've told her my name, she'll share hers. But all she says is, "Maybe we'll talk again, Sam. Or maybe not. I hope everything works out for you."

"You too," I say, but she's already hung up.

I put on side 2 of *Black Sabbath*. It's a really weird set of songs, more music than words, and listening to it gives me time to think about what might or might not be happening in my head.

Do I have a thing for Tom Swift?

It seems like a simple question. But it's not. And the answer could change a lot of things. Especially since my birthday is still eight weeks off. It's just not safe to answer yes. Especially for Tom.

But I'm afraid I can't say no.

Eight

On Friday I've had the order window at the Eezy-Freezy open for about half an hour when I hear a voice from the radio announce, "This weekend's Capital Pride Parade and Festival will culminate with a concert by Joan Jett & the Blackhearts, who will be the wedding band for more than two hundred and fifty couples who plan to tie the knot in a celebration of marriage equality."

The woman to whom I have just handed a black cherry and bubble-gum double-scoop cone makes a face. "Eww," she says. She doesn't mean the ice cream.

"Did you hear that?" my father calls out as I watch the woman walk to a picnic table where her husband and two kids are sitting. He says something to her, she says something back, and they start arguing loudly. One of the kids starts to cry.

"Yes," I shout back.

"Joan Jett," my father says. He's come over to the window area. "That's so cool. Just think, one day I can walk you down the aisle and give you away."

"Thanks," I tell him. "That's very progressive of you. Are you going to give my groom a herd of goats as my dowry too?"

"Ha ha," he says. "Seriously, this kind of thing is a big deal. This never would have happened when I was your age."

I know it's a big deal. It seems like it's all anyone's talked about for forever. Frankly, I'm tired of hearing about it. I mean, I'm glad gay people can get married now, but it's not like I have a boyfriend or anything. Still, it makes me feel good to know that someday it could happen.

"Just not for a while," my father says, and his tone is serious. "You know, because of that . . . business."

Unlike the Grands, my father won't talk about the curse. He usually doesn't talk about gay stuff either, but apparently he's making an exception for this monumental news. Normally I would be embarrassed by it, but right now I think it's kind of nice. It took him a while to be okay with me being gay. Not that he thought there was anything *wrong* with it. At least I don't think so. It's just that he had never thought about it being a possibility.

A minute later, a car pulls in and Tom Swift gets out. I haven't talked to him since the movies two nights ago, and since my conversation with Linda, which is what I'm calling the girl on the phone until she tells me to call her something else. Now my stomach knots up a little as he walks toward me.

"Did you hear about the big gay wedding thing this weekend?" he says when he gets to the window. "We should go."

"Shouldn't you propose to me first?" I joke.

"How do you know that's not why I'm here?" says Tom, which makes me feel surprisingly embarrassed.

My father pokes his head out and says, "Hey, we should give

away free rainbow snow cones today." He notices Tom standing there, and waves. "Hey, Tom Swift. How's your triphibian atomicar?"

"Running great, Mr. Weyward," Tom answers.

"Sorry," I tell him. "I guess he's read those books too."

"It's okay," says Tom. "I like your dad. I wish mine was more like him."

I try to imagine what Tom Swift's father is like. If he's anything like Tom, I imagine he's not a laugh riot. Or maybe he just needs time to get used to living with Tom instead of Jennifer, the way my dad needed time to get used to gay me as opposed to not-gay me. Sometimes it takes a while for people to process new information.

"Speaking of cars," I say. "How did you get your grandparents to let you drive theirs?"

Tom Swift gets a funny look on his face. "That's what I came over to talk to you about," he says. "I need a favor."

"A loan-me-ten-bucks kind of favor, or a help-me-hide-the-body kind of favor?"

"Sort of in the middle," Tom says. "See, I told them that you and I are maybe, kind of, going out."

I laugh, but not for the reason Tom Swift probably thinks. "Really?" I say. "Why?"

"To make them think I'm straight," Tom explains. "I mean, I *am* straight. I like girls. But they don't get that. They still think of me as"—he lowers his voice to barely a whisper—"Jennifer. And they think she should date guys."

"But you look like a—like Tom," I say.

Tom nods. "I know. But it's how they think. I don't know, maybe they're so used to seeing me as her that they still see me that way through this haircut and clothes. Maybe they just want so badly for me to not be who I am that this is better than nothing. To be honest, I don't really care. It's just that the other night I said I was going to the movies with you, and they got super excited because they assumed I meant in a date kind of way. So I let them think that's what it was."

"Good thing they didn't decide to drop by," I remark, wondering what they would have done if they'd seen Tom with his arm around Anna-Lynn.

"They don't associate with townies," Tom says. "Unless they have to."

I hate that word, so I say, "Those wacky lakies."

Tom doesn't notice the sarcasm in my voice. He just says, "So as long as they think I'm going out to see you, I think they'll let me use the car."

"Even though I'm a townie?" I say, still annoyed.

"Yeah, but you're a *boy* townie," he says. "It gives them hope."

"I still don't see what the favor is," I say.

"Oh, right. Well, I need you to be my boyfriend for this barbecue they're having on July first. My parents are coming up for the Fourth of July weekend, and they get here that day. This is like the big kickoff."

I'm tempted to tell him that I have to work. But I don't. Even if I did, I could probably get Becky to switch with me. Still, I want to say no. But I don't know if it's because I'm uncomfortable helping him lie, or if it's because I won't really be his date. Besides, I want to see what his parents are like.

"Sure," I hear myself say. "I can do that."

Tom grins. "Awesome," he says. "Thank you. You're the best friend ever. Now I've got to go pick up Anna-Lynn. We're going tubing. I'll see you Wednesday."

"I'll be there," I tell him as he walks away. "Hey, do you want a rainbow snow cone? You know, to celebrate being just like everybody else now?" The words taste bitter to me, but he doesn't notice. He's too excited about seeing Anna-Lynn.

"No, thanks," he says. "See you."

"Yeah," I say. "See you."

When he's gone, I think about what I've just agreed to. I'm going to pretend to be going out with someone who is, as far as his parents and grandparents are concerned, a girl. And even though he looks and acts like a guy, and I'm a guy, they're not going to think of us as a gay couple because they so badly want him to be normal. Whatever normal means to them.

The irony is that if it was Jennifer who was going out with Anna-Lynn, it would be a gay thing. And if it was Tom going out with me, it would be a gay thing. But Tom going out with Anna-Lynn isn't. Or maybe it is. Maybe I don't know what it is. I guess it depends on your point of view.

I decide that this trans stuff is more complicated than it looks. It was easier when it was just Tom Swift is my friend, and Tom Swift is trans, and that's that. But now it's turned into something else because of some stupid pronouns.

An hour or so later, right after I've handed four orders of

hot dogs and cheese fries to a family with a *My Kid Can Beat Up Your Honor Student* sticker on their car, it begins to rain. Torrential rain, the kind of sudden summer shower that turns everything cold and makes people run inside. I wonder if Anna-Lynn and Tom Swift are caught in it, and can't help but feel a little bit of satisfaction at the thought.

The cheese-fries-and-hot-dogs-family retreat to their car, sitting inside with the windows rolled up. We won't have any customers until this is over, so my father comes into the front of the Eezy-Freezy and we sit at the little table in the corner. I pour us two Cokes, and we listen to the rain pound on the metal roof.

My father takes a deck of cards out of his apron pocket. "Want to play War?" he asks.

I shake my head. I'm not in the mood.

"Okay," he says. "Then how about I tell your fortune?"

Although my father isn't as into magical stuff as the Grands are, he's still a Weyward. Starletta says it's in our blood; it just doesn't always manifest in the same way in every person. But my father doesn't do this kind of thing very often.

"Isn't it risky?" I ask him. "You know, with my birthday coming up?"

He shrugs and starts shuffling the cards. "The thing about fortunes is, you can change them if you try hard enough."

"Tell that to Wild Ruckus, Sam Fender, and Ezra Brown-cow," I remind him.

"They didn't know about the curse," my father says. "Maybe if they did, they could have changed things."

I hesitate a moment before asking the obvious question. "Did my mother know about it?"

My father breaks the cards into three piles. "Pick one," he says, very obviously not answering me.

I tap the pile on the left. My father puts the middle pile on top of the right pile and sets them aside. Then he turns over the first seven cards from the pile I've chosen and lays them out in a row. He looks at them for a minute. The cards are the queen of spades, the seven of hearts, the ten of diamonds, the jack of hearts, the king of clubs, the eight of spades, and the jack of clubs.

I've never learned how to read cards, so I don't know what any of these mean. I wait as my father touches one (the seven of hearts) and then another (the king of clubs). Then his finger comes to rest on the queen of spades. He looks at her for a long time.

"Well?" I ask, impatient to know what my fortune is.

My father looks up. "You got a lot of court cards," he says. "Two jacks, a king, a queen. Those usually represent people."

"Okay, but who?"

"Could be anyone," he says. "Friends. Family. Anyone. It's these other cards that are interesting."

"Interesting is a scary word, Dad," I say. "Can you be more specific?"

"The ten of diamonds is about travel," he says. "So that's cool. Maybe there's a fun trip in your future."

He sounds overly enthusiastic, so I know something is

wrong. "What about these other ones?" I ask, touching the eight of spades and the seven of hearts.

"Well, the eight of spades is about disappointment," he said. "Like a friend letting you down. And the seven of hearts is kind of a more intense version of that one."

"Intense how?"

He scratches his ear, which is what he does when he doesn't know quite what to say, the way other people go "ummmm." When he's done scratching he says, "Like someone you love betraying you."

I point to the four court cards. "Which one of them am I going to betray? Or is one of them betraying me?"

All of a sudden, my father sweeps the cards up. "They're just cards," he says as he puts them back with the others. He shuffles them quickly, as if to hide them. But I've made a mental note of what was there. I plan on asking Starletta some questions later on.

The rain has stopped. My father stands up and goes to the window. "Hey, come look at this."

I go over and look outside. In the sky, one end of a rainbow disappears behind the trees across the road.

"Looks like the big guy upstairs is getting an early start on Pride weekend," my father says.

I groan at the remark, but actually, it's kind of cool.

My father starts to hum "Over the Rainbow." Then he starts to sing it. After the first few words, I join in.

Nine

Saturday night at the Shangri-La is Pride Night. The closest actual Pride parade is hours away, so for most of the people who come to the bar, this is the only celebration they get. And they're celebrating hard.

It kills me that I have to stay in the back. I can hear the music and the voices. I can feel the walls vibrating from the bass as Madonna's "Hung Up" thumps through the speakers, and I imagine everyone dancing and want to be in the middle of them.

Farrah, dressed in rainbow-sequined hot pants and a bikini top, bursts into the dressing room. Even his (*her*, I correct myself, since she's in character big time) platform shoes are rainbowed out in Pride stripes. But she still wears her trademark blond wig.

"Glitter!" she exclaims as she shakes her head and rainbow sparkles fall out. "There is glitter *everywhere*. That queen is simply out of control."

She means Lola, who tonight is dressed like Glinda the Good Witch of the North from *The Wizard of Oz*. She's running around blowing little handfuls of glitter at people while saying, "Come out! Come out! Wherever you are! Pride is here, and we're all stars!"

Farrah looks at me slumped in the chair in front of the makeup mirror, where I've been experimenting with a look, and frowns. "Gurl, you need to be out *there*," she says, nodding at the door.

I put down the eye shadow I've been playing with. "Well, you know I can't do that."

Farrah comes and stands behind me. She looks at my face in the mirror. Then she says, "You can't. But Kandy Korn can."

"Who?" I ask.

"Kandy Korn," Farrah repeats. "With a K on both ends. She's my little cousin, visiting for the weekend from Peoria." She picks up a brush and starts applying more makeup to my face. "Her mama told me to make sure she has a good time at Pride."

I catch her meaning. "Lola will kill us," I say.

"Lola is high on gay pride happiness," says Farrah. "And nobody else is going to recognize you by the time I'm done. Now just sit there and let me prettify you."

I do sit there. And she does prettify me. Within fifteen minutes, I don't recognize myself. Farrah has given me huge eyes, a thinner nose, and lips that somehow look as though I've had them plumped up. She finds a bright yellow wig and puts it on me. I don't look like a real woman, but I look fantastic.

"I went for fabulous," Farrah says. "Nobody will recognize you under all of that. Now, let's find you something to wear."

She decides on an orange jumpsuit to go with the yellow hair and overall candy corn theme. When I'm all pulled together, I look at myself in the mirror.

"I look like Ronald McDonald's drag queen sister," I say.

"Fast-food realness!" declares Farrah.

She takes me by the hand and leads me to the door. I hesitate as she opens it. I've never been out in drag before.

"Kandy Korn, you get your ass out there and join the party," Farrah says. "And don't you worry. Your big sister Farrah will be watching your back."

For the first time ever while the Shangri-La is open, I walk down the hallway to the main room. The music is deafening, and I don't have time to worry about anything before Farrah leads me right into the middle of the dance floor.

Instantly, people are looking at me. Besides Farrah, Paloma, and Lola, there are no other drag queens here, so a new face gets everyone's attention. I freeze, gripping Farrah's hand so tightly that I'm sure I'm breaking her fingers. She squeezes back. Then she leans over and whispers one word in my ear: "Dance."

And I do. Madonna has been replaced by Nick Jonas. I move my body to the music. Actually, I move Kandy's body, because I'm dancing in a way that Sam never would. It's as if I've been taken over by a different personality. Possessed. But in a good way. Not a head-spinning-around-and-hurling-green-slime way.

I dance to one song after another: Ariana Grande, Kylie Minogue, Scissor Sisters, Mika. When I finally slow down because I'm thirsty, I go to the bar. That's when I get nervous again. Toby, the bartender, has known me ever since I started coming to the Shangri-La. But when he smiles at me and asks me what I want to drink, I realize that he has no clue who I am underneath the makeup.

"Just a Coke," I tell him, my heart still thumping in my chest.

He pours a drink for me and slides it across the bar. That's when I realize that I don't have any money on me. I start to stammer an apology, but then I hear Kandy say, "I seem to have left my purse in the limo."

Toby laughs. "No worries," he tells me. "It's on the house. Happy Pride."

I feel Kandy smile and wink at him. "Aren't you a sweetheart," she says. "Happy Pride!"

I turn and walk away, sipping on my drink. Across the room, I see Farrah and Paloma watching me. Farrah says something to Paloma, and Paloma's hand goes to her mouth. Then she gives me a big thumbs-up. I blow them both a kiss, which makes them laugh hysterically.

I dance for the rest of the night, sometimes by myself and sometimes with other people. It turns out Kandy is good at making friends. She's also a big flirt, and more than one guy gives her a kiss on the cheek after she tells him how cute he is. I can't believe how easy it is being her, how unafraid I feel, and how free.

Then the DJ plays an old song, Sister Sledge's "We Are Family." I'm surprised, because this means it's already two o'clock in the morning. Closing time. It's the song we always play to let everyone know that this is it—one last dance, one last chance to talk to the guy you've been checking out all night. I can't believe I've danced for so long. I'm disappointed, because this means it's over.

But I'm also deliriously happy. Then Paloma and Farrah are with me. Each of them takes one of my hands, and we're dancing together, singing along with the words of the song. "I've got all my sisters with me!" I shout in unison with them. Around us, everyone joins in.

When the song ends, my friends lead me back to the dressing room. I feel like I could keep dancing all night, but it's way past my curfew, and I have to get home. Just like Cinderella, my time at the ball is over, and I have to turn back into a pumpkin.

"Gurl, you were *fierce*," Paloma tells me as I start removing Kandy's face from my own.

"It was all Farrah's doing," I tell her.

Farrah shakes her head. "Uh-uh," she says. "I just did the painting. You brought her to life."

"So, is this the new you?" a voice asks.

I turn to see Lola standing in the doorway. My heart sinks.

"I should tell you to get out and not come back until you're twenty-one," she says. "You know damn well I could lose my license for letting you be out there."

"It was all my idea," Farrah says.

"I said I *should* tell you to get out," Lola continues, ignoring her. "But I'm not. Today's a special day. Besides, no one out there knew who the hell you were."

Farrah and I high-five.

"Don't push it," Lola says. "Do it again and I *will* eighty-six you."

I'm already super late getting home, so I don't rush getting out of drag. At one point, when I have one half of my face cleaned off and the other still made up as Kandy, I sit and look at my reflection in the mirror. My familiar Sam half looks happy but tired. My Kandy side looks ready to keep on going.

"You going to keep her around?" Paloma asks me.

I tilt my head, looking at what remains of Kandy. "I don't think she's *quite* who I am," I tell Paloma. "I'm really glad she came to visit, though."

"I went through a bunch of different faces before I found the right one," Paloma says. "You'll find the one that fits soon enough."

"There's nothing wrong with being Princess Langwidere," Lola says.

"Princes Whatsis?" says Paloma.

"Langwidere," Lola repeats. "From the book *Ozma of Oz*. She had a collection of heads, and would wear different ones depending on her mood."

"Well, you should know all about Oz, Glinda," Farrah jokes.

"Just because *you* don't read," Lola says. "Doesn't mean the rest of us don't."

"Oh, I read, all right," Farrah shoots back. "I'll read that pink-prom-dress good-witch drag of yours right now if you're not careful."

"Begone," Lola says, flicking her wand at Farrah. "Before

82

somebody drops a house on you."

"It would be nice to have different heads," I say. "I like that idea. I could be somebody else every day."

I remove the rest of Kandy's face, then step out of the jumpsuit and put my own clothes back on. My jeans and T-shirt feel both familiar and like they belong to somebody else. It's as if I've just shed a skin.

"All this talk about the big gay wedding this weekend," Farrah says as she undresses. "Got me thinking. Which of us is going to get married first?"

"I need to get a boyfriend before I can get a husband," Paloma says.

"What about you, Lola?" Farrah asks. "Think anyone will make you an honest woman?"

"Not in this lifetime," she answers. "You're the one with all the men."

"That's right," Farrah says. "And I'm having too much fun being a single lady to settle down with just one."

"Looks like it's up to you, Sammy," Paloma tells me. "You got anyone special in your life yet?"

I think about Tom Swift. "No," I reply.

"Not likely you'll find one hanging around this little town," Farrah says. "You need to get yourself someplace big. New York, maybe, or San Francisco."

"Right now where I need to get is home," I say. I hug Farrah. "Thank you," I tell her.

"Anytime, baby," she says.

I hug Paloma and Lola as well, wish everyone a happy Pride

one more time, then head out to my truck. There are a lot of people still hanging around, not wanting the night to end. I can feel their elation like an electric buzz, and it makes me excited to be part of something like what's happening this weekend. I think about the same thing happening in bars all across the country, in backyards and big city streets. Everywhere, people are celebrating being who we are.

When I get home at a little after three in the morning, the Grands are sitting the kitchen, playing cards. When I come in, Hank raises an eyebrow, but doesn't ask where I've been. I don't offer an explanation. Instead, looking at the cards, I ask a question.

"What do the king, queen, and jack cards mean in a reading?"

Hank's eyebrow goes up again. "Been doing readings for someone?" she asks.

"Just curious," I say. I sit down at the table across from her. Clodine and Starletta are on the other two sides. They set their cards down.

"Depends on the suit," Starletta says.

I try to remember my father's reading from yesterday. "Let's say the jack of hearts," I say.

"Young man," Starletta says. "Or girl, since there's only the one jack in a suit. Usually a good friend. Hearts are about emotional relationships. Love. So could be someone the person you're reading for is in love with."

"Or wants to be in love with," Clodine adds.

"And the jack of clubs?"

"Also a friend," Hank explains. "But you can't trust him. Or if it's you, you can't be trusted."

I'm not sure I want to know any more, but I've already started, so I keep going. "King of clubs?"

"A good man," Clodine says. "Someone like Wild Ruckus."

"Or your father," Hank says. She looks at me. "Who's next?"

"Queen of spades," I tell her.

All three of them kind of suck in their breath.

"She's a tough one," Hank says.

"Bad?" I ask.

"Not so much bad as troublesome," says Clodine. "Unpredictable. She can go either way, depending on how you approach her."

I don't entirely understand. I need an example. "Okay, so if Wild Ruckus is the king of clubs, who would be the queen of spades?"

Starletta looks at Clodine, then says, "Livvie Comstock."

I hear myself gasp. I can't believe my great-grandmother has said that name. Livvie Comstock. Former best friend of my great-great-great-grandmother Viola Weyward.

The woman responsible for the Weyward Curse.

Ten

When Tom Swift's father shakes my hand, I think for a moment that he might be trying to break it. He crushes my fingers as he pumps my arm and says, "Jennifer has told us a lot about you."

I wish I knew what Tom has told them. I haven't seen him yet. His grandmother answered the door when I knocked, and she barely said a word to me as she led me into the backyard. Now I'm standing in front of the whole family and wondering what I've gotten myself into.

"Jennifer says your father owns an ice-cream stand," Mr. McCracken says. He makes it sound like my dad sits on a corner peddling Popsicles, like those kids who set up card tables and sell lemonade in paper cups for a quarter.

"Actually, we sell all kinds of food," I say. I'm trying not to be defensive, but I already don't like this man. He looks at me as if he's sizing me up. Which he is.

Mr. McCracken is wearing blue shorts and a tucked-in white polo shirt with the buttons all done up. He also has on boat shoes without socks, and I notice that the hair on his legs ends about six inches above his ankles, as if it's been worn away from years of wearing socks that are too tight. His skin is all the same pale white, so where the hair stops it looks like a tree line on a snowy hillside.

"It must be nice living out here in the country," Mrs. McCracken says. She's small and thin and jittery, like a worried bird. Her hair is blond, but I can tell from the grown-out roots that her natural color is dark brown. She's wearing a sundress with yellow flowers on it, and her eyes are the same color as Tom's.

"It would make me nuts," Tom's father says before I can answer. "Too quiet. I bet you can't wait to get to a city when you graduate."

I can see Mrs. McCracken's smile falter for a moment, and I wait to see if she'll contradict her husband. She doesn't. I can tell she's had a lot of practice not saying what she's thinking.

"It might be interesting to live somewhere bigger," I say. "New York could be fun."

"Too many weirdos there," Mr. McCracken informs me.

Clearly, this is a trap. I get the feeling that no matter what I say, it will be the wrong thing. Tom's father is looking at me with a smug expression, as if he's just won a point in a tennis match.

"Would you like a soda?" Tom's mother says, throwing me a lifeline. "They're in the refrigerator. In the kitchen," she adds, as if I might not know where people keep their fridges. Because I'm a country bumpkin and all. She probably thinks we have an outhouse.

"Thanks," I say, and retreat into the house.

As I'm looking in the refrigerator and trying to decide between ginger ale and root beer, Tom comes in.

"Wow," I say when I get a look at him.

"Too much?" he asks.

He's wearing makeup. A lot of makeup. He has a ton of blue eye shadow on, some horrible bright pink lipstick, and two blotches of blush on his cheeks. He's tried to use eyeliner, but it looks more like the eye black that football players put on to help with sun glare.

"Wow," I say again.

He groans. "I tried to copy a picture in a magazine," he tells me. "But I don't know how to do this. I look like a clown, don't I?"

"Come on," I say, taking his hand. "We can fix it. Where's your room?"

He leads me down the hallway and into a tiny bedroom. The striped Hudson's Bay point blanket on the twin bed is covered with discarded makeup packaging, and a copy of a magazine is lying open to a picture of a girl whose face looks absolutely nothing like Tom Swift's.

"It's so hard," Tom moans.

I start by removing what he's already glopped onto his face. Of course he doesn't have anything like cold cream, so I have to use plain old soap and water from the bathroom. The washcloth looks like a paint rag when I'm done.

"Now hold still," I tell him as I apply just a little bit of brownish-gold eye shadow. I follow it with a nude lipstick I find among the pile on the bed, then add a hint of blush. A thin line of eyeliner on the lower lid finishes the job. When I'm done, I sit back and look at him.

"How do I look?" he asks.

"Hunky-dory," I say.

He laughs. "You sound like my grandmother," he teases.

"No," I say. "You look like David Bowie on the *Hunky Dory* album cover. It's number six on Ilona's list."

What I don't say is that I have a massive crush on *Hunky Dory* David Bowie. Not only is the music on the album unlike anything else that had come out before it, Bowie is absolutely gorgeous. He has this androgynous look that's part alien and part angel. The first time I took the album out of the box, I sat and stared at it for probably an hour before I even put the record on the turntable. Once I actually heard him sing, I fell in love.

And Tom Swift looks an awful lot like him right now.

"So I look like a guy?" Tom Swift says.

I shake my head. "You look great," I say. "I'll show you the album later. Go take a look in the mirror."

He gets up and goes into the bathroom. When he comes back a minute later, he's smiling. "How did you do this?" he asks.

"I'm a fairy godmother," I say. I point the eyeliner pencil at him like it's a wand and shake it. "But it wears off at midnight."

"We should get back out there," Tom says. "My father will wonder what we're doing in here."

"I don't think he likes me," I inform Tom as we walk down the hallway.

"He doesn't like anybody," Tom says. "I don't think he even likes himself."

When we open the door and step into the backyard, everyone turns to look at us. Actually, they all look at Tom Swift. I glance over at his father to see if I can tell what he thinks of Tom's new look, but I can't really read his expression. Tom's mother, though, is all smiles. She comes over and touches Tom's face.

"You look beautiful," she says. "I told you if you only tried a little makeup you would like it. Now you just have to grow your hair out." She looks at me. "Wouldn't she be gorgeous with long hair?"

"I think she's gorgeous now," I say. I feel horrible using *she*, but I can't think of any way around it. I take Tom Swift's hand and squeeze it so that he knows I'm sorry.

"And it's so well done," his mother remarks. She bends in close and stares at Tom's eyes. "You must have been practicing. I still can't get my eyeliner on that nicely, and I've been doing it for years."

Tom shrugs. "It's not that hard," he says, and I try not to laugh.

"Well, you'll have to show me your tricks later," his mother says.

Then the focus shifts to eating. Normally, this would be great. But Mr. McCracken puts himself in charge of the grill, which isn't a surprise. He cooks everything until it's either completely black (he calls this "charbroiled") or so chewy it's like trying to eat a shoe (he calls this "well-done"). Everyone pretends to love it, and maybe they do. I eat one chicken leg and part of a hamburger, wishing it was my father doing the cooking instead of Tom's. When no one is looking, I toss the rest of the hamburger into some bushes and hope it won't make whatever raccoon finds it and eats it sick.

As soon as we're done eating, Tom's father says, "Let's go swimming." It's like there's a schedule that only he knows about, and it's his job to keep us on it.

"Aren't we supposed to wait an hour?" Tom says. He sounds nervous, and I don't know why. I know he loves to swim. "Besides, Sam doesn't have a suit."

Mr. McCracken looks at me. "He can swim in his shorts."

I don't like him telling me what I can do, so I probably sound a little smart-assy when I say, "Actually, I have a swimsuit in my truck. In case of emergencies." He doesn't say anything, though, so maybe my sarcasm isn't as obvious as I think it is.

"Thanks a lot," Tom says under his breath. At first I think he's angry with his father. But then I realize that he's kind of glaring at me.

"Sorry," I whisper. I assume he's upset that I was mouthy to his dad. But before I can say anything else, he gets up and walks into the house.

I go to my truck and retrieve my suit, which is under the seat. It's kind of sandy from the last time I wore it, but I shake it out and it's fine. I think about going inside to change, but I'm still a little annoyed at Mr. McCracken, so I just change behind the open door of the truck. It takes all of ten seconds anyway. I just slip off my shorts and boxers and pull the bathing suit on. Then I go back through the house and into the backyard.

I can see everyone else already down on the beach. Everyone except Tom. I walk to where Mrs. McCracken is spreading out a towel to sit on. Tom's grandparents are in lawn chairs in the shade, and his father is waist-deep in the water. He's taken off his shirt, and is standing with his hands on his hips, looking out across the lake like he's scouting for pirates.

I go down to the water and wade in. It's cold, but it feels good because the air is so hot. I stand in the shallows and watch the water striders skimming the surface around me. Farther out, a bigger fish leaps up and then splashes back into the lake. This makes me happy for some reason, and I take a breath and dive too. The water closes over my head, and everything is golden-brown as I kick and glide farther out.

I swim until my breath runs out, then surface and shake the water out of my eyes. I turn and look back, and see that Tom Swift is standing on the shore. He's wearing an oversized T-shirt that comes down practically to his knees. Mr. McCracken is saying something to him and motioning with his hands. I tread water, watching him and listening to his father tell him to take the T-shirt off and get in the water, and I get a bad feeling.

Tom shakes his head. His mother says something that I can't hear, and Tom turns around. He pulls the T-shirt over his head and tosses it at his mother. She doesn't catch it, and it lands in the sand.

Underneath the shirt, he's wearing a brightly flowered bikini. He turns around, his arms crossed over his chest. He doesn't look my way as he stomps into the lake, his arms remaining where they are. He doesn't uncross them until the water is up to his neck. Then he swims toward me. As he passes his father, he kicks particularly hard, splashing him.

When he reaches me, he says, "I hate him. I really, really hate him."

I'm not sure what to say. The water has washed away most of the makeup from his face, but the eyeliner is running down his cheeks like black tears. Or maybe they are tears. It's hard to tell. Either way, I feel horrible. And now I know why he was mad at me for the whole swimsuit thing.

"Come here," I say. I reach for his hand and pull him to me. I put my arms around his waist and hold him. We're both treading water, so it's difficult. Our bodies keep rubbing up against each other in this awkward way, and our legs get tangled up. He puts his arms around my back.

"You look great," I tell him.

"Hunky-dory?" he says.

"Hunky-dory," I say.

Before I know what I'm doing, I lean forward and kiss him on the mouth. I guess I take him by surprise, because he sort of gasps.

And then I realize two things at once. First, Tom Swift has

breasts, and they're pressing against my chest. Second, I have a hard-on. I alternate between wondering why I never noticed his breasts before and being horrified that my dick is touching him. I know I should let go of him, but I can't. It's like my brain has locked up and won't go into gear.

"I'll race you back to shore," Tom says, pushing away from me. But it's a gentle push, not a get-away-from-me-you-perv kind. And then he's swimming.

I bob up and down for a minute, waiting for my hard-on to go away. It doesn't. The signals flashing between it and my brain are lighting up like some haywire traffic light: stop, go, slow down. I'm not sure what's happening, or how to control it. So I just float there and watch Tom Swift getting farther and farther away from me.

Eleven

On Thursday afternoon, Tom Swift calls and asks if I can drive him to Utica. "I'd go myself," he says. "But my grandfather would notice if I put that many miles on the car. He keeps track of stuff like that. He has a little notebook and everything."

"What do you need in Utica?" I ask. The city is over an hour away, and the only reason we ever go there is to catch a Comets game at the Aud a couple of times a year. Other than that, it's pretty much like any other small city.

"It's a secret mission," he says.

Of course I say I'll be right there. I mean, who can resist a secret mission? Besides, I want to see him. Although we haven't talked about it at all, I haven't stopped thinking about our kiss from the day before.

When I get to his grandparents' cabin, he's waiting out front. He's dressed in shorts and a girly top, and I can tell he's tried to put his own makeup on again. It's not as horrible as the last time, but it's not great either. He's also carrying a big purse, which hangs from his crooked arm like a slaughtered chicken.

As he walks to the truck, I see his father watching us from behind the screen door. I wave, but he doesn't wave back. When Tom gets in, he leans over and kisses me on the cheek.

"Hi, honey," he says.

"Hey, pumpkin," I say back.

I feel like we're in the world's worst school play, and that our audience is Mr. McCracken. I know he probably can't hear us, but I say, "You look pretty today."

"Bite me," Tom Swift says as he turns and waves at his father. "I look like a two-dollar hooker."

"No you don't," I tell him as we pull away. "I'd pay at least three dollars."

As soon as we're out of sight of the cabin, Tom Swift opens the purse and pulls out a T-shirt and a handful of little packaged wet wipes. He tears one open and starts cleaning the makeup off his face using the rearview mirror to make sure he's getting it all. When he looks like himself again, he pulls the shirt he's wearing over his head. That's when I notice that he's wearing what looks like a really tight white tank top underneath.

"It's called a binder," he says when he catches me looking. "It makes my chest flatter."

Now I understand why I'd never noticed his breasts until yesterday.

"I'm not very big anyway, thank God," he says as he puts the other T-shirt on. This one has a *Doctor Who* theme, showing the faces of all the different Doctors. "But this pretty much makes them go away. The only thing is, I have to wear extra-big shirts so my parents don't notice."

"Who's your favorite Doctor?" I ask him.

"Eleven," he answers. "You?"

"I'm old-school," I say. "I like Four. Probably because he's the one my dad first introduced me to."

"I haven't watched a lot of the old ones," Tom says as he combs his hair into place. "I used to call myself the Boy Who Waited, after the episode where Amy Pond waits for the Doctor to come back for her. I thought maybe that would happen to me, that someday someone would show up and take me on adventures in space."

"I used to hope my closet would turn into a doorway to someplace else," I tell him. "Like in the Narnia books. I'd open the door, close my eyes, and walk in with my hands stretched out. I always hoped I'd touch tree branches, but it was always just the wall."

"There aren't enough magic doors in the world," Tom Swift says as he puts the comb away and closes the purse.

"Speaking of adventures," I say. "Want to tell me where we're going?"

He takes out a piece of paper. "I wrote down the directions," he says. "It's a Popeyes on Genesee Street."

"We're driving to Utica for fried chicken?" I say.

"No," he answers. "We're meeting someone there."

"The Magic 8-Ball says, 'Reply hazy, try again,'" I joke.

"We're meeting a guy," he says, which is not all that helpful in clarifying things.

"A friend of yours?" I ask.

"Kind of," he says. "I know him from online."

"Okay," I say. "That sounds legit, and not at all like a good way to end up part of a missing persons story on the nightly news or anything."

Tom Swift laughs, but he sounds uncomfortable. "He's another trans guy," he says. "I know him from this online group. He's going to help me with something."

I decide not to press him for more details. This is obviously important to him, and I figure that nothing too awful can happen in the middle of the afternoon at a fast-food restaurant, except possibly a spike in our cholesterol levels. So I just drive. We talk some more about *Doctor Who*, and everything feels normal and relaxed. Then we get to Utica, and Tom Swift starts acting edgy again. His leg is bouncing up and down, and he keeps checking the directions. When we pull into the Popeyes parking lot, he's so wound up I think he might explode through the roof of the truck, like a fighter pilot ejecting from his plane.

I start to get out of the truck, but Tom swift says, "Do you mind waiting here? I told Jack I was coming alone."

"No problem," I tell him.

"Thanks," he says. "I won't be long."

I watch as he crosses the parking lot and goes into the restaurant. There's a sun glare on the windows, and I can't see inside, so I sit there wondering what Jack is like, and what the two of them are doing. I'm a little annoyed that Tom Swift hasn't told me the whole story, and is kind of treating me like a taxi driver. I figure he has his reasons, and I try not to let it bug me, but it does.

Fifteen minutes later, the restaurant door opens and Tom Swift walks out with a guy I assume is Jack. He's short and muscly, and his arms and legs are covered in tattoos. He's wearing sunglasses, and his dark hair is spiky. At the end of the walkway, he and Tom Swift shake hands. Jack says something that makes Tom Swift laugh. Then Jack walks to a black Jeep and gets in, while Tom comes over to the truck.

"I didn't know if you would want spicy or regular, so I got some of each," he says as he gets in holding a bag. He's also holding a smaller plain brown paper bag, which he tucks into the purse on the floor. "And I got you a sweet tea. I hope that's okay."

"Perfect," I tell him as he opens the bag and takes out a box of chicken.

I wait for him to tell me what's in the other bag, but he doesn't. So we sit in the truck and eat fried chicken and drink sweet tea. When we're done, we use some of Tom Swift's wet wipes to clean our fingers.

"I think *moist towelette* is probably the most disgusting term in the English language," he jokes as he collects our trash into one bag. "I'll go throw this away."

As he walks across the lot to a trash can, I think about sticking my hand into the purse and seeing what's in the bag, but I don't. It's none of my business. But it bugs me that he won't tell me, and even more that I care that he won't tell me. I think about the way he and Jack said goodbye like they're best buddies, and that makes me mad too.

Tom comes back and gets in.

"Any more secret missions?" I ask him. "Maybe a back-alley nuclear arms trade? Or stopping somewhere to sell stolen credit cards to a guy named Big Louie?"

"Not today," he says. "We can just go back to the Batcave. Which in this case means your house, if that's okay."

I start the truck without answering him. The drive back is kind of awful, because there's a lot I'm thinking about and a lot I want to say, but I don't, so I just sit and listen to Tom Swift talk about everything except what we just did. He mostly talks about Doctor Who, and I nod and agree every so often so he thinks we're having a conversation. But really what we're doing is *not* having a conversation, and an hour later when we get to my house, I'm tired of the whole thing and want to be alone.

Instead, we go up to my room. Tom Swift brings his purse with him and sets it on my bed. I get the *Hunky Dory* album and put the record on, then show him the cover, because I said I would and because I don't know what else to do right now.

"You think I look like this?" he asks me as he stares at David Bowie's face.

"Don't you?" I say.

He looks at the cover some more. "I don't know," he says. "I have this idea in my head of what I *want* to look like. Then I catch a glimpse of myself in a mirror, or in a window, and I don't look anything like that. It makes me depressed, so mostly I just don't look in mirrors and windows if I can help it. Anything reflective, really. Tinfoil. Cookie sheets. Car bumpers." He laughs, but I don't join in the joke. What he's saying makes me sad.

He hands me the record jacket, and I put it back in the cardboard box. I sit and listen to the first track, "Changes," while Tom Swift roots around in the purse. Appropriately, the song's lyrics are all about becoming someone, or something, different. I don't point this out to Tom Swift.

Ilona's note about *Hunky Dory* is written on the album sleeve. All it says is, "This record blew my mind. I think it was written by aliens. Don't listen to it—experience it." She underlined *experience* three times. The alien thing is a reference to David Bowie's Ziggy Stardust character, who was supposedly a Martian who became a rock star. But it's also totally accurate. The songs on the album are really weird, and you can't just listen to them and try to figure out what they mean, because most of them don't make a lot of sense. You have to just go with it and not think about it too much. I usually listen to the record with my headphones on and the lights off, and pretend I'm floating around in space while the aliens sing to me.

I wish I could share that experience with Tom Swift, but he's busy, and I can tell he's not listening to the music at all. He's taken the brown paper bag out of the purse, and now he's opening it. When he takes out a small glass bottle and a couple of hypodermic needles, I stop listening to the music too.

"Hold on," I say. "Did we just make a drug run?"

Tom shakes his head. "Not drugs," he says. "T."

I don't know what this means, so I keep staring at the needles in his hand.

"Testosterone," he says. "Male hormones. I decided to start taking them."

Now it makes sense. I've read a little about this. "Don't you need to get a doctor's prescription for that?" I ask.

"You're supposed to," Tom says. "But I would need my parents' permission to do that, and there's no way they would say yes. So I found another way to get it."

"Okay," I say. "But how do you know it's safe?"

"I've read a ton about it," he tells me. "And I've talked to a bunch of other trans guys about it."

"Like Jack," I say.

He nods. "Him and some other guys," he says. "They've all taken it and been fine."

He uncaps one of the needles and pokes it into the top of the bottle, drawing some liquid into the syringe. He taps it, then pushes the plunger until a little bit of the fluid comes out.

"I watched the video on how to do this like a thousand times," he tells me. "I can't believe I'm actually about to do it."

He stands up and undoes his belt, pulling his shorts down. He's wearing white briefs, and I try not to look. I'm not sure what's going on right now. "I need to inject it in my thigh," Tom says, poking around his leg. "It has to go into the muscle."

He finds a spot. He cleans it off with one of the wet wipes, then holds the needle over it. "Here goes nothing," he says, and jabs himself.

I cringe watching the needle sink into his leg. It's all happening so quickly that I'm still kind of in shock. Tom pushes the plunger down, emptying the T into his body, then removes the needle.

"That wasn't so bad," he says. Then he laughs. "I wonder how long before my superpowers kick in."

"What's going to happen?" I ask him as he caps the needle and puts everything back into the paper bag.

"Nothing for a while," he says. "But eventually my voice will deepen, my muscles will get thicker, and I'll start getting hair in all the right places."

"And what happens when your parents notice?" I ask.

He shrugs. "By then it will be too late," he says. "They'll have to deal with it."

This sounds like a shaky plan, but I don't say that. He seems so excited about taking this step. I don't want to ruin it for him. But secretly I'm thinking that maybe he hasn't thought this out as well as he could have.

"Thanks for taking me," he says. "And sorry for not telling you what it was all about. I was a little afraid you might try to talk me out of it."

"It's okay," I lie. It's not okay at all.

"Can I ask you for one more favor?" he says. "Can I keep this stuff here?" He holds up the paper bag. "I don't really have anywhere to hide it."

"How often do you have to take it?" I ask him.

"Every week or so," he says. "I have enough to get me through the rest of the summer."

I don't want to keep his T for him. I especially don't want to keep the needles for him. If anyone finds them, I'll have a lot of explaining to do. But part of me is really happy that he's asked me to help him. It's like we share this huge secret. And as much as I know that's a little fucked-up, I also like it. It makes me feel closer to him than anyone else is.

And so I say yes.

Twelve

Starletta doesn't come with us to watch the fireworks on the Fourth. Not because it reminds her of how she lost Sam, which she's had a long time to get over, but because she doesn't like the noise. We used to leave her and Millard Fillmore at home, because he was afraid of the explosions and needed someone to tell him everything was all right, but since he went deaf a couple of years ago, that hasn't been a problem. Now he sits on Clodine's lap and enjoys the show along with everyone else.

My father closes the Eezy-Freezy early on the Fourth. Everybody knows this, and they want treats to eat while they watch the show, so there's a huge rush in the hour before it gets dark. Becky and I are both working, and we're slammed from about seven o'clock on. When we finally turn the sign in the window to Closed at 8:00, we're exhausted. But we only have an hour before the show starts, so my dad and I rush home to pick up Hank, Clodine, and Millard Fillmore, then drive to the beach.

The volunteer fire department is in charge of the show, and they set the fireworks off from a floating dock in the middle of the lake. This not only makes it less likely that sparks will light something on fire, it means the explosions are reflected in the water, which is really pretty. When we get to the public beach, the shore is lined with lawn chairs, and people are standing around waiting for things to get going. Probably half of them are eating sundaes, cones, or milkshakes that I made for them.

As I help my father carry our chairs to a clear part of the beach, I notice Tom Swift and Anna-Lynn sitting on a blanket together. I'm surprised, because earlier in the day Tom told me that his parents were making him stay at home with them to watch the fireworks from their own beach. When Anna-Lynn sees me, she waves. That makes Tom turn and see me too. He gets up and runs over.

"Hey," he says.

"Hey," I say back.

Tom looks over at Anna-Lynn, who is busy rooting around in a cooler for something. "I, uh, told my parents I was hanging out with you for a little while," he tells me. "That's okay, right? Anna-Lynn called and asked me to meet her here. I texted you, but you didn't answer."

It's not all right. Not at all. Once again, he's using me as a cover for spending time with Anna-Lynn. And I haven't gotten any message from him that I know of. Still, I hear myself say, "Yeah, that's cool. Wait. When did you get a phone?"

He grins. "I picked up a burner phone," he says. "I feel like a spy. Hey, do you have the day off tomorrow?"

I nod. Then I wait for him to ask me if he can tell his parents we're doing something so that he and Anna-Lynn can hang out. If he does, I'm going to tell him no.

I'm already telling him no in my head when he says, "Let's do something, then. How about mini golf? I haven't been there yet."

"Okay," I agree. Suddenly, I'm not so angry.

"Great," he says. "I'll text you in the morning."

He punches me lightly on the arm, then trots back to the blanket and Anna-Lynn. I walk over to where my father has set up the chairs, and I unfold the two I'm carrying. My father sits in one, and I take the other. I take my phone out and look at it. Sure enough, there's a text from Tom Swift. In the rush at the Eezy-Freezy, I must have missed it.

"Tom Swift and Anna-Lynn?" my father says.

"Yep," I say.

He looks at them for long enough that I start to worry they'll feel his eyes on them. Then he says, "Huh."

"Huh what?" I ask him.

"Nothing," he says. "It's just that I thought you and he might be—"

"He likes girls," I tell him before he can finish that sentence.

"Huh," my father says again. "My gaydar is totally off."

"Did you just say *gaydar?*"

"Shit," he says. "Is that homophobic? Like ladyboy and tranny? Sorry. I didn't know it was on the list."

"What?" I say. "Where did you even hear any of these words?"

"I didn't know!" my father says again.

"Is he all right?" Hank, who is sitting on my other side, asks me. "He sounds upset."

"He's fine," I assure her. "I think."

I turn back to my father. "No, *gaydar* is not offensive," I tell him. "Relax. I was just surprised to hear you say it is all."

He breathes a sigh of relief. "I'm kind of hip, you know," he informs me.

"Okay, stop," I tell him. "And back to the original point, yes, Tom and Anna-Lynn are a thing."

"Huh," he says.

Thankfully, it's now dark and the fireworks are starting. A shell launches from the dock, shooting straight up into the sky, where it explodes in a cloud of gold stars. There are some *ooh*s and *aah*s from the crowd. These become more frequent and more enthusiastic over the next half an hour, as the fireworks become more elaborate.

I don't really notice the fireworks, though, because I can't stop staring at Tom Swift and Anna-Lynn. Every time there's an explosion, the light illuminates them. At first, they're just sitting next to each other. But after the fourth or fifth rocket goes off, they're kissing. I see them as the red, white, and blue stars fall out of the sky. I see them as the silver-and-red spinners twist and twirl over our heads. I see them as our school colors—blue and gold—swoop in comets over the water.

In between explosions, it's dark, and I can't see them. I find myself holding my breath and hoping that when the next burst comes, they'll have stopped. But of course they keep going at it. By the time the big finale comes, I'm so annoyed that I sort of wish sparks will fall into Anna-Lynn's hair and set it on fire. I know that's maybe not the most mature way to deal with what I'm feeling, but you can't always tell your heart what to do.

When the show is over, I can't get up quickly enough. I'm in such a hurry to get back to the truck before I have to talk to Tom Swift or Anna-Lynn that I practically drag Hank and Clodine down the beach. I toss our stuff in the back of the Ford while everybody crams into the cab, then pull into the line of cars trying to get out.

While we're sitting there, Tom Swift appears in the window next to me. Anna-Lynn is with him. I glance down and see that they're holding hands.

"Wasn't that a great show?" Anna-Lynn says.

"Wonderful," Hank says when I don't answer. She leans over me and pokes her head out. "The best ever. If I die tonight, I'll die happy. By the way, tell your mother I'll bring her the recipe for the Devil's Cherry Basket later this week. She asked for it at the church potluck."

Hank pulls her head back in, and I mumble a goodbye as I hit the gas.

"You owe me," Hanks says. "Jenna Burling has been after that recipe for years. And her mother and grandmother before her."

"Please," I say. "All it is is an upside-down yellow bundt cake with a can of cherry pie filling and whipped cream you dye pink with the cherry juice poured into the center. I don't even know why you call it the Devil's Cherry Basket anyway."

"Because of the rum," Hank tells me. "You soak the cake in it."

"That's why the Baptists like it so much," Clodine says. "Reverend Wittlethumb can't get enough of it."

"And you're welcome," Hank says, patting my leg. "A secret family recipe is a small price to pay for you not having to look a fool."

I kind of grunt a thank-you at her. I'm still pissed at Tom Swift, although I'm also a little excited that we're going to play mini golf tomorrow. Then I wonder if he's going to bring Anna-Lynn along. That would probably push me over the edge. So now I'm mad again, even though none of this has actually happened.

When we get home, Starletta is standing in the yard holding a sparkler and writing her name in the air with it. It leaves behind a trail of tiny silver stars. We pile out of the truck, and she hands my father the box with the rest of the sparklers in it. He gives one to each of us, but I'm not really in the mood, so I go inside and up to my room.

From my window, I can see my father and the Grands in the yard. They're waving their sparklers around and laughing. Right then I love them more than anything. But I'm still angry about the whole Tom Swift situation, so I can't bring myself to have fun. All I can do is watch for a while, until eventually they run out of sparklers and come inside.

I decide to try and calm down by listening to record number seven from Ilona's collection. It's the Rolling Stones' *Sticky Fingers*. It's one of my absolute favorites, starting with the cover, which features an actual working zipper on the model's skintight jeans. When you unzip it, there's a picture of a guy in tightywhiteys. And let's just say that he's, um, packing some major pant sausage.

The note tucked inside the record sleeve is written on the back of a concert ticket from a Stones show on September 27, 1994, at the Liberty Bowl in Memphis, Tennessee. Ilona wrote:

> You haven't lived until you've heard the Stones do 'Brown Sugar' live. This is what sex sounds like. I hope you get to see them someday.

As I haven't had sex yet, I don't know if this is true or not. But I kind of suspect it is. The music on *Sticky Fingers* is dirty, hot, and raw. Even the slow songs. It gets into your brain and into your blood, and every time I listen to it, I end up thinking about what it would be like to kiss Mick Jagger.

Only this time I start thinking about what it would be like to kiss Tom Swift. Not the kind of kiss we had in the lake, but the kind where tongues are involved and we have to come up for air. I think about his hands touching me, and mine touching him. And then my hand is slipping into my boxers and I'm hard and I'm wrapping my fingers around myself while Mick asks me over and over if I can hear him knocking.

It doesn't take long before I'm having my very own fireworks show behind my eyes. When it's over, I use my T-shirt to clean up, then get up to turn the record off. I lie down on the bed and try to decide what I'm feeling about Tom Swift. A bunch of conflicting thoughts are bouncing around in my head.

I can't get them to quiet down enough to really think about them, so I decide to distract myself. I pick up the phone and dial. This time when Linda answers, I'm not even surprised.

"Sorry it's been a while," I tell her.

"Has it?" she says. "I thought we just talked yesterday, or maybe the day before."

"It's been something like ten or eleven days," I tell her.

"That long?" she says, but she doesn't sound upset or shocked or anything. "I guess the days all kind of run into one another."

"Did you do anything for the Fourth?" I ask her.

"The fourth what?" she replies.

"Of July," I say. "You know, Independence Day? The birthday of the U.S. of A.?"

"Oh," she says. "No, I didn't do anything. Did you?"

I tell her about the fireworks on the lake, and about Tom Swift and Anna-Lynn.

"I know I shouldn't be so into him," I tell her. "I know he doesn't like guys. But I can't help it. There's just something about him."

"Feelings don't always make sense," she says. "If they did, nobody would fall in love with the wrong people."

"Have you ever been in love?" I ask.

She's quiet for a long time before she answers. "Once," is all she says when she does speak.

I can sense that she doesn't want to talk about it, but I ask anyway. "What happened?"

"I lost him," she says.

"Like the Weyward Curse," I say.

"The what?" she asks.

And so I tell her.

"When my great-great-great-grandmother, Viola Weyward, was a girl, her best friend was Livvie Comstock. Livvie had a crush on a boy named Otis Cattermole. She waited and waited and waited for him to ask her out. Like for years. From the time they were twelve or so. Finally, one day when they were in high school, while Viola and Livvie were sitting on Livvie's front porch, drinking grape Nehis, Otis came walking right up and said, 'I would like to invite you to accompany me to the Harvest Dance.' Because that was a big thing back then. Well, Livvie got all excited, and she started to say yes, but Otis said, 'I beg your pardon, but I was speaking to Miss Viola Weyward.'"

"Oh no," Linda says. "He'd liked her all along."

"Apparently," I say. "And of course Viola said no, because Livvie was her best friend and she didn't want to hurt her feelings. But Otis kept coming over to Viola's house and begging her to go to the dance with him. Livvie had already decided she wasn't going, on account of how her heart was broken, and Viola said that she wouldn't go either, because it wouldn't be any fun without her best friend. And she meant it. But Otis kept asking, and eventually Viola said she would go if he would leave her alone after that. You can probably guess what happened."

"Viola fell in love with Otis."

"According to Clodine, who heard the story about three million times growing up, Otis was a fantastic dancer, and Viola couldn't resist a man who could dance. So she kept on seeing Otis, and a month later, he proposed and she said yes."

"Poor Livvie," Linda says.

"Viola felt terrible about it," I say. "But love is love. She couldn't help how she felt any more than Otis could help how he felt, or Livvie could help how she felt. Not loving him wouldn't make him love Livvie. So they got married. They didn't invite Livvie to the wedding, but she showed up anyway. She walked in at the part where the minister asked if anybody had any reason why Otis and Viola shouldn't get married right then and there."

"What did she say?"

"That's when she put the curse on them," I say. "She said that if Viola went through with it, if she took Otis's last name, that their love would be doomed. She also said that if Otis and Viola had any children, those children would inherit the curse, and if they fell in love before their seventeenth birthdays, the people they fell in love with would die."

"Why seventeen?" Linda asks, which is a logical question.

"Because that's how old Livvie and Viola were when all of this happened," I explain. "And magic works best if you're specific."

"But why make the person the cursed person falls in love with die?" Linda says.

"So that the cursed person feels guilty. Not only will the person they love be dead, it will be their fault, and they'll have to live with that for the rest of their life."

"That's some curse," Linda remarks.

"I know. And it worked. Viola didn't believe it at first. Her father and brothers dragged Livvie out of the church, and Viola and Otis went ahead and got married. A couple of months later, Viola was pregnant. A couple of months after *that*, Otis fell into a smelter at the ironworks."

"Ouch," Linda says.

"When my great-great-grandmother Clodine was born, Viola thought she could maybe trick the curse by giving her the last name Weyward instead of naming her Clodine Cattermole."

"But that didn't work, did it?" Linda asks.

"No," I say. "But it became kind of a tradition anyway. That's why Starletta, Hank, and my father are all Weywards. And why the curse is called the Weyward Curse."

"So all of them fell in love before they were seventeen?" Linda says.

"All of them," I say. "That's the really horrible thing about the curse. You can't help falling in love. It either happens or it doesn't. It's not like Sleeping Beauty, where all she had to do was not touch the spindle on the spinning wheel. You can *try* really hard not to fall in love, but in the end it's just dumb luck whether you do or not."

"Whatever happened to Livvie?" Linda asks. "Did she ever marry?"

"No," I say. "Clodine says working up the curse took all the good out of her, and her heart shriveled up. She lived in town for a few more years, but then she disappeared. No one knows what happened to her."

"And you've never found a way to break the curse?"

"The Grands have tried," I say. "But curses cast by someone with a broken heart are especially strong. Usually only the person who cast it can break it, and Livvie is probably long dead by now."

"So if you were to fall in love with Tom Swift, that would be bad for him," Linda says.

"And for me," I say.

"That sucks," Linda says.

I can't help but laugh. "Yeah," I agree. "It does."

Because, really, that's all you can say about it. It sucks.

"Hey," Linda says. "Do you want to hear another song?"

"Will it make me feel better?" I ask her.

"Probably not," she says. "But maybe. It's worth a try."

"Okay then," I say.

Just like last time, I hear her set the phone down. Then she's playing the guitar. She plays for a little while, then sings.

Astronaut of Love

i let you boldly go where no one's ever gone before
so you took me up to heaven and then left me wanting more
you got everything you wanted, then climbed back into your
    ship
now i might never get home, but I'm still glad i took the trip

i'm an astronaut of love
floating weightless in the dark
while the planets spin around me
and the universes spark
the power of your gravity
has pulled my world apart
one small step for a girl
one giant leap for my heart

i wore a red shirt for you, i was glad to play the part
you set your phaser to kill, i was doomed from the start
now you've charted a new course, found another number one
left me like a piece of space junk to get burned up in the sun

i'm an astronaut of love
floating weightless in the dark
while the planets spin around me
and the universes spark
the power of your gravity
has pulled my world apart
one small step for a girl
one giant leap for my heart

like a little Russian dog who went up in a silver ball
i was never coming back, i never had a chance at all
now i'm chasing meteors and wondering what it's all about
how long do i have left until my air runs out?

i'm an astronaut of love
floating weightless in the dark
while the planets spin around me
and the universes spark
the power of your gravity
has pulled my world apart
one small step for a girl
one giant leap for my heart

they say the light from here will take a hundred years to fly
by the time it reaches home our love and i will both have died
but a century from now when gazers look up at the stars
they'll see a new constellation in the shape of my heart

i'm an astronaut of love
floating weightless in the dark
while the planets spin around me
and the universes spark
the power of your gravity
has pulled my world apart
one small step for a girl
one giant leap for my heart

"Well," she says when she's finished. "Did it make you feel better?"

"Sort of," I tell her. "It's funny, because of the *Star Trek* references, but it's also sad, especially because you mention Laika, the Russian space dog."

"Oh, you caught that," she says. She sounds pleased. "Great. Most people wouldn't."

"She's kind of one of my heroes," I tell her. "But that's such a sad story. So it's a strange mix of funny and sad. Which is pretty much how I feel right now. I like that about it."

"But?" she says.

"But it's not really hopeful," I say. "At the end, the person who is in love is still floating around, waiting to die."

"True," she says. "But she's also looking at all the stars and thinking about how beautiful they are. That's something, right?"

"Yeah, it's something," I say. But what I'm thinking is, it's not enough. I don't want to be floating around, alone. I want to be with someone else, sharing the experience.

I'm suddenly really tired. "I should probably get to sleep," I tell Linda.

"Sure," she says. "Morning is wiser than the evening, and all that."

"What's that from?" I ask her.

She laughs. "I can't believe I said that," she tells me. "It's something my mother used to say whenever she caught me up late at night worrying about something. It's an old Russian saying. From folktales about Baba Yaga and Ivan the Fool and all of those. It means things that look bad when you're awake at night thinking about them often don't seem quite so bad in the morning."

"Your mother is Russian?"

"The youngest of twelve daughters of the tsar," she says, obviously dodging the question. "Every night, she and her sisters turned into swans. My father is a peasant boy who stole her feather cloak and made him marry her to get it back. I should get to sleep too. Good night. Thanks for calling."

"Thanks for talking," I say back. "And for the song."

She hangs up. I lie there, thinking about what she said, and about Tom Swift, and about a million other things. After a while, I realize that I'm singing the chorus of her song over and over in my head. *One small step for a girl, one giant leap for my heart.* That's a good line. And that really is how love is, isn't it? You take this huge risk, then wait to see what happens.

Then I think about Laika, the little dog the Russians sent into space in 1957. She was the first living creature to orbit the earth. They knew they couldn't recover the spacecraft she was in, and that she would die, but for years the Russian government claimed that she died peacefully from a serving of dog food with an overdose of tranquilizers in it, and that made people feel a little bit better about it. Finally, they admitted that she'd died a horrible death from overheating. The scientist in charge of the mission said that her death wasn't worth what they'd learned from the experiment.

In Laika's case, taking the chance totally wasn't worth it. She should have just stayed home. Not that she had a choice in the matter. But if she had, would she have gone? If someone had said, "This is really risky, and there's a good chance that you'll die," would she still have gone? A lot of human astronauts have answered yes to that question. And some of them have died. If we could ask them, would they say it was worth it?

I bet some of them would. Maybe even all of them. The people they left behind might have a different opinion on the subject, though.

I turn off the light. Tomorrow I'm going to play mini golf with Tom Swift. That's all. Mini golf. Not going into space. Not risking my life. Just mini golf.

So why do I feel like I'm about to be launched into orbit and the countdown is almost to one?

Thirteen

"Jesus H. Christ," Tom Swift says.

We've just gotten out of the truck at Rising Son Mini Golf & Bait Shop. Tom is staring up at the sign, which depicts Jesus holding a golf club in one hand and a fly rod in the other.

"Is this for real?"

"Oh yeah," I tell him. "Wait until you see the holes."

Rising Son has been in Midgeville for just about forever. Well, forever to anyone under the age of forty. It was started in the 1970s by a Methodist minister who figured he could combine his two favorite things into one and make a business out of it. And he was right. It's totally weird, but it's also totally awesome.

When we get to the counter where you pay, we're greeted by the owner himself. Reverend Prater has to be close to ninety, but he still runs the place. He looks at me and Tom and says, "You fellas go to church this morning?"

"Sorry, Reverend," I answer. "Not today."

"In that case, it's seven dollars apiece," he says. "Would have been five, but I'm charging you the sin tax for skipping services.

Oh, and your friend here gets dinged another dollar for taking the Lord's name in vain." He chuckles when Tom Swift looks embarrassed. "Didn't think I heard that, did you?"

Tom Swift reaches into his pocket and pulls out some bills. Reverend Prater takes them, then hands us each a putter. "Have fun, boys," he says. "And remember the rules—no picking up the ball once it's been played, no smoking, and no cussing." He looks at Tom Swift when he says this, and his eyes are twinkling.

"Absolutely, Reverend," I say, trying not to laugh.

I pick up a score sheet and a pencil, and while we walk to the first hole, I explain to Tom Swift how the course works. "Every hole is based on a Bible story," I tell him. "You work through the Bible until you get to the last hole, which is Jesus rising from the dead. This first one is the Garden of Eden."

"That explains the naked people."

He points his club at the plywood cutouts of Adam and Eve. They have fig leafs strategically placed over their crotches, and Eve's painted hair covers her breasts. Between the two figures is a plywood tree covered in painted apples. A snake twists around the trunk. Real potted plants make up the Garden, and you have to get your ball down a crooked path and into a hole at the base of the tree.

I let Tom go first. It takes him four shots to get his ball in. It takes me three, but that's because I've played before and know how to bounce the ball off the tree of knowledge of good and evil so that it falls in. I write our scores on the slip of paper, and we move on to hole number two, which is all about Noah's Ark.

"You have to get the ball up the ramp and into the ark," I explain. "There's a path between the animals walking up it two by two. But watch out. The hippos are wider than the others, so you have to get it just right."

He doesn't get it just right. The ball hits one of the hippos' butts and rolls back down. Tom Swift starts to swear, then stops himself. He tries again, and this time he makes it. His ball goes into the ark, then rolls out a hole in the back deck and into the cup.

As I line up my first shot, I say, "I guess things are going okay with Anna-Lynn." I get so anxious waiting for Tom's answer that I miss the ramp going into the ark, and my ball ends up in an awkward position.

"Yeah," Tom says. "I think she likes me."

I steady my nerves and try again. But I guess I still don't quite have it together, because this time, even though my ball starts up the ramp, I haven't hit it hard enough. It rolls back down and ends up back at the starting point.

"Great," I say sarcastically. I'm not talking about my bad golf playing.

"It's a little weird," Tom Swift says as I make a third attempt. This time, my ball goes right up the ramp and into the ark. I imagine Noah giving me a thumbs-up sign and saying, "Way to go. But you're still going to drown when the rain starts. Sorry about that."

"What part is weird?" I ask Tom as we walk to the third hole. This time it's Daniel in the lions' den. You have to get your ball between the legs of three plywood lions, which sounds easy except that they aren't spaced evenly. You have to hit your ball at an angle, or you'll get stuck between two lions.

"She's the first girl I've gone out with," Tom says. "Well, the first straight girl. I fooled around with this girl at camp last summer, but that's when I was still Jennifer and thought I must be gay."

"How is this different?" I ask.

Tom hits his ball, and it passes through the three lions with no problem. He's better at this than I expected him to be, and now I feel pressured to get a hole in one too.

"It's just different," he tells me as he watches me line up my putt. "I don't know how to explain it. Girls kiss other girls different than they kiss boys, I guess."

"Really?" I say, watching my ball go underneath the lions and into the hole. I'm not sure I understand what he means.

We collect our balls and head over to where Moses is parting the Red Sea. Plywood Moses stands at one end with his arms raised. Behind him is a small, shallow pond. A narrow bridge goes across it to the hole, and you have to hit the ball through an opening between his feet and over the bridge.

"Haven't you ever kissed a guy who was really into it?" Tom asks me.

I shake my head. I don't tell him that he's the only guy I've ever kissed.

"I guess maybe it was me," he continues. "I mean with Kelly. The girl from camp. I was into her because she was a girl and she was pretty and I liked her. But I think she was just trying it out, you know? She wasn't into me because of me. With Anna-Lynn, I can tell she likes kissing me because she likes kissing boys. And because she likes me. I don't know. This probably all sounds really stupid."

I think about it while he takes his shot. His ball goes through Moses's feet, but halfway down the bridge, it veers to the side and plops into the water. This is the one hole where you're allowed to pick up the ball, though, so he plucks it from the water and tries again. This time, it gets almost all the way across before falling in. On the third try, he finally gets it into the hole.

I figure this is a good time to ask, "Do you think Anna-Lynn would be as into it if she knew?"

"Knew what?" Tom says.

He knows very well *what*. But apparently he's going to make me say it so that I look like the horrible friend that I guess I am. Because if I was a good friend, I wouldn't bring this up.

I pretend to be concentrating really hard on getting my ball across the Red Sea. This buys me about fifteen seconds. Then my ball is rolling over the bridge and I'm holding my breath, praying it will make it.

It does. I take it as a sign, and say, "If she knew you haven't always been Tom Swift."

Tom shrugs. "I don't know," he says. "But she's not going to find out, so it doesn't really matter. This is just a summer thing. It's not like I live here and we're going to date or anything. Come September, I'll be gone. So why tell her?"

The next hole is all about Jonah and the whale. I guess Reverend Prater figured that since he had the pond there, he might as well make the most of it. We walk around to the other side of it and face the whale. The trick is to get the ball into his open mouth. But you have to hit it hard, because inside there's a loop that the ball has to go around. If you do it right, your ball comes out the whale's blowhole, then runs down a groove in his tail and onto the green behind him.

"Where's Jonah?" Tom Swift asks.

"He used to stand on top of the whale," I tell him. "But a couple of years ago, someone knocked him right off with his putter."

I think about things while Tom Swift takes two tries to get his ball through the whale. What he's said about not telling Anna-Lynn is bugging me. I know it's his life, and his business, but something about it feels off to me.

"You don't think you'll keep in touch with her?" I ask.

"Maybe," he says as he makes the short putt into the hole. "I don't know. Does it matter?"

Three minutes ago, it didn't matter. But now, weirdly, it does. It matters a lot. But I don't really know why, and trying to figure it out quickly enough to give him an answer isn't going to happen. Instead, I concentrate on my ball. I hit it just right, and it goes into the whale's mouth and rattles around his insides. As it comes out the blowhole, I walk around to the green.

"You think I should tell her?" Tom Swift asks me as I get ready to putt.

I don't say anything as I tap the ball. I overdo it, and the ball goes wide of the hole. It should have gone in, but I can't concentrate. I feel Tom waiting for me to answer him. But I don't want to. I know what I want to say, but I'm not sure *why* I want to say it.

"That's up to you," I tell him. It's a cop-out, but it's the best I've got right now.

Tom Swift knows it, and he points his putter at me as he says, "But what do you *think* I should do?"

I stand there looking ahead to the next hole, which is based on the story of David and Goliath. Goliath, the giant, is lying on the ground, where he's fallen after David whacked him in the forehead with a stone from his slingshot. There's an actual hole in his head, and you have to get your ball through it in order to get to the green. I stare at the hole and pray for a miracle to save me from having to answer Tom Swift's question.

Here's the thing. I think who Tom Swift is is Tom Swift's business. If he says he's a guy, then he's a guy. Never mind whatever it is he's got or not got in his underpants. But I also have the benefit of knowing what he's got, at least in theory, so I get to decide whether I would want to be with him based on having all the information. Anna-Lynn only has part of the information. Does she deserve to know it all? Does she have a *right* to know?

This is where everything gets weird and stupid and (sorry, Reverend Prater) fucked-up. In a perfect world, we would be attracted to people because of who they are, not because of what bits and pieces they have or don't have. And I know there are some people who *don't* care about those bits and pieces. But a lot of people do care. Maybe Anna-Lynn isn't one of them. But maybe she is.

Then again, maybe Tom Swift has a point when he says he doesn't plan on things going any further than they already have. Maybe it is just a summer thing. And if he's not going to, you know, get to the point where Anna-Lynn will find out firsthand what's inside his boxers, maybe it doesn't matter. Maybe all that matters is that she likes him, and that once he goes away she has some nice memories of the summer she spent making out with the cute summer boy.

I still don't know how to answer him, though, because—and here's where it gets ironic—even though Tom Swift thinks no one should care about what he used to be or what he's got in his underpants, he apparently does care what someone else has in theirs.

And that makes me angry.

And then I'm angry that I'm angry. Because if I was a good friend, or even just a good person, I wouldn't be angry. I wouldn't be standing here in front of a giant with a hole in his head trying to think of something to say that doesn't (1) make me a liar and (2) make me an asshole for wanting Tom Swift to play by a set of rules that he didn't invent and that nobody should have to play by anyway.

That's when my phone vibrates. I feel it skitter against my butt cheek. I reach for it, thankful for a momentary reprieve from having to answer Tom Swift's question. When I look at it, I see that I have a text from Farrah: *Lola is in the hospital.*

It's not the miracle I was hoping for. It's about as far from that as you can get. But it has the same effect.

"I'm sorry," I tell Tom Swift. "This is an emergency."

I text Farrah back. *Is he okay?*

The answer comes back almost immediately. *Don't know yet. Waiting to talk to the doctor. Will let you know.*

"Is everything okay?" Tom Swift asks me.

I shake my head. "My friend is in the hospital," I tell him. "I don't know why."

"We should go," Tom says.

I nod. "Probably," I say. "I'm sorry."

"Don't be," Tom says as he picks up my ball and hands it to me. "This is more important. We can finish our game another time."

It's not the game I'm thinking about. It's our conversation. I know there's more to say. But now I'm worried about Lola.

"It's going to be okay," Tom Swift says. Then he hugs me.

"Thanks," I tell him. I don't want him to let go. And I want to believe he's right. I think that maybe if we stand here like this forever, it will be.

But then he lets go.

"Come on," he says. "We don't want to give the reverend a stroke."

Despite my worry, I laugh. Tom really is a good friend. Which makes me feel even worse for how jealous I've been about him and Anna-Lynn. I promise myself that I'm going to let it go, and just be happy that I met him and have gotten to know him.

When we hand our putters and balls to Reverend Prater, he looks surprised and says, "You boys giving up already? What's the matter, you scared of the giant Philistine?"

"No, Reverend," I say. "There's kind of an emergency. A friend of mine is in the hospital."

"I'm sorry to hear that," he says. "Tell you what. When you're ready to finish your game, you just come back and start where you left off. And bring your friend to celebrate."

"Thanks," I say. I try to imagine what Reverend Prater would do if I showed up with Lola. Especially if Farrah and Paloma came too. I imagine them all trying to get their balls past the three wise men and into the manger on hole eleven. When you do, the angels on top light up and sing "It Came Upon a Midnight Clear." I know the three of them would adore it.

As Tom and I walk to the car, I promise myself that I *will* bring Lola and the girls here. As soon as Lola is able to. Maybe we'll even come in drag. Inspired by my vision of hole eleven, I decide I can call myself Christmess Eve, and make a horrible, tacky dress out of a velvet tree skirt, tinsel, and a bunch of cheap decorations from the dollar store.

Thinking about this makes me feel better. Now that there's a plan, Lola has to be okay. Like Tom Swift said, everything will be fine. Everything.

I think.

Fourteen

It's Thursday before I actually get to see Lola. He's been in the hospital for four days. Four days that I haven't been allowed to see him, because he's been in the ICU. But today Farrah told me to meet him here.

When I arrive at the hospital, Farrah is arguing with a nurse. Actually, Brandon is arguing with her, but it's Farrah's voice and attitude coming out of him, so it's all a little confusing.

"How many times does he have to ring the buzzer before you bring him a damn cup of ice?" he's saying as I approach the desk he's standing in front of. Behind the desk, the nurse is looking at him with a weary expression. She picks up a clipboard.

"And who, exactly, are you in relation to Mr. Beatty?" she asks. "Only relatives are allowed to visit him right now."

"Brandon Thomas. It's right there on that paper. We already went through this when they brought him in here on Sunday."

The nurse scans the sheet again. "Brandon Thomas," she says. Then she looks up. "You're Mr. Beatty's *son*?" she asks. She sounds skeptical, and it's obvious why.

"What?" Brandon says. "You don't think I can be his son because I'm black? You never heard of interracial marriage? What is this, 1958?"

The nurse sighs. "Somebody will bring Mr. Beatty a cup of ice as soon as possible," she says.

"Thank you," Brandon says. Then he turns to me. "Come on. *Grandpa* will be very happy to see you." He looks back at the nurse, as if daring her to say something. She doesn't.

"You told them you're Lola's son?" I ask as we walk down the hall.

"Gurl, it was either that or pretend she's my husband, and as much as I love that old queen, we all know I can do a lot better."

"So if you're his son, and I'm his grandson, that must make you my father."

"Do I look old enough to have a child your age?" Brandon says as we stop in front of room 427. "Paloma can be your mother."

"But Paloma is younger than—"

"Don't you even finish that sentence," Brandon snaps. "Not if you want to live to be seventeen. Now listen. Lola looks pretty rough. But you just pretend you don't even notice, okay?"

"Okay," I agree.

"And we'll keep this visit short," Brandon adds. "She needs to rest. But she's been asking about you, so I told her you'd come in to see her."

He pushes open the door, and we go into the room. It looks pretty much like every hospital room I've ever seen before, except that now someone I know is in it. Lola is propped up in the room's one bed. He's wearing a pink robe with a furry collar, and he's watching something on the television mounted on the wall. He looks exhausted, but when he sees me come in, he smiles.

"Hey there," he says, holding his arms out.

I walk over to the bed and he hugs me. As I hug him back, I can't help noticing that he smells funny. Kind of musty and, well, old. It makes me sad.

"You're just in time," he says as he lets me go. "They're about to get on the plane." He nods at the television, and I see that he's watching *Lost Horizon*.

Brandon sits down in one of the two chairs in the room, and groans. "I never should have brought that DVD over," he says to me. "She's watched it a hundred and eighty-nine times since Monday."

"When *you* have a heart attack, you can watch whatever *you* like," Lola says. He reaches over and picks up a rhinestone tiara that's sitting on the table beside the bed, then puts it on his head. "Need I remind you that I am literally the queen of broken hearts?"

He turns up the volume on the TV as Brandon looks at me and shakes his head. Then we sit and watch the movie. It's a little boring, since I've seen it before, and I'm sort of relieved when, twenty minutes into it, the door opens and a nurse comes in.

"We need some blood from Mr. Beatty," he says. "I'm kicking you two out."

Brandon and I get up. Lola motions for me to come over to

him, so I go over and stand beside the bed. He takes my hand. "James is just trying to get rid of you so he can give me a sponge bath," he says in a loud whisper. He glances at the nurse, who laughs. "Promise me you'll come see me again."

"I will," I tell him.

I lean over and kiss him on the cheek.

"Careful," he says. "You're going to make James jealous."

Brandon and I leave Lola with James, and go downstairs to the hospital cafeteria. Brandon is going to stay a little longer, so we get something to eat before I head home.

"Is Lola really going to be okay?" I ask him.

"That queen will live forever," Brandon says. "They just need to patch her up, and she'll be good as new."

I've been thinking about something ever since the scene with the nurse at the desk. Now I ask Brandon, "Does Lola not have any real family?"

"You don't think we're a real family?" he asks me. "You, me, Paloma, Lola?"

"You know what I mean," I say. "Real as in related."

Brandon looks at me as he chews a bite of the chicken salad on his plate. For some reason, it makes me nervous.

"Your mother left when you were born, right?" he says.

I nod.

"Technically, she's your *real* family," he continues. "Her blood is in you. Her genes are why you look the way you do. She's why you're here in this world. But you don't think of her that way, do you? Not like a *mother*."

"She's more like the idea of a mother," I tell him. "I never got a chance to know her."

"No, you didn't. And that's a sad thing. But you got a whole lot of people in your house who love you, so the fact that your mother isn't one of them, well, it's still sad, but it's not as sad as it could be. There're a whole lot of people who have to deal with worse."

I'm not sure what any of this has to do with my question, and I kind of feel like I'm being lectured. But I don't say anything. Not that Brandon gives me a chance to.

"My point is, sometimes *real* family isn't much family at all," he says. "You and me, we're lucky we've got blood that does love us. Sure, they make us crazy sometimes, but we know that if we need them, they'll come through. Not your mama, but the others. Lola, she doesn't have any of that. She's alone. But she still has people who care about her. You're here. I'm here. Paloma will be here when she gets off work. That's *real* real. And that's *family*. So yeah, Lola's got real family."

He still seems upset, and I'm afraid it's my fault. I don't know why, though, so I just sit and eat my sandwich as quickly as I can.

"I should go," I tell Brandon. "I've got to work at the Eezy-Freezy tonight. I'll come back tomorrow, if that's okay."

"Lola would like that," he says. "And don't worry. That heart of hers is big. It can take a beating. She'll be fine."

I drive, thinking about Lola. I get what Brandon was saying. But it's still sad. I wonder how his life got like this. Then I feel bad that I've never really paid all that much attention to what his life is like outside of the Shangri-La. I just assumed he had, well, some kind of family besides the one at the bar.

I head straight to the Eezy-Freezy. It's not super busy, and my dad is chatty. I really want to talk to him about what's going on with Lola, but that would mean talking about how I know Lola, and where I go sometimes, and how I like to do drag. And those are things I just don't want to talk about yet. Luckily, he's got a lot to say himself, and doesn't notice that I'm only saying things like "yeah" and "uh-huh" in response.

When customers do come in, I find myself looking at them and wondering what their lives are like. I mean really like, not just how they appear at first glance. The man who orders five soft-serve cones for the family waiting in the car, for example. Does he like being a dad? Does he like being married to the woman sitting in the passenger seat? Is this what he wanted his life to be when he was my age? Or the three teenage girls who flirt with me while I make their cheese fries. Are they really as happy as they seem? What do they worry about when no one else can see them?

I remember something Lola said to me once: "There are all kinds of drag. Sometimes it looks like wigs and makeup; sometimes it's just a face someone shows you when they're afraid to show you their real one."

I didn't know what he meant at the time. Now I get it. You can't know who someone is just by looking at her. And maybe you can never really know. Maybe people always have secrets

137

that they don't tell a single other person. Which of course makes me think about Tom Swift. He has a pretty big secret. And I know what it is. But maybe he has other, even bigger ones that he hasn't shared, and never will.

When I think about what I want *my* life to look like, I think about having someone who does know everything about me. Someone I'm not afraid to tell everything to. Someone who knows what I look like underneath all the drag I put on for the rest of the world. And I wonder if that even exists.

By the time we close up for the night, I'm actually pretty depressed. I drive home more quickly than usual so that I can beat my father there. I barely say good night to the Grands, who of course are gathered around the kitchen table, drinking Nehi and playing cards. I go straight to my room and shut the door.

I pick up the telephone without even thinking about it. When Linda answers I say, "Is your life the way you thought it would be?"

She laughs, which takes me by surprise. "Is anybody's?"

"Sure," I say. "I mean, there must be some people who have the lives they always imagined having."

"Maybe," she says. "I must not know any of them, though."

It occurs to me that I've never asked Linda how old she is. So I do. "How old do you think I am?" she answers.

"Why do you always answer my questions with another question?" I say.

"Do I?" she asks. "Anyway, I'm seventeen. Cheating at solitaire and inventing lovers on the phone and everything."

"What?" I say. "Am I missing something?"

"From the song," she says. "Janis Ian? 'At Seventeen'?"

"I've never heard it," I tell her. "I'll look it up later. I'm a little preoccupied with other stuff right now."

I tell her about Lola's heart attack, and about how it makes me sad that he's sort of alone. "I just wanted to tell him it would all be okay," I say. "That's it. Just that it would be okay."

"I get it," Linda says. "Here. Listen to this."

There's a clattering sound as she apparently drops the phone on a table. "Sorry," she shouts. Then I hear her strum her guitar a couple of times.

Blanket Fort

i want to be your blanket fort
your safety net, your first resort
where you can always come inside
and hang out when you need to hide

i want to be your lucky charm
your rabbit foot, your falling star
the one who can reverse the curse
when things have gone from bad to worse

i want to be your weekend shirt
the one that's ripped and stained with dirt
but you still wear it anyway
because it feels like Saturday

i want to be the jumping sheep
you lie and count when you can't sleep
the blanket you wrap round you tight
when something scares you in the night

i want to be the wish you make
on candles on your birthday cake
and when you cast your magic spells
and drop your pennies into wells

i want to be the song you play
when you have had the worst of days
and turn up high as it will go
when it comes on the radio

i want to be your favorite book
about Peter Pan and Captain Hook
with dog-eared pages, underlined
that you have read a thousand times

i want to be the special gift
you write atop your Christmas list
and when it's underneath the tree
the tag will read to you from me

i want to be the drug you score
the leaf you smoke, the drink you pour

to fly your soul across the sky
and leave me here to wonder why

When she's done I say, "That's a little happier than your other ones."

"I guess I can't be sad all the time," Linda says.

"I didn't mean it like that."

"I know," she says. "It's okay. And actually, it is pretty sad. I wrote that for someone who was having a bad day. I wanted to make him feel better. But it didn't help him much."

"What happened to him?"

"It doesn't matter," Linda says. Her voice sounds funny, though. "I'm sure your friend will be all right."

"I hope so too. I think he will."

"I should go," she says. "I've got some stuff to do."

"Okay," I say. "Thanks for the song. And, hey."

"Yeah?"

"I bet we can have the lives we want."

There's a long silence. Then Linda says, "Yeah. Maybe we can."

Fifteen

Saturday night, Tom Swift calls while I'm working at the Eezy-Freezy and asks if I want to hang out when I get off. I tell him sure, and he says he'll come by my house later. I'm getting out of the shower after washing off the smell of grease and sweat when he shows up. I haven't even changed into my clothes yet. I'm just wearing boxer shorts and a T-shirt.

He seems a little bit hyped up, and as soon as I shut my bedroom door he says, "Where's my T?"

This explains why he wanted to come over. I'm a little disappointed, as I thought maybe he wanted to spend time with me. I get the bag with his T and syringes from my closet and toss it to him.

"Thanks," he says, sitting on my bed and opening the bag.

"Is it doing anything?" I ask. "Do you feel any different?"

He nods. "Yeah. I can't really explain how, exactly, but I do. For one thing, I'm super horny."

I pull on a pair of jeans. "Right now, or just in general?"

He pulls the leg of his shorts up and feels around on his

thigh. "In general. But I was hanging out with Anna-Lynn earlier, so I'm kind of more worked up than usual."

While he injects the T, I go over to the record player and put on record number eight from my mother's list, the New York Dolls' first album.

"What is this?" Tom asks as the first song starts and David Johansen wails crazily.

I take the record jacket over and hand it to him. The photo on the cover is the Dolls dressed up as women. Kind of. They don't look anything like real women, but they're wearing wigs, makeup, jewelry, and platform heels.

Tom looks at the cover for a minute. "Ugh," he says as he hands it back. "I hate fake trans shit. They look like that guy from *Rocky Horror*."

I look at the photo of the band. "I don't think they were pretending to be trans," I say. "I think it was just a gimmick."

"That's even worse." Tom sounds angry now. "And what a stupid name. Dolls? Like being trans is about playing dress-up or something. And the music is shitty."

"It was 1973," I remind him. "I don't think they even really knew what being trans was back then. This is more about being glam or punk. Trying to shock people and make them think about how dumb their ideas of what people should look and act like are."

"Whatever. They could still take off the wigs and makeup and live their lives without people giving them a hard time. Not like real trans people, who get harassed every day if they look like that."

I decide it's not worth arguing with him about this. I doubt listening to the Dolls' lyrics will change how he thinks. And anyway, maybe he's right. Maybe nobody who ever saw the Dolls perform or heard their music thought anything about trans people and their lives. Maybe they just saw a bunch of guys dressed up like women and thought it was funny, or weird, or cool.

I turn the record off. Tom is lying on his back on my bed. I go and lie next to him.

"So, Anna-Lynn got you all worked up, huh?" I ask. I think maybe if I can get him to talk about something else, he won't be so angry.

He groans. "We did a little kissing," he says. "Okay, a lot of kissing. I really wanted to do more."

His voice trails off, and I know he's not saying something.

"But she didn't want to?" I ask.

"Oh, she wanted to," he says. "We both wanted to. I just . . . couldn't."

I'm not sure what he means, exactly, but I don't want to ask too many questions. I decide to let him talk if he wants to talk. We lie there for a while. Then he says, "What's it like having a dick?"

I laugh.

"Why's that funny?"

"Sorry," I say. "It's just that I've never really thought about it."

"How can you not think about it?" Tom sounds genuinely surprised. "If I had one, I'd think about it all the time."

I can't think of anything to say, so I just say, "Huh."

He rolls over and props his head up on his hand. "Don't tell me you've never thought about what it would be like to have a pussy."

I make a face.

"You have too," he says.

"I really haven't," I tell him.

He sighs. "If you knew you should have been born with one, you would."

Now I feel bad. I decide to try to answer his question. "It kind of gets in the way a lot."

"What do you mean?"

"Well, for one thing, it's always getting hard at the wrong times."

Tom laughs. "Aww, poor baby," he teases.

"I'm serious. You don't know. You'll just be sitting there in class, looking at some guy's butt or arms or even his ear, and the next thing you know—boing! And it never goes down on its own."

"Right," Tom says. "You have to *beat it* into submission."

"Ha ha," I say. "But, well, yeah."

He pauses a second, then asks, "What's that like?"

I groan. "I'm not going to talk about this."

"Come on," he says. "I know you do it. Everybody does it. I just want to know what it feels like."

I shrug. "It feels great," I say. "What else do you want to know?"

"What does it feel like when you shoot?" he says. "And don't say 'great.'"

I can't believe he's asking me this. I almost tell him I won't talk about it. Then I figure, why not? We're friends. And I can tell that it's important to him. So I think about how to describe it.

"It's like sneezing," I say.

Tom snorts. "That's not all that sexy."

"No, really. You know how when you sneeze, it's not just this instant thing? There's a buildup. You can sense that it's going to happen, and you know what it's going to feel like when you finally do it, and that it's actually going to feel kind of amazing, but you sort of try to make it not happen. It's like that. You feel yourself start to tense up, because you're getting close. And you want it to happen, but you also don't want it to be over quite yet because the best part is that moment right before you come. Your whole body tingles all over. If you could stop time right then, it would be the greatest superpower ever. So you try to make it last as long as you can. But you can't. You have to let go. And that's really good too, just giving in and letting it happen. Messy, but good. After that it's like the part of a roller coaster ride where the car is coming back to the start. The feeling you got dropping down the hills is still there, but it's going away, and all you can think about is riding it again."

Tom doesn't say anything, so I ask a question. "Isn't that what it's like when girls come? Or, you know, people with girl parts?"

"Maybe," he says. "I don't like to touch myself there."

"How do you not?" I ask. "If I didn't jerk off, I'd go nuts. Seriously, I think I would explode."

He sighs. "It's not like I never do," he says. "It's just that putting my hands down there reminds me that something's wrong. I'm a guy, and guys are supposed to have dicks. When I reach down and feel this other thing, it's like I've had an accident. It reminds me that my body isn't really the one I should be living in."

I try to imagine what this must be like for him. It's one thing to think about being a different kind of person. But to know that you're one person and be constantly reminded that you don't look like that person would be horrible. I mean, it's not like wishing you had hair that was a different color, or more muscles, or something you can change.

"I dream about it," Tom says. "A lot. I dream about holding it, and peeing standing up, and putting it inside someone." He looks at me. "Have you ever done that? Put it inside someone? Or, you know, had someone suck it?"

I can't believe the room isn't glowing from the heat of the blush I know is all over my face. "Uh, no."

"I thought guys were always playing with each other," he says. "Even straight ones."

I immediately think back to a night two years ago. It was the middle of August, super hot, and John Sudderline and I had set up a tent behind the house. We were lying on top of our sleeping bags, reading comic books by the light of a lantern. John was on his stomach, looking at an issue of *X-Men*. He said, "Man, would

I love to do it with Psylocke." Then he rolled over, and I could see he had a hard-on.

"One time my friend and I jerked off together," I tell Tom. "Well, sort of. We both jerked off, but we didn't touch each other."

"You just watched?"

"Kind of. I definitely watched him. But I think he was too freaked out to really look at me."

"That must have sucked for you," Tom says. "Sorry. I mean, it must have been hard for you." He laughs. "Jesus, everything I say sounds porny."

I laugh too, even though thinking about it makes me a little sad. "I really wanted to touch him," I say. "I mean, he was *right there*. I'd been thinking about touching another guy for forever. But I wasn't out to anyone then, and I was afraid if I made the first move, he would freak out and tell everybody."

"Do you think he wanted you to do something?"

"Not really. I think he was just horny and wanted to get off. It's not like we talked about what we were doing. He pretended he was still looking at his comic. But his hand was moving up and down, and I could see it. That made me hard, so I did it too. Only I was jerking off to him and he was jerking off to Psylocke."

"As far as you know," Tom says. "Maybe he was watching you too."

I've never actually considered this possibility. I don't think Tom is right, but I say, "Maybe."

"I bet having balls is fun," Tom says. "If I had balls, I'd play with them all the time."

"They're fun until someone kicks you in them," I tell him. "Or you nail them on the bar of your bike."

"Ouch," he says. "Still, it would totally be worth it." He sighs. "MTFs have it a lot easier in the equipment department."

I'm not sure what he means. "MTFs?"

"Male-to-female trans people. It's a lot easier to turn an outie into an innie than the other way around. T gives you facial hair, deepens your voice, and helps build muscle, but it doesn't grow a dick and balls."

"Having a dick doesn't make you a guy," I say.

"Oh yeah?" he says. "Cut yours off and tell me how you feel about things."

I don't know what to say to this. He's right. If I somehow lost my dick, I'd be pretty upset about it.

"I know what you're saying," Tom says a minute later. "And you're right. Mostly. But it's easier to believe that when you don't really have any great options. If getting a dick was as easy for trans guys as getting a vagina is for trans girls, you can bet we'd all have them. And nights like tonight just remind me all over again."

"You mean because of Anna-Lynn?"

"Yeah. Like I said, the kissing is fantastic. But it makes me want to do more, and I'm afraid the things I can do aren't going to be enough. I have these," he says, holding up a hand and wiggling his fingers. "And I have this." He sticks out his tongue. "But I don't have that." He points to my crotch.

"Maybe she wouldn't care," I say.

"Maybe she wouldn't," Tom agrees. "But I do. I want to know what it feels like to be inside of her. Not just rubbing against her. Which right now is all I've got."

When I don't respond to this he says, "Do you think I'm selfish for feeling like this?"

"No," I tell him. And I don't. But I do wonder how long he can keep not telling Anna-Lynn about himself.

"I should go," Tom says, sitting up. "My grandparents will be pissed if I stay out too late."

I say good night, and he leaves. When he's gone, I put the New York Dolls record on again. Despite Tom Swift's comments about them, I love the songs. They're simple and raw, and David Johansen's voice is like cigarette smoke. The music is everything music now isn't. It feels real, not manufactured in some factory somewhere, like almost everything on the radio.

I'm curious now about whether any of the Dolls were actually trans, or even gay. I go to my computer and start searching for information. It's easy enough to find. And it turns out they weren't. I'm a little disappointed, but I still love the music.

Then I start searching for other things, and pretty soon I'm learning all kinds of stuff about trans people, and in particular the different kinds of surgeries they can have. It's fascinating. And of course Tom is right about how much more difficult it is for trans men. The pictures I find are interesting, but it also makes me sad how painful it must be.

One thing leads to another, and when the Dolls record ends

42 minutes later, I've seen and read all kinds of things. I've also landed on a site that has given me an idea. Something that might help Tom Swift get what he wants. I stare at the screen for a while, going back and forth. Then, with the click of a few keys, it's done.

I turn off the computer and the stereo, strip down to my boxers, and lie down on my bed. I replay my conversation with Tom Swift in my head, which gets me to thinking about what happened that night with John Sudderline. Was he watching me? Did he want to touch me as badly as I wanted to touch him? Were we both too afraid to make the first move?

I close my eyes and imagine what might have happened. As I stroke myself, I pay attention to how everything feels. And after I come, I know that this is something I hope Tom Swift gets to experience one day.

Sixteen

When the sound of a dog barking interrupts my dreams, at first I think it's Millard Fillmore having an argument with the moon. I sit up in bed and start to yell out the window for him to be quiet. Then I see something flashing in the darkness, and I realize it's my phone blurting out the new ringtone I downloaded.

The only person I can think of who might call me in the middle of the night is Tom Swift, and only if he's in some kind of trouble. I stumble out of bed, trip over my clothes where I left them on the floor, and snatch the phone from my dresser.

"Hello?"

"Hey, Sammy." It's Farrah's voice. "I know it's late. Or early. I don't even really know what time it is."

There's something odd about the way he sounds. The usual spark is missing.

"What's wrong?"

There's a little hitch, as if he's trying not to cry. "Lola died."

At first I think I must still be asleep and dreaming. I know he didn't just tell me that Lola is dead.

"Sammy? Did you hear me?"

I shake my head. I'm awake, not dreaming. "I thought he was going to be okay?"

"I hoped she would be," Farrah says. "But it didn't work out that way. Turns out there were complications."

Complications. That's what they always say on the medical shows on television. They never really say what it means. Just complications, like that's some kind of disease all by itself. "Sorry, Mr. Smith, but your tests results are back. I'm afraid you have complications."

"When did he die?"

"About an hour ago."

"Were you there?"

"Yes. The hospital called me when things weren't looking good. I got here around midnight." His voice breaks a little bit again. "I was holding her hand when she went. I sat with her for a while before they came and took her. Then I called Paloma and you."

Paloma and me. I remember my conversation with Farrah in the cafeteria, when he said we were family. "Isn't there anyone else?"

"A few cousins," Farrah says. "Nobody that would want to be woken up to hear about it. I'll call them in the morning."

I don't know what to say next. It seems like this should be a bigger deal somehow. This is the first time I've had someone I know die. I feel like I should be doing something. Boiling water, or getting towels, or I don't know what. Something more than standing in my bedroom.

"Sammy?" Farrah's voice brings me back. "It's gonna be

okay. I've got to go now, but we'll talk later on today, all right? I love you, baby."

"Yeah," I manage. "Me too."

He hangs up. I set the phone down and just stand there for a while. I don't know what to do. I don't even really know what I'm feeling. Lola is dead. I'm not going to see him again.

Her. I hear Farrah's voice in my head. *You're not going to see her again.*

Him. Her. Both of them. Either of them. Neither of them. They're gone.

The darkness in my room suddenly feels too black, too cold, too much like it wants to swallow me up. I pull on a pair of shorts and get out of there, going downstairs, heading toward the light that shines up the stairwell.

The Grands are, as usual, in the kitchen, sitting around the table and playing cards. When I come in, Starletta looks at me and says, "Hank, get another Nehi."

My grandmother gets up and goes to the refrigerator, while I take one of the empty chairs at the table. Starletta and Clodine look at me over their cards.

"Who died?" Starletta asks.

I look at her, although I'm not actually surprised, more curious. "How'd you know?"

Starletta points to the kitchen door. "There's a luna moth hanging on the screen. Showed up a couple of hours ago."

"Plus, the milk turned," Clodine adds. She sighs. "And Jimmy just brought it this morning."

Hank hands me a Nehi, then sits. "So, who was it?"

I take a drink of the orange soda. It occurs to me now that the Grands don't know anything about Lola, or the Shangri-La. They especially don't know that I go there, and why. If I tell them about Lola, it will bring up a whole bunch of other stuff. But then I remember that they *do* know Lola, just not by that name.

"Garrison Beatty."

Starletta lays her cards down. "Well, I'll be. He wasn't even on my list of possibilities."

"Garrison Beatty," says Clodine, her mouth puckering as she sucks her teeth and thinks. She looks at my great-grandmother. "You went out with him once upon a time."

"Not really," Starletta says. "Not seriously, anyway."

"Lucky for him," says Clodine.

I'm waiting for them to ask me how I know Garrison, but they don't seem concerned about this. Hank picks up her cards, and they go right back to their game. Hank places three cards facedown on the table. "Three queens," she says.

"Bullshit," Clodine exclaims. She looks very pleased with herself.

Hank turns over the cards, revealing the queens of spades, hearts, and diamonds. Clodine sighs and reaches out to sweep up the pile of cards. "I just like saying that," she says as she adds the cards to her already full hand. "How did Garrison pass?"

"Heart attack," I say. "Complications from one, anyway."

"He must have been close to seventy," Starletta remarks as she places some cards on the table. "Two kings."

"Bullshit," Clodine barks.

Hank sighs. "Would you stop that? You're taking every hand. We might as well just stop now."

"No, this time she's right," says Starletta as she turns over the cards to reveal the two of clubs and the eight of spades. But there's no pile of cards for her to take, so she just puts her own two cards back into her hand.

"I wonder how Eulalie's going to take it," Clodine says as she examines her cards and chooses some.

"Who's Eulalie?" I ask.

Clodine puts down four cards and declares, "Four aces."

Nobody calls bullshit, so the cards stay and now it's my grandmother's turn. As she's trying to decide what to lay down, Starletta says, "Eulalie is Garrison's mother."

"Mother?" I'm shocked. "His mother is still alive?"

"Yes, she's still alive," says Clodine. "And she's no older than I am." She looks at me meaningfully, as if I've just said she was long past her expiration date.

"I just didn't know," I explain. "He never talked about her."

"One two," says Hank as she slaps a card down. "That's probably because they haven't spoken in, oh, about forty years."

"Because he's a fairy," Clodine announces. Then she notices my grandmother and great-grandmother looking at her. "What?"

"We don't say *fairy* anymore," says Starletta.

Clodine harrumphs. "It's a perfectly good word. And what's wrong with fairies anyway? Some of my best friends are fairies. What are we on now?"

"Threes," Starletta says as she puts three cards on the table. She and Hank look at Clodine.

"I know you're lying, but I'm not saying it," Clodine says. "Those cards can just sit there."

"Then I'll say it," Hank says. "Bullshit."

Starletta reveals the jack, ten, and six of hearts before scooping up the pile. "She's going to regret not making amends," she says. "Her only child is gone."

I'm still waiting for one of them to ask me something about how come I was friends with an old man. An old *gay* man. A fairy, as my great-great-grandmother would apparently say. Do they think there was something between us? Do they simply not care? Or are they afraid to ask because they don't want to know the answer?

They play a few more rounds of cards without asking me anything else about Lola's death. Garrison's death. I sit there, watching them and drinking my Nehi, thinking about the new information I have about Lola's mother. I can't believe I've never heard about her before now. Even if Lola never mentioned her, our town just isn't that big.

"How come I've never heard of Eulalie Beatty?" I say, unable to stand the suspense anymore.

Hank, who has just been caught lying about the number of sevens she put down, answers me. "Because she's not Eulalie Beatty," she says as she rearranges the cards in her hand. "She's Eulalie Householder."

"Mrs. Householder is Lola's mother?" I exclaim. Mrs.

Householder taught math at my school for about a thousand years before retiring when I was in ninth grade. I never knew her first name. When you're a kid, teachers don't have first names.

"I don't know about being Lola's mother," Hanks says. "But she was definitely Garrison's mother."

When I realize that I've used Lola's other name, I panic for a moment. But the Grands just keep on playing cards as if I haven't said anything peculiar. I think about explaining, but don't. Besides, I'm too busy wondering how someone could live in the same small town as her son for so long without speaking to him.

"Beatty was Eulalie's maiden name," Starletta says. "Garrison took it on when they had the falling-out."

I recall the story Farrah told me about the uncle who left Lola money. He must have been Eulalie's brother, and Lola must have taken his name as a way to remember him. To keep his name alive, as if he had been the uncle's child and not Eulalie's.

"One eight," Starletta says, putting a single card down. "And I'm out."

Clodine, who is holding most of the cards, looks at Hank. "Want to keep going for second place?"

Hank shakes her head. "It'll be dawn soon."

Clodine puts her cards down and stands up. "Better go fetch an egg, then."

"An egg?" I say. "What for?"

Starletta takes my hand. "This is your first death," she says, pulling me up. "Come on."

The four of us go out into the dark yard. The moon is barely a sliver, so everything is wrapped in shadows. Hank has a flashlight, though, and she uses this to light the way as we go into the backyard and walk to the chicken coop out behind the barn. As we pass the Airstream, Def Leppard's "Pour Some Sugar on Me" comes from the open window, along with the sound of my father's snoring.

When we get to the henhouse, Hank opens the door and steps inside. The chickens, still asleep, *buk-buk-buk* softly, but nobody comes flying out into the yard. Then Hank reappears, holding an egg in her hand. She hands it to me. It's still warm.

"It's from one of the black ones," Hank says. "There were a bunch under the reds and white, but I had to check three of the blacks before I got one."

"Does it matter?" I ask.

"It doesn't hurt," Starletta says as we return to the house.

Back in the kitchen, Hank takes a bowl out of a cupboard, fills it with water from the tap, and sets it on the table. Starletta takes the egg from me. Using a large sewing needle, she makes a hole in one end of the egg, then another in the opposite end. She hands the egg back to me.

"Blow it out," she says. "Into the bowl."

I hold one end of the egg to my mouth and blow into it. A tiny drop of yolk appears through the hole in the other end. I blow harder, and the drop gets bigger, almost like I'm blowing up a balloon. Then it slowly falls into the bowl of water, forming a long, glistening string of raw egg.

I blow again and again until the contents of the egg are floating in the bowl of water. When I'm sure that the last drops are out, I hold the empty eggshell in my palm.

"Now what?"

Clodine takes the bowl with the water and egg in it and holds it in her hands, looking into it.

"Any blood?" Starletta says.

Clodine shakes her head. She sniffs. "No smell either."

Hank comes to the table with a small piece of paper and a pencil. "He was your friend," she says to me. "You should do this part."

"What do I do?"

"Write his name on the paper," Hank says. She takes the egg from me and gives me the pencil. "Printing is best. It's easier to read."

I have no idea why we're doing this, but I do it. I write G-A-R-R-I-S-O-N in neat capital letters. Then I hesitate. "What last name do I use?"

"Use the name he wanted," says Clodine. "That's his real one. Doesn't matter what it says on his birth certificate."

I debate with myself for a few seconds, then add L-O-L-A B-E-A-T-T-Y to the paper. I put the pencil down.

"Now roll the paper up tight," Hank says. "It has to fit through one of the holes."

I roll the paper into a thin tube. Hank hands me back the egg, and I push one end of the tube into it. It's a little tight, but the paper slips inside. I shake the egg gently, feeling the paper move around.

"Now whisper his name into the egg," says Starletta.

Again I hold the egg to my mouth. I whisper, "Garrison Lola Beatty" into it, feeling a little silly.

Clodine nods. "Let's go put it back."

We go outside, me carrying the egg. The sky is a little lighter, but it's not quite dawn. We troop back to the henhouse. My father is still snoring, and now AC/DC is playing "Back in Black."

"Better let Hank take the egg," Starletta says when we arrive at the coop. "They take better to her."

I hand my grandmother the egg, and she goes inside. She comes back out a minute later. "Well, that's done," she says. "Didn't make a bit of fuss."

"Now can somebody tell me what this was all about?" I ask.

Clodine puts her arm around me. "We're sending Garrison's spirit on," she says as we walk.

"On to where?"

"To wherever it wants to go next," says Hank.

I get it. The egg is a symbol of birth. Or, in this case, rebirth. But do they really think Lola's spirit is inside the egg now? And that the hen is going to somehow hatch it so that it can move on? The Grands believe a lot of strange things, so I wouldn't be surprised.

I almost ask. Then I realize, it doesn't matter. I actually do feel a little less sad. Maybe it's being with the Grands. Maybe I'm tired from not sleeping. Or maybe it just hasn't hit me yet that Lola is really gone. Whatever it is, I feel like we've done a little magic together, even if I don't understand it.

As we reach the kitchen door, Clodine stops. "Look at that," she says.

The screen door is covered with luna moths. A dozen of them. They hang there, their wings very slowly moving up and down. Then the sun breaks over the trees, and a glimmer of light slides across the lawn, gilding the grass. It hits the door, and for a moment the moths are bathed in light. Then, all together, they rise up and flutter away across the yard like scraps of paper.

Clodine steps onto the porch and takes hold of the door handle. "Well," she says as she pulls the door open and goes inside. "Now we know it worked."

Seventeen

"I've been working on a song."

Linda sounds almost happy.

"What's it about?"

"Fairy tales. I've been thinking about them a lot lately."

"Any one in particular?"

"All of them, really. You want to hear it?"

Of course I do. And so she sings it for me.

When she sings the final lines of the chorus, "*ever after, happy ending, true love wins and never dies, am i cursed or are the stories, nothing but a pack of lies?*" I say, "So much for happy endings."

"That's the point. Fairy tales promise us all kinds of happy endings, but life doesn't work like that. You might have some happy moments, but they don't last. Not forever, anyway. Not happily ever after."

"So you're happy because you wrote a song about how life doesn't have happy endings the way fairy tales do?"

She laughs. "I'm happy because I'm telling the truth. So, what's up with you?"

"Lola died," I say, my voice sticking in my throat.

She gasps. "Oh, shit. No."

I take a breath. "Like you said, in real life people don't get happily ever after endings."

"I'm really sorry," Linda says. "And here I am making you listen to my stupid song."

"It's not stupid," I say. "It's good. I'm glad you're writing. And it's nice to think about something other than Lola being gone. That's all I've been doing for the past couple of days."

It's Wednesday night. Almost Thursday morning. Lola's funeral starts in a little more than nine hours, and I can't sleep. Which is why I picked up the phone and dialed Linda's number. I don't even think about it anymore. My fingers automatically find the right holes, as if she's the only person the phone can call now. I've stopped thinking it's weird.

"Tell me about him," Linda says. "Wait. Sorry. You said you were trying not to think about it so much."

"That's okay. I'd like to talk about him."

I tell Linda about the first time I saw Lola.

"I'd heard about the Shangri-La," I begin. "I mean, everyone here knows about it. You can't have a gay bar in a place like this without it being a big deal. My dad let me start driving the truck around town to practice when I was fifteen. I couldn't even get a learner's permit yet, but I'd been driving it around our house for a couple of years already. Besides, a town this small, nobody pays attention anyway, not even the cops unless you cause an accident. As soon as I could get away with taking the truck, I would drive by and just look at the Shangri-La. I'd never stop.

Not at first. Just go by and hope I might see someone coming in or out. Like a real live gay person." I laugh. "That sounds so weird. But I really had never seen one. Only on TV or online. Anyway, one night I drove by like usual. It was a Saturday. I was supposed to be on my way home from helping my dad at the Eezy-Freezy. I was—" I stop, not sure I want to say what I'm about to.

"You were what?" Linda says.

"I was horny," I admit.

She giggles, like I've just told her a really dirty joke. This makes me laugh too. "Well, I was. It was a super-hot night, and a bunch of guys came by the Eezy-Freezy wearing shorts and no shirts. I was a little worked up. I mean, I was fifteen. I thought about guys all the time. So I was driving home and took a little detour. When I drove past the Shangri-La, I thought I saw one of the guys who had come to the Eezy-Freezy going inside. Before I could even think about it, I pulled into the parking lot. Then I freaked out because I thought someone would recognize my truck, so I drove around back and parked there."

"Why didn't you just leave?"

"I was going to, but another car was pulling in, so I decided to wait. Also, I wanted to see if that guy would come out. He'd been really nice to me when I made him his cone earlier, and I don't know, I guess I hoped maybe he was flirting with me. It's stupid, I know."

"No, no. Totally understandable. And then?"

"Um, well, then I decided to have a cigarette. Because I was nervous. Only I was afraid to have the window open in case anyone saw me, so I rolled it up."

"Smoking in an enclosed truck," Linda says. "Probably not the smartest thing."

"Yeah, I know. But my mind was all over the place. So there I am, smoking in the truck and it's getting stupid hot and I can't really see anything, and the next thing I know, someone knocks on the window."

Linda snorts. "Oh shit."

"Right? Then I turn my head, and there's this woman looking right at me through the window. She taps again and motions for me to roll it down. I'm terrified to do it, but I'm also terrified not to do it, because she looks like if I don't, she'll kick my ass. So I roll it down, and she says, 'Little gay white boy, do your parents know you smoke?'"

Linda howls, and I start to break up remembering my first encounter with Farrah. I can picture exactly how he looked that night. "He was wearing his Diana-Ross-in-*Mahogany* dress, although I had no idea then that it was an actual thing. I just saw a pretty woman in a long purple dress with one purple fur sleeve and a turban."

"I know that dress!" Linda squeals. "It's gorgeous. Wait. You just said *he*."

"Sorry. I'm always doing that. Farrah would kill me. But yeah, he's a guy. A drag queen."

"Like Boy George," Linda says. "I love him." She starts to hum the Culture Club song "Do You Really Want to Hurt Me?"

"I'm not sure Boy George was really a drag queen," I tell her.

"Farrah's more like RuPaul."

"I don't know who that is."

"From *RuPaul's Drag Race*? The TV show?"

"I don't think my TV gets that. I mainly watch *Scarecrow and Mrs. King* and *Fame*. I wish they would show new episodes, though. They keep playing reruns."

"Probably for the summer. I haven't seen any of those, though. But I don't watch much TV. Anyway, it took me a minute to realize that Farrah was a guy."

"Does he really look like Diana Ross?"

"He does," I say. "But I didn't even know who *she* was. I didn't know any of the classic stuff. Farrah and Paloma and Lola taught me everything later."

I'm getting way ahead of myself, so I back up. "Okay, so he asks me if my parents know I smoke, and I say, 'I only do it every so often. And I don't have a mother.' And he leans in and says, 'I'm sorry about your mama.' Then I started to cry."

"Because you were sad about your mother?"

"No. Not really. More because I could tell he really meant it. Also, because it was the first time I'd talked to another gay person. Like really talked to one. Have you ever seen *Close Encounters of the Third Kind*?"

"Sure. It's really good."

"Yeah, it's one of Paloma's favorites. He likes sci-fi and fantasy stuff. Well, you know the scene where Richard Dreyfuss finally meets the aliens and he's so happy because he's been thinking about them for so long and now he knows for sure that they're real? That's how I felt meeting Farrah."

"Like she was going to take you away in her spaceship and show you the universe," Linda says.

"Pretty much. Only her spaceship was the Shangri-La. She opened the truck door and took me by the hand, and before I knew what was happening, I was inside. Not in the bar, but in the back. Farrah knew I was too young to be there, but she didn't care. Lola did, though. At first, she told me to get out. She and Farrah had a big argument about it. But Farrah won. I still don't know what she said to Lola, but whatever it was, it worked. That first night I just sat there watching them put on their makeup and costumes. I was terrified to say anything. I couldn't believe how beautiful they were, and how funny. In a weird way it was like listening to the Grands talk. It felt like home. Like I was someplace I belonged. And that's how I started hanging out there."

"It must be nice to have friends like that. People who understand you and want you to be happy."

"It is. Do you have any like that?"

"I thought I did," Linda says. "But it turns out I was wrong." She stops talking, and I hear her playing on her guitar. A minute later she says, "Do you mind if I hang up? I think I have an idea for a song, and I want to work on it while it's still in my head."

She sounds kind of sad. I hope I haven't upset her by asking if she has any friends.

"You can call me later, though," she says. "If you want to."

"Sure," I say. I'm feeling really tired anyway, and know I

should get some sleep before Lola's funeral. "I can't wait to hear what you're writing."

"We'll see if it's any good," she says. "You never know with songs until they're done. Sometimes, not even then."

I hang up and lie in the darkness. According to the clock, it's about to be three. The witching hour. I know everyone thinks that's midnight, but it's not. Or, at least, it didn't used to be. It was always from three to four in the morning, apparently because that's the one hour the Catholic church didn't set aside for prayers, and creatures like ghosts and witches and devils were free to do their thing until the priests started up again at four. I don't know if the Catholics set it up that way on purpose because they figured if they didn't give the ghosts and whatever a chance to run around every now and then they would cause even more trouble later, or if the ghosts found the loophole and went with it, or what. But that's how it was.

When the numbers on the clock read 3:00, I wait to see if Lola's ghost will make an appearance. I'm still not sure how the Grands' ritual with the egg is supposed to play out, but I figure nothing will happen until after Lola's funeral later today. If his ghost is going to do any haunting, now would be the time. Although why he would haunt my house, and not the Shangri-La, or his own house, I don't know.

Maybe he should be haunting his mother. I'm still surprised that Mrs. Householder is Lola's mother. And I'm still sad that they didn't talk for so long. Forty years is forever. I can't imagine not talking to my father, or to the Grands, for that long.

Especially not just for being gay. I know that happens, and that it happened more when Lola was younger. Still, it's extreme.

I wonder if my mother would be upset that I'm gay. My father took a little time to get used to it, but I never worried that he would stop talking to me or anything. But I don't know about my mother. Based on the music she liked, I think she'd be okay with it. I mean, she loved Bowie and the New York Dolls. Not that they were gay, although I've heard Bowie was bisexual. Still, I think she was pretty cool.

Suddenly, I wish I could tell her. I've never thought about it like this before, but I guess Lola was kind of the mother I didn't get to have. Or maybe Lola, Farrah, and Paloma are another version of the Grands. My fairy godmothers. And now one of them is gone.

I think about losing one of the Grands, and how awful that would be. Clodine is eighty-five, which is pretty old, but there's nothing wrong with her. Someday, though, there will be. Or, knowing her, one day she'll just turn into a pile of dust at the kitchen table. But one way or another, one day, they'll be gone.

I can't think about this. Losing Lola is enough. I wait a little longer for his ghost, in case he has something to say to me. But he doesn't show up, and when the 3 on the clock turns to a 4, I figure he's not going to. Still, I can't sleep. Instead, I watch my window.

When the first lemony light coats the glass, I think of the phrase Linda's mother taught her, "Morning is wiser than the evening." Is it true? I don't really feel much better. Lola is still dead. But the sun is a reminder that the world keeps turning and life goes on. So is the sound of the chickens clucking in the yard. Then I hear, just barely, the chorus of Ratt's "Round and Round" coming from the Airstream where my father is probably still asleep.

My life is still here, even though Lola is no longer in it. Nothing I do will reverse time. The world is going to keep turning, and the days are going to keep going forward. All I can do is move forward with them or be left behind. I don't want that to happen, so I get ready to say goodbye to my friend.

Eighteen

When I walk into the kitchen, the Grands look up.

"You're not wearing that," Clodine says. "Go put on a white shirt."

I look down at my black shirt, confused. "White? Why? It's a funeral."

That's when I realize that *they* are all wearing white. Then the door bangs open and my father walks in wearing khakis and a white shirt.

"What's going on?" I ask. "Why are you all dressed like this?"

"For the funeral," Starletta says. "Now hurry up. We don't want to be late."

"You're all coming?"

"Of course we're coming," Hank says.

"But—"

"Change," Clodine orders. "Now."

I know better than to argue with her. As I go back upstairs to my room, though, I wonder why my entire family is coming to Lola's funeral. Farrah said it was going to be a small thing, just for us. I worry that he'll be angry if I show up with the Grands. And what about my father? How does he even know about this? And what questions is he going to ask?

I try not to think too much about it as I look in my closet for a white shirt. I find one and put it on, still unclear on exactly *why* I'm not wearing black. I check my hair in the mirror, then go back to the kitchen.

"Okay?" I ask the Grands.

"Much better," says Clodine. "It would be better if you had white pants too, but nobody wears white pants anymore, except maybe sailors."

"We'll need to take two cars," Hank announces. "John, you ride with Sam in the truck. We'll take my car."

As the Grands pile into Hank's ancient Buick, my father gets into the passenger side of the Ford.

"You want to drive?" I ask, but he waves away the question, so I get in and start the engine.

With nobody to take charge of Lola's funeral, Farrah has done everything. And according to him, Lola didn't want any kind of church service, so we're going right to the cemetery. As we drive there, the question I want to ask my father hangs over me like a storm cloud. I keep hoping he'll say something, but he doesn't. Finally I blurt out, "You're probably wondering how I know Garrison."

He grins. "I wondered how long it would take you to say something. I was about to put you out of your misery." He runs his hand through his hair. "I know all about you going to the Shangri-La, Sam."

He doesn't sound angry. Still, I feel a knot form in my stomach. "I didn't know how to tell you," I say. "I know I'm not old enough to—"

"It's okay. Garrison told me when you first started going there."

"He did?"

"He didn't want there to be any trouble about it," my father explains. "I guess you had already told him that I knew about you being gay, so he wasn't afraid of outing you or anything."

I don't know what to say. My father has known about me going to the Shangri-La for almost two years and hasn't said a word.

"So, are you into the whole drag thing?" he asks.

"Um, sort of. I mean, I've tried it out a little." This is as much as I can admit to him right now. I'm still processing things.

My father is looking at me. "You'd be a pretty girl, I bet."

"Dad!"

He laughs. "I'm just saying. Anyway, you know you can do whatever you want. And I'm sorry Garrison is gone. What did you say his drag name was?"

"Lola."

"Like the Kinks song," he says. "That's perfect." He starts singing, "Lo-lo-lo-lo-looooola."

He keeps singing, and I keep driving. He's on the line about walking like a woman and talking like a man when we reach the cemetery. It's a small one, tucked behind the old Methodist church that almost no one goes to anymore. I pull into the gravel parking lot, which is empty except for Farrah's little red Kia Soul. Hank's Buick pulls up next to me like a battleship docking.

We all get out and make the walk past the church and up the small hill behind it. The cemetery is on top of the hill. There's a fence around it, with a gate in the center. The gate is open. As we pass through it, Clodine runs her fingers over the bars and says to me, "Iron. To keep the ghosts in. Doesn't always work, of course, but you can't make a fence out of salt."

Inside the cemetery, I see Farrah and Paloma. Not Brandon and Ricky, but their drag selves, all done up. And not in black or white, but in colorful outfits. Farrah is dressed in her favorite, a gold-and-red beaded number she wears when she performs as what she calls Afro Cher and sings "Dark Lady," complete with a giant blond puffball wig. Paloma looks like an escapee from a Katy Perry video in a getup she made herself, with giant peppermint-swirl breasts and candy glued everywhere. Her hair is blue, and her eyelids sparkle with pink glitter. She's holding a bouquet of daisies.

When Farrah and Paloma see me, they come over and hug me. I introduce them to my family, watching the Grands for their reactions, but if any of them think Farrah and Paloma are a little over the top, they don't show it.

"Thank you for coming," Farrah says to my father as she shakes his hand.

I glance at the ground, expecting but not wanting to see

freshly dug dirt. Farrah, seeing me looking, says, "Lola wanted to be cremated. Most of her ashes will be kept in an urn at the Shangri-La so that she can keep an eye on all of us as usual. But she also wanted to be buried here next to her grandma, so we put a little of her in a rum bottle."

Paloma holds up a small, dark brown bottle and shakes it. "Because she loved mai tais."

"Naturally," Starletta says as the other two Grands nod approvingly.

Sitting on the ground is a foam head. I recognize it as one of the wig stands from the Shangri-La, the one that usually holds Lola's Dolly Parton wig. Written in black marker across the forehead is GARRISON LOLA BEATTY.

"The real one won't be ready for a couple of weeks," Farrah says. "It's not exactly standard procedure, but I don't think the Lord will mind."

"He certainly will not," Clodine says.

Next to the foam head is a real, older stone. This one reads ERMENGARDE HORSFELD BEATTY January 3, 1887– March 9, 1961.

"Shouldn't Lola's have the dates on it too?" I ask.

Farrah shakes her head. "A lady never reveals her age," she says. She glances at Ermengarde's stone. "Not if she can help it, anyway."

Paloma produces a small trowel, the kind you use to plant bulbs with. "I can't bend in this dress," she says as she hands the trowel to me. "Sammy, it's up to you."

I kneel in the grass and start digging a little bit in front of the makeshift headstone. The earth is soft, and comes up easily, and it doesn't take long until I have a hole deep enough. When I'm done, Farrah hands me the rum bottle. I lay it in the hole on its back, as if it's really a person. Then I shovel the dirt back over it until the hole is filled in again and pat it down. When I'm done, I stand up and wipe my hands on my pants.

"Now what?" I ask.

Farrah takes out a piece of paper and unfolds it. "If you all don't mind, I'd like to read a little something." She clears her throat and recites:

> *This is thy hour O Soul, thy free flight into the wordless,*
> *Away from books, away from art, the day erased, the lesson*
>   *done,*
> *Thee fully forth emerging, silent, gazing, pondering the themes*
>   *thou lovest best,*
> *Night, sleep, death and the stars.*

"Walt Whitman," my father says. "*Leaves of Grass.*"

Farrah nods. "He was one of Lola's favorites."

The Grands and I are all looking at my father.

"What?" he says. "I'm not allowed to know poetry? You gave me *Leaves of Grass* for my thirteenth birthday," he adds, pointing at Clodine.

"I remember," she says. "I just didn't know you actually read it."

My father snorts. Then *he* recites.

I wish I could translate the hints about the dead young men
    and women,
And the hints about old men and mothers, and the offspring
    taken soon out of their laps.
What do you think has become of the young and old men?
And what do you think has become of the women and
    children?
They are alive and well somewhere,
The smallest sprout shows there is really no death,
And if ever there was it led forward life, and does not wait at
    the end to arrest it,
And ceas'd the moment life appear'd.

All goes onward and outward, nothing collapses,
And to die is different from what any one supposed, and
    luckier.

When he finishes, he looks at us with a smug expression.
"And you thought I could only quote Ozzy Osbourne lyrics." He
makes the sign of the horns and sticks his tongue out.

"Smart *and* handsome," Farrah says, and my father blushes.
"Now I know where Sammy gets it."

Paloma leans over and places the bouquet of daisies in front
of Lola's makeshift gravestone. Then we all stand there silently.
I'm not sure what's supposed to happen. I wonder if maybe we

should sing, or recite more poetry. But I don't know any poems, and for some reason the only song I can remember is "Lola," which is still running through my head. That doesn't seem totally appropriate, though, so I hum it to myself and wait for someone to say something.

A moment later, I see Farrah turn around. She gets a puzzled expression on her face, so I turn to see what she's looking at. Behind us, an old woman is walking through the gates of the cemetery. She looks familiar, but it takes me a minute to realize that it's Eulalie Householder. She's wearing a long black dress and a little black hat. She even has on black gloves. And she's carrying something. At first I think it's a stuffed animal, but then I realize that it's a rag doll.

She walks up to us, and we part to let her through.

"Eulalie," Clodine says. "I'm sorry for your loss." Mrs. Householder nods at my great-great-grandmother, but doesn't say anything.

Lola's mother doesn't even glance at Farrah or Paloma. She goes to Lola's grave marker, bends down, and leans the rag doll against it. It's an old doll, stained and worn. It has yellow yarn hair, buttons for eyes, and a dress made out of blue-and-white-checked material with a white apron over it. One foot has a black felt shoe on it; the other one is bare.

Eulalie straightens up. "My mother made that doll," she says. "Garrison always wanted to play with it. I told him dolls weren't for boys; they were for girls. He kept taking her, so finally I put her away and told him I'd thrown her out. He cried for a week."

Her voice is fragile, like the glass in a very old window, and sounds as if it might break at any second. Eulalie clasps her hands together as she stares at the doll sitting on Lola's grave. Then she says, "I'm sorry," practically whispers it, and turns around. We watch her leave the same way she came, without a word to any of us. She passes through the cemetery gates and appears to sink into the grass as she descends the hill, until her hat is the only thing visible. Then that disappears too, and we all stand there in the silence she's left behind.

"Well," Starletta says after a minute. "How about we all go back to the house for some lunch?" She looks at Paloma and Farrah. "You can tell us stories about Lola. Hank is making her fried chicken, and my mother made a lemon pie. You don't want to miss that."

She doesn't wait for an answer, as if the matter is settled, and leaves with Clodine and Hank. My father, Paloma, Farrah, and I come behind them. I feel sad leaving Lola in the cemetery by herself, but then I remember that most of her is going to be in a jar at the Shangri-La, and the part of her that's here has her grandmother to keep her company.

Farrah's Kia follows me as we drive back to the house. When we get there, the Grands start cooking, shooing my father and me outside but letting Farrah and Paloma help them. My father and I set up the picnic table and lawn chairs and bring things out as Hank opens the door and hands them to us. Plates, napkins, utensils, and glasses come first, followed by the food: potato salad, Jell-O with mandarin oranges and whipped cream mixed in, watermelon, pickles, dilly beans, a whole crate of Nehi. The chicken comes last, carried out by Hank on a big platter. Starletta and Clodine come behind her with smaller plates of steamed corn on the cob and biscuits. They look like the three wise men bringing gifts to the baby Jesus in the manger.

With all the food out, we fill our plates and take our seats in the lawn chairs. Despite their outfits, Paloma and Farrah look right at home with my family, and the Grands chat with them as if they've known them forever. We listen to stories about Lola, each one funnier than the last, and there's a lot of laughter.

It's while we're sitting around eating pie that my father says, "What's going to happen to the Shangri-La?"

This is the first time I've even thought about this. I just assumed that the bar would go on as it always has. But with Lola gone, maybe it won't.

"Well," Farrah says. "That's something we need to talk about. Before she died, Lola gave me a copy of her will. Just in case anyone tried any monkey business. And she left the Shangri-La to us."

The anxious feeling in my chest evaporates. "That's great!" I say. "So you and Paloma own it now?"

Farrah shakes her head. "Me, Paloma, and *you* own it now."

"Me?" I laugh, thinking she must be joking.

"Remember how Lola got the money for the Shangri-La from her uncle?" Farrah says. "Well, she wanted to pass it on, and since she doesn't have any real children, she decided to leave it to her drag children. That's us."

What she's saying still isn't really sinking in. "I can't own a bar," I say. "I'm not old enough."

"Lola set it up as a partnership," Farrah explains. "With the three of us as the partners. You can own it; you just can't work in it yet. But that's getting ahead of ourselves. First, we have to decide if we want to keep it or not."

"Why wouldn't we?" I ask.

"The Shangri-La doesn't make a lot of money," Farrah says. "Leastways not enough to support all of us. But the *building* is worth a lot. Lola owned it outright. She had a couple of offers over the last few years, but she turned them all down."

"How much are we talking about?" my father asks.

"Enough to send Sam to college and give me and Paloma a chance to maybe do something bigger than what we're doing."

My father whistles. "That's something to think about, Sam."

"But the Shangri-La was Lola's life," I object.

"Lola's life," Farrah says. "But maybe not ours."

I find that I'm angry at Farrah for even suggesting that we sell the Shangri-La. We just buried Lola, and now she's talking about giving up the one thing that meant the most to her. Something that means a lot to us. Or maybe, I think, just to me. Maybe Farrah and Paloma don't feel the same way.

Paloma hasn't said anything. I look at her. "Is that what you want to do?"

She takes a while to answer. Then all she says is, "It could change our lives."

"Maybe I don't want mine to change," I say. I know I sound

angry, and I don't want to. I don't want Lola's death to start a fight.

Farrah puts a hand on my arm. "We don't have to decide anything today."

I don't say anything. I just sit there with Farrah's hand on my arm. I don't want her to touch me, because I'm mad at her, but I also don't want her to let go, because now I'm scared. I want time to think and figure things out.

But I'm afraid that time is running out.

Nineteen

On Saturday, I work with my dad and Becky at the Eezy-Freezy. It's a blisteringly hot day, all blue skies and no clouds, and apparently everyone in the known world has decided to go to the lake. We've spent all day making shakes and sundaes. My hands are sticky from the ice cream, and my nerves are shot from the screaming kids and their frazzled parents. I'm watching a family of five devour their dip cones (of course each of them wanted a different coating) while I say to Becky, "If one more person asks me to tell them what flavors we have, when the sign is hanging right there on the wall beside the window, I'm going to answer, 'Chicken fat, booger, upchuck, and ass.'"

Becky groans. "Seriously, the woman who wanted to know if we have carb-free slushies?"

We're wiping off the counter for the eight millionth time when the door opens and the Grands walk in.

"What are you doing here?" I ask.

My father appears from the kitchen area, sees the Grands, and says to me, "Come on. You and I are cutting out early."

I don't understand. The Grands rarely come by the Eezy-Freezy. They certainly don't work here. But now they're all putting on aprons.

"Go on," Starletta says to me. "Git. We're taking over for the rest of the day."

"You don't even know how to operate the soft ice cream machine," I protest.

Clodine comes over and eyes the SaniServ. "How hard can it be? It's only got one lever." She pulls on it, and ice cream burbles out. "See?"

"I think we can make some hamburgers and hot dogs," Hank assures me. "And anything we don't know how to do, we'll just tell them the whatchamathingy is broken and we're real sorry about it."

I look at my dad, still unsure.

"Becky's here," he reminds me. "Come on."

I take off my apron, hang it up, and leave with him. We get into his Chevelle, and he starts it up.

"Are you going to tell me what's going on?"

My father shakes his head. "I'll give you a hint, though. Look under your seat."

I reach underneath and pull out a plastic shopping bag. Inside I find two makeup kits, the kind they sell around Halloween, containing tubes of colored greasepaint. The kit has a clown on the packaging, grinning at me with a creepy red smile. I stare at it for a minute, then look at my dad. "What is this?"

"What?" my father says. "I thought you liked clowns."

"Don't you remember what happened at the circus when I was four?"

My father chuckles. "Hey, balloon giraffes are terrifying. Okay, I'll give you another clue."

He reaches under the seat and pulls out a beat-up 8-track cartridge. Without showing me what it is, he pushes it into the player he's mounted under the dash. The old tape clicks and whirs for a few seconds, and then out of the speakers a man's voice says, "You wanted the best, and you got it. The hottest band in the land, Kiss!"

There's the sound of an explosion, accompanied by the opening guitar riff of "Deuce." The album is *Alive!* I know it really well, and not just because it's one of my father's favorites. It's also number nine on my mother's list. I've listened to it dozens of times, maybe even hundreds.

My father drums his hands on the steering wheel as he pulls out of the parking lot. I lean back in my seat and let the music surround me. The note my mother scrawled on the liner of her *Alive!* album says that Kiss is a band you don't just listen to. You experience them. And that's what the album is like. It's like being at a Kiss show. Not that I've ever been to one myself, but my father has seen them a bunch of times.

"You know, they played the Utica Aud on this tour in '76," my father says, right on cue. "Of course, I wasn't even born yet." He sounds disappointed, as he always does when talking about not being alive to see Kiss when they were first starting out. "Man, that would have been amazing."

The song "Strutter" begins, which happens to be both of our favorite. I turn the volume up, and my father and I sing along. I still don't know what Kiss has to do with anything, but it's nice just being in the car with the windows down and the music blasting.

Then I get it. "Wait a minute. Are we—"

"Going to rock and roll all night?" my father says. "And party every day?"

"No way! Where are they playing?"

"Saratoga," my father says. "I can't believe you didn't know."

"I haven't even looked to see who's going to be there this year," I admit. I've had other things on my mind, but I don't tell him that.

"I figure we can stop somewhere, get something to eat, and paint ourselves up," my dad says. "Who do you want to be?"

There's no question about this. "Gene," I tell him. "The Demon." I stick my tongue out the way Gene Simmons does. I already know his answer too. "You're going to be Ace, right?"

"The Spaceman himself," my dad says. Then he sighs. "I wish he was still in the band."

I groan. "Don't sound like one of those internet whiners," I tell him. I switch to a high-pitched, complaining voice. "The band's not the same. Tommy is an impostor, even though he's been in the band for twice as long as Ace was. Gene and Paul are just in it for the money. Wah, wah, wah."

He answers me back by singing really loudly. We ride like this through the rest of the album, not talking, singing and pretending to play guitars and drums. As the last song fades away, we pull into the parking lot of a Burger King.

The food isn't as good as what we serve at the Eezy-Freezy, but it doesn't matter. I'm too excited about the concert. Then we go into the bathroom and break out the makeup kits, spreading the contents on the counter beneath the mirrors.

"I should have picked Paul," my father says as he applies white makeup to his whole face. "He just has the star on his eye."

I take a black grease pencil and start to draw Gene's Demon makeup on one side of my face. It's tricky, especially as I'm doing it from memory, but when I'm done, I like how it looks. I draw the flipped design on my other eye.

"I guess all that drag queen stuff comes in handy, huh?" my father says as he wipes away a mistake in his Spaceman makeup and tries again.

I look around, hoping nobody has heard him. Two of the three stall doors are open, but the third one is closed, and in the gap at the bottom I see a pair of feet in scuffed-up work boots.

My father is oblivious to the fact that we have company. "There's no blue in the kit," he says. "I don't suppose you brought any eye shadow?"

I knock him in the arm with my elbow and, when I have his attention, jerk my head toward the occupied stall. My father makes an "oops!" face, but I can tell he thinks it's pretty funny.

"I'll just go with all silver," he says loudly.

While I'm putting the final touches on my makeup, I hear the sound of flushing. The stall door opens, and a man comes out. He's probably fiftysomething, dressed like a construction worker in worn jeans and a faded red work shirt. He comes over to the sink and washes his hands, not saying a word. Then he reaches into his shirt pocket and pulls out what looks like a pencil. He hands it to my father.

"Grease pencil," he says. "Blue. I use 'em to mark tiles on site. Should work."

My father takes the pencil and applies it to his skin. "Perfect!" He quickly colors around both eyes, then starts to hand the pencil back.

"Keep it," the man says as he opens the door. "It's gonna be a hot night. You might need to do a touch-up."

We finish our makeup and head back to the car. This time we listen to *Alive II* as we make our way to the Saratoga Performing Arts Center. As we get nearer to the venue, we see other cars filled with other people dressed as members of Kiss. Each time, we wave or pump our fists or give the rock-and-roll horns sign. It's silly, but fun, especially when at a stoplight a girl made up as the Catman leans out the window of the car beside us, yells, "God of Thunder!" at me, and I yell back, "And rock and roll!"

The parking lot is filled with fans made up as their favorite Kiss members, and as we make our way into the venue, I think about how underneath the makeup, each one of us is different. Probably, a lot of us wouldn't like or even speak to each other under other circumstances. But for tonight, we're all part of the Kiss Army, and everybody is getting along.

One of the nice things about SPAC is that even the lawn

seats are fantastic. That's where we're sitting. My dad spreads out the blanket he's brought, and we sit there watching the crowd and waiting for the show to begin. We sit through an opening band I've never heard of, then during the set changeover we visit the merch tables and get ourselves tour shirts, which we put on.

Finally, the lights go out. Everyone in the amphitheater stands up, screaming, as the loudspeakers crackle and a voice says, "You wanted the best, you got the best. The hottest band in the *world*, Kiss!"

The black curtain that has been hanging in front of the stage drops amid a cannon blast and a burst of confetti, revealing a huge metal structure that looks like a giant spider. Standing in the middle of it, way up near the overhead lights, are the members of Kiss. As the spider's legs extend and the platform lowers to the stage, they play the opening of "Detroit Rock City."

From those first notes on, the concert is a full-on thrill ride. Paul wails. Gene breathes fire and spits fake blood. There are explosions and flames and videos. When Paul gets onto a small platform and sails out over the crowd, everyone goes insane. And at the end, as the band plays "Rock and Roll All Nite," giant fans blow a storm of confetti out over the audience and we all sing along until the very last note and Paul smashes his guitar to pieces. When he asks, "Have you had a good time?" we scream. When he asks, "Can we come back and see you again?" we scream louder. And when he says, "Good night. We love you," I feel as if it's only been fifteen minutes since the show started, and I want to do it all over again.

We're sweaty from dancing and the mugginess of the mid-July nighttime heat, but we're also high on adrenaline and excitement. As we walk back to the parking lot, I say, "For guys who are almost as old as Starletta, they sure can rock."

"Maybe the Grands should form a Kiss tribute band," my father suggests.

This cracks me up, as I picture Hank, Starletta, and Clodine in kabuki makeup. "Clodine would totally be the Starchild," I say. "But we're missing one member."

"Too bad your mother isn't around," my father says as we get into the car. "She would be the perfect Demon." He laughs.

My good mood vanishes instantly. I know my father didn't mean to say anything to make me upset. But he doesn't know what I know, which is that my mother is dead. He starts the car and pops in yet another Kiss 8-track, this time the *Destroyer* album. He sings along as he inches the car into the traffic trying to get out of the parking lot, and doesn't seem to notice that I'm not saying anything.

I look up and catch a glimpse of myself in the rearview mirror. My makeup is smudged a little from all the sweating. As I look at myself in the Demon makeup, I wonder what my mother would look like wearing it. The thing about the Kiss makeup is that anybody can put it on and become the characters. It's easy to imagine yourself in the band because it's easy to look like any one of them.

It's a lot like drag. When you put on the makeup, you become someone else. Maybe that person is a lot like who you are normally, the way Farrah is a more exaggerated version of Brandon. But maybe that person is someone completely different, like when Ricky becomes Paloma. Or maybe it's something in the middle, like Lola was. I feel different with the Demon makeup on, but it's hard to say how. Which part of this is me, and which part is a character? And am I like my mother? Is that why my father said she would make a great Demon? Or is he just saying she's kind of evil?

I want to ask him about her.

"Dad," I say.

"Yeah?"

He's tapping on the steering wheel, singing along to "King of the Night Time World." He's so happy. I know part of it is having seen one of his favorite bands. But it's also because he's with me. I don't want to ruin that. The questions rush to the tip of my tongue. I close my teeth, trap them there, swallow them down.

When they're gone, I open my mouth again and say, "I had a great time tonight."

Twenty

"You got a package."

Hank hands me the box as I come into the kitchen. I take it from her. I heft the box in my hand. It's heavier than I expected.

"You've got the house to yourself tonight," Hank informs me. "We're going to bingo night over at the VFW. Starletta found ants in the sugar bowl, so she's feeling lucky."

"First prize this week is a gift certificate to Hair of the Dog," Starletta announces.

Hair of the Dog is a combination biker bar and dog grooming parlor. It's probably the only place you'll see a little old lady talking to a tattooed Harley-Davidson enthusiast while waiting for a Pekingese to finish getting a shampoo and blowout. And you never know which one of them is there for the dog and which one of them just likes the buck-a-bottle Budweisers and jukebox filled with Foreigner and Lynyrd Skynyrd songs.

"I'm going to win it for Millard Fillmore," Starletta says. "He told me he needs some pampering."

Millard Fillmore, who happens to be lying under the kitchen table, thumps his tail against the floor.

"Have fun," I tell the Grands, and head upstairs with my box,

I'm actually thrilled that they're not going to be around. I have plans. Tom Swift is coming over. We were just going to listen to records or watch a movie or something. But the arrival of the box has changed that in a big way.

I shut the door to my room, find a pocketknife in my desk drawer, and use it to slice open the tape on the box. What's inside is even better than I was hoping, which is both a relief and kind of unnerving. I put it back in the box, shove it under my bed, and go take a shower to wash off the grease smell from the Eezy-Freezy.

Now comes the second part of my plan. The part I've been thinking about for a while but also trying not to think about *too* much because I'm afraid if I do, I'll talk myself out of it.

I sit down at my desk and get to work. First, I set a small mirror up. Then I lay all the makeup out on the desk and start painting my face. I go for a more realistic style so that I look more like an actual girl than a glammed-up drag queen. When I'm done, I examine myself in the mirror. I look good, if I do say so myself.

I put on a blond wig. Then I get dressed: a red bustier and panties, stockings, and a garter belt. It would probably look even better if I made myself breasts, but even without them, I'm a good-looking girl. I even have heels, tall ones that make me stand so that my butt is pushed out.

I practice walking in the heels, tottering over to the record player and taking Blondie's *Parallel Lines* out of its sleeve and putting it on the turntable. As "Hanging on the Telephone" starts, I try dancing. I almost tip over as my ankle buckles, but I grab the edge of the dresser to stay upright. I try again, and this time I manage to move around a little.

I'm attempting a twirl when I hear Tom Swift's voice calling up the stairs. "Anyone home?"

I go to the door. "Come on up!"

As he tramps up the stairs, I take the package and put it on the bed. I also take his bag of syringes and T from the closet and place them beside it. Then I go into my bathroom and shut the door. My heart is beating in my chest, but it's too late to back out now.

"Where are you?" Tom's voice cuts through Debbie Harry informing me that she's gonna get me, get me, get me, get me.

"In here," I call. "Your T is on the bed. And I got you something else. It's kind of a present."

I lean against the door and wait to hear something. It's difficult over the sound of the music, and for a minute there's nothing. Then Tom Swift says, "What the fuck?"

I can tell he's opened the package.

"Sam," he yells. "What the hell is this?"

"What does it look like?" I yell back.

"A dick."

"That's what it is."

"What am I supposed to do with it?"

"There are instructions."

I wait another couple of minutes, getting more and more anxious. Blondie moves on to "Picture This," then "Fade Away and Radiate." It's during the end of this song that Tom Swift comes and knocks on the door.

"Are you coming out, or what?"

"Yeah," I answer. "Just a second."

I take a deep breath. Then I open the door and step into my bedroom. Tom Swift is standing there, his hands on his hips. He's wearing a Totoro T-shirt and white boxer shorts. A dick is sticking out of the fly of his boxer shorts.

Tom looks at me. "Whoa."

"Do you like it?"

He looks at me some more, his eyes moving from my high heels to my wig. "It doesn't even look like you."

I'm not sure if this is good or bad. I point to his dick. "Thanks. I think. But I meant that."

Tom looks down. His dick wiggles back and forth. He doesn't say anything.

"It's called a Mr. Stiffy," I say. "It's for, you know, trans guys. They make a regular version too. I mean one that's not hard. But you said you wished you could feel what it's like to have a hard-on, so I thought this would be better. It's not quite the same, I know, but . . ." I stop talking. Tom hasn't said a word, and I'm afraid he's mad at me.

He wraps his hand around his dick and strokes it a little. "It feels so real," he says. "I mean, I guess it does. I've never touched one."

"Was the harness easy to figure out?"

He nods. I can't see it under his boxers, and his dick is sticking out like a real one would, so I guess everything is working the way it's supposed to.

The record comes to the end of side 1. I go turn it over. Tom is still playing with his dick. He's got a smile on his face. He sits on the bed, takes out his T and a syringe, and prepares to inject himself. His dick flops against his leg, and he laughs.

I watch as he pushes the needle into his thigh. When he finishes, he caps the syringe and puts everything back in the bag. Then he lies back on the bed. His dick sticks up.

Before I can lose my nerve, I walk over, drop to my knees, and reach out, taking his dick in my hand. Then I lean forward and put my mouth on the head. It slips between my lips. It tastes like licking a beach ball.

Tom Swift doesn't move. He doesn't say anything. I push more of his dick into my mouth. It's weird, but it's also exciting. I've never had a real one in my mouth, so I don't have anything to compare it to, but it *feels* real. Tom's skin is warm, I can feel him shifting around, and it's easy to pretend that I'm really sucking him.

Like I said, I've never done this before. But I've seen a lot of videos, and I try to do what I've seen the guys in them do. They must have a lot of practice, though, because I only get about half of Tom's dick in my mouth before I start to gag. It's a good thing his isn't real, or I would probably be scraping him with my teeth.

I pull back, then try again. This time, I manage to get more of him into my mouth. I move up and down his dick slowly. I have no idea if I'm doing it right or not.

Tom Swift moans. At first, I think I've hurt him somehow. I take his dick out of my mouth.

"Don't stop," he says.

I try again. Tom Swift reaches down and touches my wig. His fingers brush against my face. He seems to like what I'm doing. I like making him excited, and giving him what he's always wanted. It's what I've wanted too. And I want more.

I stand up and crawl onto the bed, straddling Tom's body. I start rubbing myself against him, and he opens his eyes.

"What are you doing?"

"I want you inside me," I say.

I can feel Tom pressing against me. I press back, and he groans. His fingers reach for the waistband of my panties, and he starts to pull them down. Then he stops, and the expression on his face changes.

I look down and see that the head of my erection is sticking out. Tom Swift is staring at it. I quickly tuck it back inside.

"Just pretend," I say.

He shakes his head. "I can't."

I try rubbing against him some more. I lean down, letting my hair fall in his face. I want so badly to make him happy. To make us both happy.

He moves his hands away. "Sam, I can't."

I climb awkwardly off the bed, trying not to touch his dick. My own is still hard, refusing to go down, and I'm ashamed.

Tom sits up. He reaches for his shorts, which are on the floor, and pulls them on. He has trouble stuffing his dick inside them.

"Now I know what you mean about it getting in the way," he says. He laughs a little, but I can tell he's embarrassed. So am I. I don't say anything. In the background, Debbie Harry is singing "I'm Gonna Love You Too." I wish she would shut up.

Tom says, "I'm sorry, Sam. I'm just not into guys. You look really pretty, but it's just not the same."

I look up. "Yeah, well, I'm not into girls, so I guess I get that."

Tom looks as if I've slapped him. "I'm not a girl, Sam. I'm a guy."

"Right," I say. "I forgot. I guess I was fooled by the fake dick."

As soon as I say it, I regret it. Tom's face hardens. He unzips his shorts, reaches inside, and pulls out the Mr. Stiffy. He yanks on it, hard, and it comes loose. He tosses it at me. It hits me in the chest. I flinch, and it falls at my feet.

Tom stalks by me, bumping me with his shoulder. "Have fun playing dress-up," he mutters.

He storms down the stairs. The bag with his T and syringes is still sitting on the bed, but I don't call him back or try to follow him. When I hear the screen door slam shut, I kick the Mr. Stiffy. It slides across the floor. I fling myself onto the bed and press my face into a pillow. I can still smell Tom Swift's aftershave on it, and this makes me start to cry.

The last song on *Parallel Lines* is called "Just Go Away." It's an appropriate ending to the disaster that's just taken place. I sing the lyrics to Tom Swift, trying to forget about what a fool he's made of me. What a fool I've made of myself.

I get it. He's a straight guy. He likes girls. But I like guys, and I was willing to pretend a little. Why can't he?

I feel like an idiot all over again. I need something to help me forget. I go downstairs and open the cabinet over the sink where the Grands keep the bottle of gin they use to make gin and tonics sometimes. I don't bother getting a glass. I take the gin back to my room, unscrew the cap, and take a slug.

It tastes terrible, like chewing on pine needles, and makes me gag. But I also like the way the alcohol hits the back of my throat. And I really like how after a few more sips, I can feel things getting a little fuzzy.

I go over to the record player and put the needle at the first track on the album. As Debbie Harry sings, I start to dance. I sing along with her, using the gin bottle as a microphone. The jittery, punkish music is fun to move to, and the pissed-off lyrics reflect exactly how I feel. I toss my head around, hair flapping in my face, and pretend I'm fronting Blondie at a concert in some small club in New York or someplace else far away from where I really am. I imagine the crowd watching me, wishing they were as cool as I am. But I don't care what they think. I don't care about anything except the music.

I dance and drink right through the second side of the record, then turn it over and play side 1 again. All the songs start to run into each other as the gin makes everything a hazy, tipsy blur. I'm trying to remember the words to "Pretty Baby," and can't.

"Pretty baby, I peed on your shoes," I sing, knowing it can't be right but completely unable to recall the real lyrics.

I step on something and look down. The Mr. Stiffy is under my foot. "Sorry," I apologize to it. "I didn't see you there."

I reach down and pick it up. I hold it up, and notice that there's lipstick all over the tip. This strikes me as hysterically funny, and I start laughing. I take another drink from the bottle of gin, but nothing comes out. I upend it, tilting my head back. Still nothing. I don't know where it all went, but it doesn't matter. My head is twirling around, and I don't care about anything. I know I was upset earlier, but I can't remember why.

Then I do.

Tom Swift. Mr. Stiffy. What Tom and I said to each other. All of it comes rushing back into my cloudy mind, and suddenly I know I'm going to be sick. I drop the gin bottle, throw Mr. Stiffy onto the bed, and run into the bathroom. I barely have time to lean over the toilet before everything comes up.

I retch and retch, each new wave of nausea cramping my stomach like a sucker punch to the gut. It seems to go on forever. My throat burns, and the taste in my mouth is enough to make me gag again. When I'm fairly sure that there's nothing more that can come out, I manage to get up and get to the sink, where I rinse my mouth out before going back to my room.

The bed seems really far away. Also, the floor seems to be pitching like the deck of a ship in a storm. I close my eyes and lurch forward. I hit the bed and tumble onto it. I spread my arms out, clinging to the blankets as the mattress rises up on a wave.

Just hold on, I tell myself as I wait for the storm to die down. *Just hold on. Just hold on.*

Twenty-One

sleep and dream your heart's desire
sleep and dream the face of love
when you need me, call my name,
i'll come to you and keep you safe

The voice cuts through my troubled dreams, bringing me out of the fog I've been wandering in. My mouth tastes terrible, and I feel as though I've been wrestling with a bear. A really big, really angry bear. I struggle to open my eyes, which are stuck together and sticky.

I reach up and pull at the thing holding my eye closed. It comes away in my fingers. At first I think it must be some kind of weird insect. Then I remember. My fake eyelashes. I flick it away and open my eyes.

My father is sitting on the end of my bed. He's holding the cover of *Parallel Lines* in his hands and looking at it.

"Did you know 'Heart of Glass' was originally written as a reggae song?" he says.

I nod. "I listened to it on YouTube. Was that you singing a minute ago?"

"Was I singing?" he said. "Old habit, I guess. I sang that to you the first few nights. It was the only way you would go to sleep."

"I thought Ilona sang that to me," I say.

My father puts *Parallel Lines* down. "Ilona?" He laughs. "Ilona can't sing a note. No, that was me."

I wait for him to say more about this. Instead, he looks at me for what seems like forever. Then I remember that I'm still dressed up in my drag from the night before.

"It must have been some party," my father says.

I reach up and pull the wig from my head, trying to shove it under my pillow. "I, um. I was . . ."

"It's okay, Sam," my father says. "I came up because you were supposed to be at the Eezy-Freezy two hours ago. I thought you might be sick."

I am sick, or at least feel like I'm going to be.

"I'm fine," I say. "I just overslept."

I get out of bed. Then I see the Mr. Stiffy lying on the floor. I quickly kick it under the bed, hoping my father hasn't seen it. I'm still wearing the heels, and I almost trip and fall on top of my father. He reaches out to catch me, but I wobble-dodge him and race past him for the safety of my bathroom. When I'm inside, I shut the door, lock it, and sit down on the toilet.

I take off the heels and toss them in the corner. Then I pee, flush, and stand up. I'm still not ready to face my father, so I spend some time washing the makeup off my face. I also take off the lingerie and pull on the boxers and T-shirt lying on the floor. When I look like my normal boy self, I open the door.

My father is walking around my room. He's put a record on the stereo. Elvis Costello's *This Year's Model*. Number 11 on Ilona's list.

"I haven't listened to this in years," he says. "I'd forgotten how good it is."

"His lyrics are like poems scribbled on the backs of cocktail napkins in lipstick."

My father laughs. "Oh, that's good."

"It's what Ilona wrote in the liner notes," I tell him.

I go to my bed and sit down. My father comes and sits next to me. He's looking at the sleeve of the Elvis Costello album, reading Ilona's note.

"Did she do this on all of them?" he asks.

I nod. "You never looked at them?"

He shakes his head. "She left them for you," he says. "Besides, I was kind of pissed at her. The last thing I wanted to do was listen to her records. I stuck the box in a closet until you were old enough to have them."

I wait a minute before I say, "I think she's dead."

"What?" he says. "Why would you think that?"

"She left a suicide note," I tell him. "Inside record number five."

"I forget which one that is."

"Black Sabbath. The first album."

He rolls his eyes. "That sounds like Ilona. Did she really say she was going to kill herself?"

I shrug. "I might have misinterpreted it. Do you want to see it?"

To my surprise, he shakes his head no.

"I probably should have mentioned it a while ago," I say.

"Why didn't you ever ask me?"

"Why didn't you ever talk about her?"

"Fair enough," he says.

"This is fucked-up," I say. "You know that, right?"

He stands up. "I don't know what to tell you, Sam. Am I sorry this is how it played out for you with your mother? Of course. But you can't change the past. You can only deal with the present and look to the future."

"You should have the Grands needlepoint that up for you," I say.

He sits back down. "I know you're angry at her."

"What else should I be?"

"Nothing. I'd be angry too if I were you."

"Shouldn't you be angry anyway? She left you too."

His eyes grow sad. "I never really expected her to stay."

"So naturally you made a baby with her."

He starts to respond, then stops. I can tell he's wrestling with what to say next. And all of a sudden, I'm not sure I want to hear it.

"I met your mother at the carnival," he begins. "She was working at one of those booths where you try to toss a Ping-Pong ball into little bowls of water to win a goldfish. A quarter for each ball. I thought she was pretty, so I put down five dollars and took my time, just so I could talk to her."

This is literally the most he's ever told me about my mother. Ever.

"I don't even remember what we talked about. Stupid shit. I was trying to impress her, but I couldn't land a throw in any of those bowls. I blew through all twenty of my balls and never came close. Then I found one last quarter in my pocket. I told her I wanted one more ball, but that she had to kiss it for good luck. And then I said that if the ball landed in a bowl, she had to go out with me."

"What did she say?"

"She said that her kisses were cursed, and that if she kissed the ball, it would be sure to miss. But she did it anyway. I closed my eyes and tossed it, and when I opened them, she was staring at a bowl. The ball was sitting right inside it. She told me later that it shouldn't have been possible. The openings to the bowls are a little too small for the balls to fit in, so they usually bounce off. But this one didn't."

"So, she went out with you."

My father nods. "After her shift. We rode all the rides and ate a bunch of junk. Then I took her for a drive and got her pregnant."

I expect him to laugh and say that he's joking. He doesn't.

"We didn't know she was pregnant for a while, of course," he continues. "We found out a few months after that."

"Then why did she stay?" I ask. "If she didn't know she was pregnant, I mean. Why didn't she move on when the carnival did?"

"She said it was because I landed that ball in the goldfish bowl. Said it was a sign that I was the guy who could fix her bad luck. Then I told her about the curse, and she said maybe we had crossed each other's bad luck out. I thought maybe she was right."

"But then she left when I was born."

"But then she left when you were born," he agrees.

"And you really haven't heard from her in all this time?"

He shakes his head. "Not a word. But I know she isn't dead."

"How?"

"Because Dokken is still alive."

At first, I don't understand. I think he's talking about the metal band Dokken. Then I realize that he's talking about the bubble-eyed black fish that lives in a bowl on the kitchen counter in the Airstream.

"You don't expect me to believe that that's the goldfish you won that night at the carnival. He'd be almost eighteen years old. Goldfish live like six months, especially with how often you change the water."

"That's him," my father insists. "When Ilona left, she said that as long as he was still swimming, so was she."

I want to argue with him, because this is simply not possible. But now that I think about it, I can't remember a time when Dokken wasn't sitting in his bowl in the trailer.

Then I think of something else.

"If Ilona isn't dead, then the curse didn't get her," I say.

My father looks sad again.

"What?" I say.

"The curse only works if you fall in love," my father says.

"Yeah," I say. "And you and Ilona were in love. Ergo, she should be dead, and Dokken should have been belly-up years ago."

"I don't think I was ever in love with Ilona," my father says. "Not really. I think I *wanted* to be. But I didn't really know what being in love was. Not until I held you for the first time, anyway."

I have no idea what to say. A lot of things I've always thought were true apparently aren't. I keep opening my mouth, starting to say something, then closing it again. Finally I say, "Don't you ever wish we were a normal family?"

"What's normal?" he says, standing up. He walks to the door, then turns back and looks at me. "I'll see you downstairs."

Twenty-Two

It's Saturday night—four days since the disaster with Tom Swift—and I'm working at the Eezy-Freezy with Becky and my dad. Normally, Saturdays are not my favorites, because there's a steady stream of customers from the time we open until the time we close. But today I'm thankful for the distraction.

I haven't seen Tom Swift since the night I made an idiot of myself, but I've been thinking about him. I know I went too far. I know I need to apologize. But I haven't been able to make myself dial his number. I decide I'll do it when I get home.

Then I look up and Anna-Lynn is standing in the order window. Tom Swift is behind her, his arms around her.

"Hey, Sam," Anna-Lynn says.

"Hey."

Tom Swift doesn't say anything to me, but he nuzzles the back of Anna-Lynn's neck. She laughs, and Tom smiles.

"Can we get a banana split?" Anna-Lynn says.

"Sure."

I start making the sundae. Anna-Lynn and Tom stay

standing in the window, so it's like watching a television show starring them. Tom keeps kissing Anna-Lynn's neck and cheek, and she keeps laughing and pretending that it's making her crazy. I can't help but think that Tom is doing this to prove something, but to who, I'm not sure.

I put the banana split on the counter. Anna-Lynn takes it, dips a spoon into it, and holds it up for Tom Swift to take a bite from. He does, then licks the end of the spoon.

"I think I got some whipped cream on my nuts," he says.

Anna-Lynn giggles at the stupid joke.

"You'd have to have nuts for that to happen."

I don't even realize I've said it out loud until I notice Tom looking at me. He's not smiling. We stare at each other for a second before he says, "Fuck you, Sam."

He slaps a five-dollar bill on the counter. "Keep the change," he says. "Maybe you can use it for some new lipstick and wigs."

He stares at me, as if daring me to take the money. Anna-Lynn is still holding the spoon in her hand. "What's going on?"

"You'll have to ask her," I say, looking at Tom Swift.

Tom's face tenses. Then he turns and stalks off. Anna-Lynn looks at me. "What the hell, Sam?"

I don't know how to answer her. I didn't mean to out Tom Swift. It just happened. And maybe Anna-Lynn didn't get what I was saying anyway.

"Forget it," I say. "And give him back his money. I don't want it."

Anna-Lynn sets the banana split down. I want to apologize

to her, but she leaves before I can. The banana split and the five-dollar bill are still sitting there, and now a woman is waiting to give her order. I see her staring at the counter, waiting for me to clear it.

"Hang on a minute," I say, and go into the back, where Becky has been helping my dad in the kitchen.

"I'm feeling kind of sick," I say. "Can you guys cover for me?"

Becky wipes her hands on a towel. "Sure. I'll go up front."

"What's wrong?" my dad asks when she's gone.

"My stomach," I tell him. And I'm not lying. My guts feel all knotted up. But it's not because I'm sick. "I think I'm going to go home."

He looks at me for a moment. Then he nods at the door. "Go on," he says. "Have Starletta whip you up a glass of her tummy tamer."

I cringe. Starletta believes that any stomach ailment can be soothed with a mixture of milk, Coca-Cola, and a raw egg.

"It works!" my dad yells as I leave.

Thankfully, Tom Swift and Anna-Lynn are nowhere to be seen as I go to my truck. I wonder what kind of conversation they're having. Will Tom Swift tell her about what happened the other night? Will she tell him that she knows his secret? Or will they just pretend everything is okay? Whatever happens, it's my fault. And that makes me feel like crap.

I drive home, park, and sit in the truck for a while. I can hear the Grands in the kitchen, talking. I feel like smoking, so I risk it and light up a Camel, blowing the smoke out the open window. Part of me hopes someone comes out and says something so that I can pretend I don't care what they think. I'm kind of pissed off at everybody at the moment. Mostly myself.

I finish the cigarette, get out, and go inside. The Grands look up as I come in. "You're home early," Hank says.

"I just need to get something," I say, walking past them and going upstairs to my room. I take the paper bag with Tom Swift's T and syringes in it out of my closet. I add the Mr. Stiffy to it, then go back downstairs.

I don't look at the Grands. "I'll be back later," I mumble as I leave.

I get back into my truck and drive. My anger at Tom Swift is growing hotter, like a coal someone is blowing on. The feeling radiates through me, filling up every bit of empty space. All I can think about is how he looked at me with such disgust, like I was something he'd found on the bottom of his shoe.

Fuck you, Sam.

I hear his voice in my head.

Fuck you.

I drive until I reach the little bridge outside of town, the one that crosses over Coldwater Creek. I pull my truck to the side of the road and park it there. I take the paper bag and walk to the center of the bridge. The quarter moon illuminates the water passing beneath me, streaking the surface of the creek with silver threads that shimmer as they wind around the rocks.

I hold the bag out over the edge of the railing. For a moment,

I hesitate. Then I picture Tom's eyes looking at me as if he hates me more than anything in the world, and I let go. The bag tumbles through the night, and there's a soft splash as it hits the water. The creek gurgles in surprise, then swallows it up and carries it away.

"Fuck you, Tom."

I walk back to my truck, get in, and pull back onto the road. The bridge rattles under my tires as I cross it and head out of town. I'm not ready to go home yet, so I drive. I don't even think about where I'm going. I just follow the road, one arm on the wheel and one hanging out the open window. I drive away from Tom Swift. I wonder what it would be like to keep going, to get on the thruway and drive all night, to head west, maybe, until I end up somewhere totally different. Somewhere new.

What I want is to go home. But home doesn't feel safe anymore. Tom Swift is roaming around my world like some kind of dangerous animal I don't want to run into. I need somewhere new. Somewhere safe.

But there is nowhere safe. Not now.

In the end, I turn around after about fifty miles and drive back. It's after midnight, and I'm getting tired. My anger at Tom Swift is fading to sadness, which is much, much worse. I don't want to miss him. Not so soon.

When I get back to the house, I go inside and barely acknowledge the Grands, who are now playing Yahtzee. I go up to my room and take a shower to get rid of the lingering smells from the Eezy-Freezy and the cigarettes and my unhappiness. Only two of those things wash away. Then I sit on my bed with the telephone and dial Linda.

"Everything is fucked-up," I say when she answers.

She laughs. "You're just figuring this out?"

"I mean here, specifically," I say. "In my life. Tom Swift hates me."

I explain about the other night.

"Wow," Linda says. "Plot twist. I'm sorry."

"It's not your fault." I sigh. "I was wishing tonight that I could run away from everything. Go somewhere totally new. Have a different life. Be a different person. You ever feel like that?"

Linda says, "That's what Dorothy wished for, and remember what she learned."

"Dorothy?"

"In *The Wizard of Oz*. But what did she end up figuring out?"

"That a pair of pretty shoes isn't always worth the trouble?"

"That there's no place like home."

"Oh, that. I don't know. I think she should have stayed in Oz. I've never understood why she wanted to go back. From what I can tell, Kansas kind of blows."

"I should do a tarot reading for you," Linda says. "Hold on. Let me get my deck."

I hear Linda moving around. Then she comes back. "Sometimes when I'm feeling a little lost, I pull one card and let it tell me what I should be focusing on," she says. "Let's see what card comes up for you."

I hear the sound of shuffling. Then Linda says, "Okay, I've spread them out. I'm moving my hand across the cards. When you want me to stop, say 'stop.'"

I don't really know how I'm supposed to decide, so I wait awhile. Then, weirdly enough, I feel a kind of tingling in my body. "Stop!"

"I've got your card," Linda says. "I'm turning it over."

There's a short silence, then she says, "Interesting."

"Interesting how?"

"You pulled the Eight of Swords."

"Is that bad?"

"None of the cards are necessarily bad. Some are maybe more challenging than others."

"Is this one of them?"

"That depends on how you look at it."

"Well, I'm not looking at it at all, so I have no idea."

"Oh, right. Sorry. Well, the card depicts a woman standing up, wrapped around with rope. She also has a blindfold over her eyes. And there are eight swords stuck into the ground around her."

"Swords and rope sound not good," I say. "What does it mean?"

"Like I said, it depends. Some people interpret it to mean a person who is feeling outnumbered and helpless, powerless to do anything."

"And some people don't?"

"I prefer to think of it as someone who feels overwhelmed,

but just needs to take off the blindfold to see things more clearly. To change her way of thinking and see other ways of dealing with the situation."

"But how can she when she's tied up?"

"That's the thing. She's tied up. But has someone else tied her up, or has she tied herself up?"

"It's kind of hard to tie yourself up."

"It's a metaphor," Linda says. "Just go with it."

"Okay, so I can totally relate to the feeling outnumbered and overwhelmed thing. What do I do about it?"

"That's up to you."

I snort. "I thought the point of tarot cards was to tell you your future."

"Not really. They show you how things are. What you do with that information is up to you."

"I think I want my money back," I tell her.

She laughs. "Sorry. No refunds. We can do a larger reading, though, if you want to."

I'm tempted. But I'm also feeling exhausted by everything that's going on. "Another time?" I say.

"Sure."

"Thanks for listening to me. I should probably get some sleep now. Morning is wiser than the evening. Isn't that how it goes?"

"You remembered!"

"Yeah, well, it's good advice. Your mom is smart."

"She is," Linda agrees. "I wish I'd listened to her more."

"Is she dead? I'm sorry. I don't remember you saying anything about it."

"She's not dead," Linda says. "We just haven't talked in a while. It's a long story. I'll save it for another night."

"You sure? I'm not *that* tired."

"I'm sure."

"Okay. Well, thanks for listening. And for the tarot reading."

"Anytime. Good night, Sam."

Twenty-Three

The inside of Lola's house is airless and hot. The first thing Farrah does is open the windows in the living room. A small breeze comes in, but not enough to drive out the stifling heat.

"This place is like a museum," Paloma remarks as we look around.

She's right. The room is crammed with antique furniture, and every shelf, table, and mantle is covered with knickknacks: china figurines, glass vases, teacups. On the walls, portraits of stern-looking women and men look out at us, as if we've invaded their home and woken them from two-hundred-year-long naps.

But the weirdest thing is the Christmas tree. In one corner of the room, a huge artificial tree looms. Paloma touches a switch on the wall beside it, and it comes to life. Hundreds, maybe thousands, of small white bulbs begin to twinkle, illuminating the ornaments that crowd the branches. An elaborate tree topper almost grazes the ceiling.

"This thing must be twelve feet tall," Farrah says.

I go over and look at the ornaments. There are hundreds

of them, each one different, all made of glass. I see snowmen, angels, a dozen different Santas. Glass birds with real feather tails perch on the branches. Strings of tiny glass beads are strung around the tree, and strands of perfectly placed tinsel dangle airily.

"I guess somebody liked Christmas," I say.

Farrah goes over to an old phonograph and picks up a record that's sitting on top of it. *"Holiday Sing Along with Mitch,"* she says. "Mitch Miller and the Gang. Old-school."

"She told me once that the only time she was happy was at Christmas," Paloma says. "I guess she decided to make it Christmas all year long."

"Like Miss Havisham and her wedding day," Farrah says. When she sees Paloma and me looking at her with clueless expressions, she adds, "From *Great Expectations?* Charles Dickens? Don't you bitches read? Woman got jilted as she was getting dressed for her wedding. Found out her fiancé had swindled her and run off. She kept everything just the way it was for the rest of her life. Wedding dress. Wedding cake. Everything."

"Sounds like she needed to let some things go," Paloma says as she investigates a hanging cabinet lined with tiny spoons commemorating the fifty states.

Farrah puts the record back. "You two need to brush up on your literature. Let's go upstairs. Maybe we'll find Santa Claus tied up in the guest room."

We walk up to the second floor. There are two guest bedrooms, each one overflowing with more collectibles. We leave them without looking too closely, then go into the third bedroom, which was Lola's.

Over the bed there's a framed poster for the film version of *Damn Yankees*. It shows Gwen Verdon wearing the famous black merry widow costume. Against one wall is an antique makeup table with a lighted mirror. It's covered in pots and tubes and brushes. Tucked into one edge of the mirror is a photo of Lola wearing a costume very similar to the one Gwen Verdon is wearing in the poster. And on a stand to one side of the table is a hat shaped like a big pink rose, just like the one she wears in the film.

"More records," Paloma says, holding up the cast album from *Damn Yankees*. She looks through the rest of the stack sitting near the phonograph that rests on top of a small table. Unlike the one downstairs, this one looks like something a kid would have in his bedroom sixty years ago, and it occurs to me that it's probably the one Lola had when she was little.

I'm looking at another framed item. It's the playbill from *Sweet Charity*. Across the white part of the magazine cover is an inscription: "To Garrison, Whatever you want, you get! Best Regards, Gwen Verdon."

"It's like a shrine," Farrah says. She opens the door to the room's closet, then whistles. "Stuffed with girl clothes," she says. "I wonder where she kept her boy clothes?"

"Probably in one of the guest rooms," Paloma suggests. "I think this room is like the Christmas tree. It was how she wanted her life to be."

I sit down on the edge of Lola's bed. For some reason, the room makes me incredibly sad. "She spent her whole life wishing she was somebody else."

"Most people do," Farrah says.

"Is that what we're doing?" I ask. "Doing drag? Are we trying to be people we're not?" I think about the time Lola commented on Farrah being a little black boy who named himself after a white woman, and how hurt Farrah looked when she said it.

Farrah turns around. "Lola was not the happiest person on the planet," she says. "I think he really would have preferred being a woman. And it looks like that's how he lived when he was alone."

"You think he was trans?"

Farrah shrugs. "I don't know what he would have called it."

"Now you're calling him 'he.' What happened to 'she'?"

Farrah shuts the closet door. "You know I almost always say 'she.' But right now we're talking about Lola the person. Not Lola the character. And what I'm saying is that I don't know what Lola—what Garrison—thought about who he was. Maybe she was trans. Maybe he just liked to dress up. People aren't always one thing or another. You know that. Lola was from a different generation. Things were harder then for queer people. They didn't have as many options. What I *do* know is that he did the best he could with what he was dealt."

"Can I ask you guys something?" I say. "It's kind of personal."

Farrah snorts. "Honey, you've helped me tuck my boy bits

up inside my butt crack and tape 'em in. How much more personal does it get?"

"Do you ever want to be real girls? Like, go the whole way?"

Farrah shakes her head. "Uh-uh. I like having a ding-dong."

"Ding-dong?" Paloma says. "What are you, four?"

"More like eight and a half," Farrah says, cracking up. "That's why it takes so much duct tape."

Paloma rolls her eyes. "I've thought about it," she says.

"Really?" I ask.

She nods. "I'm a lot happier as Paloma, so for a while I thought, why not be her all the time?"

"But?" I say.

"But I'm not a woman," she says. "It's one thing to dress up as one a couple of nights a week. It's another to know you're one. I might not be all that happy as Ricky, but being Paloma full-time wouldn't change that."

Farrah sits down in the chair at Lola's dressing table. "May I ask what brought this up? It's not just all this, is it?" She gestures around the room.

I'm embarrassed to tell them about what I did, dressing up for Tom Swift.

"Sammy, are you thinking you might be trans?" Farrah presses. "Cuz you know we're your sisters and would be fine with that."

"No. I'm not trans. I don't know what I am." I take a breath, then tell them about what happened with Tom Swift. I tell them everything. Well, not quite everything. I leave out the part about throwing Tom Swift's T and his dick into the creek. But I do tell them about outing him to Anna-Lynn.

"Maybe the girl didn't get your meaning," Paloma says when I'm done.

"Maybe," I say. "But that's kind of not the point. The point is, I shouldn't have said anything at all."

"True," Farrah agrees. "You shouldn't go blurting out people's business like that. But I know how it can be. One time I was dating this guy and he was all, 'I love you' and 'I want to be with you forever.' Then one day I was at the mall and ran into him with his girlfriend. They were looking at *engagement rings*. I had a couple of things to say to the both of them. But in that case, I don't think I was wrong."

"No, you were not," says Paloma, and they nod at each other.

"That's the thing, though. Tom Swift and I were never going out. He never promised me anything. Nothing. This is all me."

"Friends fight," Paloma says. "You'll make up and get over it."

I can tell they don't really understand. Or maybe I'm the one who doesn't understand. Either way, talking about Tom Swift with them isn't helping. Thankfully, there's something else to talk about, and now Farrah brings it up.

"I don't know about you two, but I don't see myself taking up residence here," she says.

In addition to leaving us the Shangri-La, Lola has also left us the house and everything in it. That's why we're here, to decide what to do with it.

"Me neither," says Paloma. "I say we sell it."

"Sammy?"

Having to decide whether or not to sell a house is not something I thought I would be doing at sixteem. I've lived with the Grands my whole life, in a house that my dad lived in his whole life and that the Grands have lived in for almost forever. I can't imagine us ever selling it. So having to make that decision about Lola's house is a big deal for me.

"I guess," I say. "What else are we going to do with it?"

"That's settled, then," Farrah says. "Now I know we've put off talking about it, but this is as good a time as any to do it. What about the Shangri-La? As you know, we each own a share of the bar. As you also know, we've had a very nice offer to buy the place. We've all had a little bit of time to think about it, so I want to see what we're all thinking. Paloma, what about you?"

"I think we should keep it," Paloma says. "If we sell the house, that will be a little bit of money for everyone. And I don't have anything else going on, so I'm happy to work at the bar."

Farrah sighs. "Is that really what you want to do with your life? I thought you were thinking of going to cosmetology school. You want to work at a bar in the middle of nowhere, or do you want to go out on tour with Ariana Grande and make her beautiful every night?"

"That's not going to happen," Paloma says. "The most I can hope for is opening my own salon."

"You need to dream bigger."

"Oh yeah?" says Paloma. "What about you? What are your plans?"

"I say we sell the place. I'll use the money to send myself to school."

"And what are you going to study?"

"Filmmaking," Farrah says.

"Filmmaking?" Paloma says, and laughs. "Gurl, you going to be the next Steven Spielberg?"

"More like the next Ava DuVernay," Farrah says. "And what's so funny about it? I already filled out my application to NYU."

Paloma laughs again. "New York University?"

I can see that Farrah is getting mad. She looks at me, "That makes one for selling and one for keeping. Looks like you're the deciding vote, Sammy."

Any relief I felt at not talking about Tom Swift anymore disappears instantly. I don't want to be in this position. Farrah and Paloma want different things, and I want them both to be happy. But one of them isn't going to be, and which of them it is depends on what I decide.

"I still don't know," I mumble.

They both groan.

"Come on, Sammy," Farrah says. "What are you going to do with a bar you can't even legally work in yet? You can't expect us to run it and just give you a third of the profits when you can't even help out. No offense. It's not your fault. But it's how it is."

"We can always work something out," Paloma counters. "Don't worry about working, Sammy. The Shangri-La will be there when you're ready."

"So you expect him to stay put in this backwoods little bit

of nothing?" Farrah says. "Just like Lola did? Why? What's here for him?"

"His family, for one thing."

"Family doesn't pay the bills," Farrah snaps. "And family isn't all there is. There's a whole big world out there. Maybe he wants to see some of it. Just because you're afraid to take chances—"

They start arguing. I tune them out, staring at the mirror over Lola's dressing table. I see my face reflected in it. Next to it is the photograph of Lola dressed as the other Lola. Sitting in her bedroom, surrounded by her dreams, makes me feel trapped. Farrah is right. I don't want to end up like Lola. I loved her, but I don't want to be like her.

I also don't want to disappoint either of my best friends. I've already disappointed Tom Swift, and myself. I don't want to add anyone else to that list. I stand up.

"I've got to go. I'll talk to you guys later."

"Sammy!" Farrah calls as I leave the room.

I ignore her and go downstairs as quickly as I can without running. I walk past the Christmas tree and through the living room. I go outside, then remember that I drove there with Farrah and Paloma in Farrah's car. I don't have a ride.

So I walk. Lola lives in town, and our house is a couple of miles away. It's a long walk, but I've done it before. Besides, it will give me time to think. I half expect Farrah and Paloma to come after me, but they don't. Part of me is relieved, but another part—the part that's mixed-up and angry and wishes somebody would just tell me what to do—is mad at them for not coming.

But that's typical of how I feel lately, so I'm kind of getting used to it.

It's hot as anything, and as I walk past the Bi-Rite, I want to go in and get something to drink. But through the doors I can see Anna-Lynn standing at the register, and I can't deal with seeing her right now. So I keep going. Sweat starts to pour down the back of my neck and soak my T-shirt, and I wish there was a breeze or something to cool me off, but the afternoon is completely still, like even the weather doesn't want anything to do with me.

I have to walk over the bridge out of town, which of course makes me think about throwing Tom Swift's T away. I don't look at the water as I cross the creek, even though I'd really love to walk down to the edge and stick my feet in.

I'm about halfway home when I hear a car coming behind me. I turn around, thinking maybe Farrah and Paloma have decided to come looking for me. Instead, I see Tom Swift's grandparents' car coming toward me. Tom is behind the wheel. For some reason, I decide it's a sign. Like the universe is arranging things so that we have to talk to each other.

I put my arm out, my thumb extended up like I'm a hitch-hiker looking for a ride. I wiggle my hand back and forth. The car approaches, but doesn't slow down. As it speeds by, Tom Swift doesn't even turn his head to look at me. He keeps his eyes straight ahead as he hits the gas and disappears around the bend.

Twenty-Four

On Wednesday night, the Grands go to movie night in town. The VFW is doing something they call Shh!: A Silent Film festival. Every night is a different movie, and tonight it's the Harold Lloyd film *Safety Last!* It's one of Clodine's favorites. I kind of want to go, but I want to be alone more than I want to see the movie.

I got a wicked sunburn walking home from Lola's house on Monday, and it's at the ouch stage, where touching it makes me wince. I've slathered some of the Grands' homemade lotion on it, and it feels a little better, but I still feel hot all over, and all I want to do is sit in my room with a fan blowing on me and drink the bottle of beer I swiped from the fridge downstairs. I've got the Cramps' *Songs the Lord Taught Us* on the stereo. The muddy, swampy sound of their music perfectly fits how I'm feeling.

Songs the Lord Taught Us is number 12 on Ilona's list. It's weird and punky, and the songs are about things like UFOs, teenage werewolves, and cutting off your lover's head and putting it in the refrigerator. It sounds gross, but it's actually a lot of fun.

Since no one is home, I have the music turned up louder than I usually do. I'm listening to my favorite song, "Strychnine," when I hear a car pull into the driveway. At first I think it's the Grands coming back early. Then I see Tom Swift standing outside the screen door.

"Hey," he says.

"Hey. Come on in."

He opens the door and comes into the kitchen. I've been thinking so much about what I want to say to him, but now that he's here, I forget all of it. "Want a beer?" I say.

"No, thanks," he says. "I just came by to get my T."

My stomach drops. "Uh," I say. "Don't you want to talk about what happened?"

He shakes his head. "Not really."

"I didn't mean to out you to Anna-Lynn," I say anyway.

"She already knew."

"You told her?"

"No. But she knew. She's not stupid."

"I never said she was."

What I want to ask him is how she feels about it, and whether they're still a thing. But now I'm getting angry again, and I don't want this to turn into a fight.

Unfortunately, it's kind of doomed to turn into one anyway, because now I have to tell him about his T. "I don't have your T."

"Where is it?"

I consider lying and telling him that one of the Grands found it. But something inside me wants to hurt him, to make him feel bad for how he's acting, and so I say, "I threw it away."

"You what?"

I take a drink from the bottle of beer. It's mostly gone now, and it's making me feel less worried. I swallow, set the bottle down, and say, "I said I threw it away."

I watch his face, and it's like watching a film speeded up. His emotions register so clearly, moving from disbelief to shock to anger in about five seconds.

"You had no right to do that," he says, his voice shaking.

I shrug. Inside, I'm a tornado of emotions: anger, fear, sadness, a little bit of happiness. I'm glad he's upset. Now he knows how he made me feel. A small part of me understands that what I'm doing is cruel, but I bury it beneath a pile of anger.

"So, go get some more," I say.

He turns red. "It's not like it's a can of soda," he says. "You can't just go pick some up at the store. You know that. Do you know how much that T cost me?"

I don't say anything. Tom Swift's hands are balling up into fists, and I wonder if he's going to attack me. I kind of want him to. A physical fight would be less painful than the one we're having. But he just stands there, his hands clenching and unclenching.

"You stupid little fag," he says, and wrenches open the kitchen door. It slams behind him, leaving me staring at the spot where he used to be.

His words slap me harder than any hand ever could. They ring in my ears, echoing as they bounce around, growing louder and louder. I want to scream something after him, but I can't think of anything.

I hear a car start up. A second later, I hear another sound, a loud yelp. Then a kind of high-pitched yowl. I leap up and go outside. Tom Swift is leaning out the window of his grandparents' car, looking behind him. In the driveway, Millard Fillmore is lying on his side. His mouth is open, letting out the horrible screaming sound.

I run to Millard Fillmore and kneel down. His eyes are open wide, and he's trying to move. But something is wrong. His sides are heaving, as if he's having trouble breathing.

"I didn't see him," Tom Swift says. "He must have been behind me."

I ignore him. I know I need to get Millard Fillmore to the vet. I try to pick him up, and he lets out a piercing howl. I stroke his head and whisper, "It's all right. It's going to be all right."

Tom Swift has gotten out of the car and is standing behind me. "Is he okay?"

"What do you think?" I snap.

I slide my hands underneath Millard Fillmore. He yelps as I lift him up, and his body twitches. I know it must hurt, but there's nothing I can do. I carry him toward my truck. Tom Swift follows me.

"What can I do?"

"Open the door."

He does, and I set Millard Fillmore down on the seat. He's whining and panting, and now I see blood on his tongue. I shut the door, then run back to the house for my keys. Tom Swift stands in the yard, staring at the truck. When I come back out, he says, "I didn't see him," again.

I ignore him, getting into my truck and starting it up. I leave Tom Swift standing there and take off. I keep petting Millard Fillmore as I drive. His whimpering is softer now, and his eyes are closed. I'm terrified that he's dying, and I keep my hand on his side so I can feel whether it's moving or not. It is, but barely.

There's only one vet in town. Dr. Stavin is closed for the day, but I know where she lives. I drive to her house, breaking about fifteen different traffic laws, and pull up next to her truck. "I'll be right back," I promise Millard Fillmore.

I run to the door of the house and bang on it. It seems to take forever for anyone to answer, so I bang again. Then it opens, and Dr. Stavin looks out.

"Millard Fillmore was hit by a car."

She follows me to my truck, where she examines Millard Fillmore. He barely opens his eyes, but he does thump his tail weakly against the seat.

"Is he going to be all right?"

Dr. Stavin doesn't answer me, instead saying, "I need to get him inside."

I let her carry him. He doesn't even yelp as she picks him up, which worries me. It's as if he doesn't even have enough life left in him to hurt. I hover around Dr. Stavin as she carries Millard Fillmore into the house, opening the door for her and waiting for her to tell me what to do.

"I need to see if there's any internal bleeding," she says. "I can do that here, but if anything shows up, we'll have to take him to the office."

"What can I do?"

"Wait in the living room. He'll be calmer if you're not in there worrying."

I sit down on a couch and watch as she takes Millard Fillmore through a doorway and into another part of the house. I have no idea what to do with myself. It feels weird being in Dr. Stavin's house, as if I'm here for a visit. And I can't concentrate on anything because I keep replaying the sound of Millard Fillmore crying in my head.

I know Tom Swift didn't mean to hit him. I know this. But I'm angry at him anyway. I keep telling myself that he should have looked behind him. He should have paid more attention. He shouldn't have come over in the first place. But of course he *wouldn't* have come over if I hadn't fucked everything up.

If Millard Fillmore dies, I'll never forgive Tom Swift. Or myself. I can't even imagine having to tell the Grands that he's dead. He's been part of our lives for as long as I can remember.

I stand up and walk around. Not that there's really anywhere to go. But sitting feels like being trapped. The problem is, walking doesn't get me away from the thoughts in my head. Lola and the Shangri-La. Tom Swift. Now Millard Fillmore. It's all happening at once.

And then I think, maybe it's the Weyward Curse. Maybe that's why all this is happening. I know it usually works by killing the person you fall in love with, but isn't that kind of what it's doing, attacking *everything* I love? Maybe it's somehow gotten stronger, or I've made it stronger, and now that my birthday is getting closer, it's working overtime.

"You can't take Millard Fillmore," I say.

"I'm afraid I'll have to," a voice says. "At least for the night."

I turn to see Dr. Stavin standing behind me.

"Sorry," I say. "I didn't mean you. I meant the cur . . . Is he okay?"

"I don't know," she says. "I don't see any signs of internal bleeding. But he's old, and you can't always tell what's going on inside. I want to keep him overnight so I can watch him."

I can't help but think about Lola and the "complications" that killed him after we thought he would be okay. What if the same thing happens to Millard Fillmore? What if tomorrow Dr. Stavin calls and says, "I'm sorry, but there were complications"? I couldn't take it.

"Can I stay with him?"

She opens her mouth to answer, and I know she's going to tell me it would be best for me to go home, so before she can, I say, "Please."

"Okay," she says, giving me a little smile. "We can make a bed for him on the floor, and you can lie next to him if you want to. That might make him feel better."

I know she means it will make *me* feel better. And she's right. I reach for my phone so I can call my dad and let him know what's happened and where I am, but I've left it at home. "Can I use your phone?" I ask Dr. Stavin.

She shows me to the phone, and I call my dad. He's upset, but I make it sound as if everything really will be okay. I ask him to tell the Grands not to worry, and he says he will. While I'm on the phone, Dr. Stavin brings out a bunch of blankets and a sleeping bag, and we make a soft bed for Millard Fillmore on the floor in the living room. She carries him out and lays him on it.

"I gave him a sedative, so he'll sleep," she says. "Watch him, and if anything seems off, you come get me, all right? I'll be upstairs."

When she's gone, I unroll the sleeping bag next to Millard Fillmore and lie down. I get as close to him as I can, so that his back is against my front. I put my arm over him, holding his paw. My face is pressed into the fur of his neck. He doesn't smell particularly good, but he smells familiar, like home. I close my eyes and breathe him in.

"Good dog," I whisper, over and over. "Good dog, good dog, good dog."

Twenty-Five

"We should be at home."

My father ignores me. He's wrestling with his fishing pole. Somehow, the line has gotten all snarled up in the reel, and he's trying to untangle it.

It's been two days since Millard Fillmore was hit. He hasn't died, but he's not a whole lot better either. Dr. Stavin can't find anything seriously wrong with him, and says he's just old and tired and his body might not be able to recover from the trauma. She sent him home, and now all we can do is wait and see.

"The Grands can take care of Millard Fillmore for a little while," my father says, taking out a pocketknife. He cuts the knotted fishing line, then pulls the string through the guides on his pole. He roots around in the tackle box, pulls out a lure, and ties it to the end. "There."

He's taken me fishing to give me a break from worrying. Unfortunately, being away from Millard Fillmore is making me worry *more*. I'm terrified that he's going to die while I'm gone. Like Lola did.

"Are you sure Becky can handle cooking at the Eezy-Freezy?" I ask, thinking that maybe if I can get my dad to worry about the shop, he'll call this off.

"She'll be fine," he says, casting his lure into the creek.

I sigh. Apparently, he's not going to give in on this. I toss my own line into the water and wait. It's another hot day, but we're standing in the shallow water in the shade of some trees along the creek bank. Dragonflies are skimming along the top of the water, and minnows are darting around my toes. If I wasn't a ball of worry, it would be pleasant.

I'm also edgy because I think my father wants to talk about what happened the other day, about how he found me in bed in drag. I'm afraid we're maybe going to have The Talk we've never had, and I don't think I'm ready for it.

"You know, we haven't talked very much about what you want to do with yourself," he says, and for a second I panic, thinking this is it. Then he continues. "This is your last year of school coming up. I assume you don't want to hang around here and work at the Eezy-Freezy for the rest of your life."

My heart calms down. This conversation I think I can handle.

"I don't know," I say. "Eight bucks an hour and all the ice cream I can eat. Sounds pretty perfect to me."

The truth is, I haven't really thought about life after graduation. Partly this is because of the Weyward Curse, where nobody thinks beyond turning seventeen because they don't want to jinx it. Partly it's because nobody in our family has ever gone to college. But also, I don't want to think about leaving the Grands, or my father, or even Millard Fillmore. I know that there's not a lot happening for me in this little town, but this little town is my entire life.

"There's the Shangri-La," I say. "I could help run that. Or we could sell it and use the money for something else."

"You have options," my father says. "That's more than a lot of people have."

I know he's right. A lot of the kids in my class don't have options. Their families don't have money, or they're needed to work on farms, or they simply don't have the grades. They'll stay here, getting dead-end jobs and living here until they die. Some might join the military as a way out, which is great and everything, except for the part where we seem to always be fighting wars in horrible places and the chances of coming back with pieces missing is pretty high, if you even come back at all.

So yeah, having options is nice. Still, I feel like whatever decision I make, someone will be unhappy about it. I don't like that reaching for my dreams (whatever they are) means someone else might not get to have theirs come true. And I don't like that the main reason I have options is because Lola is dead. That's a big price to pay, and I'd rather have her alive again.

"Hey," my father says. "I think I got something."

His line is taut. He tugs on it, and the bobber sinks a little.

"Whatever it is, it's pretty heavy."

I watch as he reels in his catch. It's not darting around like a fish would, so I suspect he's accidentally caught a turtle, or even a small log. But he's having fun, so I don't say anything. I wait for the hook to come in, bringing his catch close enough to see.

Something rises up through the brown creek water. It's pale, and it jiggles in the water, and for a moment I think maybe it *is* a fish. Then my father lifts it clear of the water.

"What the hell?"

The Mr. Stiffy is hanging from the hook, which is embedded in one of its balls. It dangles in the air, water dripping from the tip, as my father reaches out and grabs it.

I'm so horrified at seeing the thing that I can't even laugh. Of all the things he could have fished out of Coldwater Creek, he had to go and hook Tom Swift's fake dick.

He takes the hook out of the dildo and waves the Mr. Stiffy at me. "Think it's legal size? Maybe I should toss it back so it can get bigger." He laughs like a mad person and waves it again.

I wish he would stop. I can't even look at it. I remember dropping it off the bridge and hearing the splash. The paper bag must have ripped open. I wonder if Tom Swift's vial of T and the syringes are also hanging around at the bottom of the creek. They might actually float, which now that I think of it would be pretty horrible. I don't want anyone tubing down the creek to find them.

My father tosses the Mr. Stiffy onto the creek bank, where it lies like a beached perch. He laughs again. "I don't even want to know how that got into the creek. I mean, did someone toss it out the window while they were driving over the bridge? Did it fall out of—"

Mercifully, his musing on the origins of the dong is cut short by Twisted Sister's Dee Snider yelling, "I wanna rock!"

It's the ringtone on his phone. Dee keeps telling us that he wants to rock while my father scrambles up the bank to where his phone is sitting on top of the cooler. He picks the phone up and answers it.

"Shit," he says a few seconds later. "All right. We'll be right there."

I spin around, panic rising. "Is Millard Fillmore all right?"

"It's not Millard Fillmore," my father says. "It's Clodine. She collapsed."

"Collapsed? How? Why?"

"That's all I know right now." He sounds scared, though, and I wonder if there's something he's not telling me.

I know there's something I'm not telling him. It's about the curse, and how I think it's changing, expanding. Ever since the night Millard Fillmore got hit, this has been on my mind, this worry that the curse is reaching to touch everything I care about. Now I'm sure something is happening. I want to blurt it all out, but I also don't want to say it out loud, like maybe if I keep it to myself, it won't really happen.

We gather up our stuff, including the Mr. Stiffy, which we stick in the cooler, and head back to the truck. I let my father drive. We don't talk, but I can tell he's anxious. So am I. The dark clouds that have been gathering over me for the past few days seem to be getting even darker, like the storm brewing inside of them is about to unleash itself.

When we reach the house, there's an ambulance in the

driveway, but the yard is empty. We run inside and discover everyone in Clodine's room. Clodine is lying on the bed, Hank and Starletta are standing at the foot of it, and two paramedics are attending to Clodine.

"What happened?" my father asks.

"We were working up some magic," Starletta says. "We should have known better. The curse is too strong."

Hank glances at me, then nudges Starletta, who looks at me as if she's just realized that I'm there.

"What are you talking about?" I say.

"Nothing," Hank says a little too quickly. "We were out gathering milkweed, and Clodine got a little too much sun, that's all."

"You said you were working up some magic," I argue.

One of the paramedics, a woman, says, "We're going to need to take her to St. Anne's."

"I don't need a hospital," Clodine says. Her voice is weak and raggedy. She tries to sit up, then falls back against the pillows.

"Miss Weyward, you might have had a stroke," the paramedic says. "We need to get you to the hospital and get you checked out."

"All I need is some of Starletta's rainwater tonic," Clodine says.

"Mom, I think the young lady is right," Starletta says. "Let's just get you checked out, okay?"

"You know doctors don't know anything," Clodine says. "You go into the hospital, you don't come out again."

Starletta takes her hand. "Please, Mom. I'll feel better."

Clodine sighs. "Fine. But bring some of that tonic too."

"Sure," Starletta promises, and nods at the paramedics, who leave the room.

"What did you mean about the curse being too strong?" I ask again.

"You never mind that," Starletta says. "I was just talking."

I start to argue, but my father puts a hand on my shoulder. "Not now," he whispers.

The paramedics come back in with a gurney. They lift Clodine onto it, then strap her in, ignoring her protests. As they wheel her out of the house and into the ambulance, a debate about who is going to go with her begins. In the end, we decide that Starletta will ride in the ambulance with her while the rest of us wait here for an update.

"It's not like I'm going to die on the way there," Clodine hollers from the back of the ambulance. "I'll give you fair warning when it's time."

When they're gone, my father goes to the Airstream and I corner Hank in the kitchen. "What was all that about magic and the curse?"

My grandmother takes a Nehi out of the refrigerator. "I already said, it wasn't anything. Starletta was just talking."

"You're lying."

Hank slams the Nehi down on the counter so hard that soda splashes out and over her hand. "Don't you talk to me like that!"

My grandmother has never yelled at me before. Ever. Now she looks as if she'd like to smack me.

"I'm sorry," she says as she turns on the tap and rinses the

Nehi from her hand. "I'm worried about Clodine is all."

"She's mine too," I say.

"I know she is."

"You think she took sick because of the curse, don't you?"

There. I've said it out loud, the thing I've been keeping to myself. I want my grandmother to tell me I'm being ridiculous, that it doesn't work that way. I want her to tell me that this is all just a bunch of horrible coincidences.

Hank leans against the counter. "It's a possibility."

I feel my throat tighten. "Because of Lola, and Millard Fillmore," I say. "You think it's trying to take the things I love." I don't mention Tom Swift, but his face flashes through my mind.

I can tell that Hank doesn't want to confirm my suspicions. I wonder how long she and the other Grands have been talking about it. "What kind of magic were you doing?"

"Nothing big," Hank says. "A little poppet magic."

"Poppet?"

"A kind of doll," she says. "Made from leaves and twigs and whatnot. We wanted the milkweed for hair. We were walking out into the field to get some when Clodine had her spell."

"I don't get what a doll—a poppet—has to do with the curse."

"It's symbolic," Hank explains. "A representation. You make the poppet and then you bring it to life, in a manner, and tell it what you want it to do."

"And what did you want it to do?"

"You're not supposed to talk about it," Hank says. "It undoes the magic."

"But you didn't do the spell," I say. "Did you?"

Hank hesitates. "Not yet," she says.

"You mean you're still going to? After what happened to Clodine?" I shake my head. "Uh-uh. No more magic. Not if it's pissing off the curse."

Hank doesn't say anything.

"Promise me you won't," I say.

Hank shrugs. "We'll see."

"Do you want Clodine to die?" I ask. "Do *you* want to die? Because that's what's going to happen. The curse is going to take everything I love. That's how it works."

"That's not how it works," Hank says. "It only takes the one you fall in love with."

"Not anymore. I don't know why, but it's gotten bigger. Now it's taking everything."

I wait for her to tell me that I'm wrong. When she doesn't, I know that she thinks I might be right. "I'm going to go check on Millard Fillmore," I say. "Hopefully it hasn't gotten him yet."

I go up to my room. Millard Fillmore is sleeping in the blanket nest next to my bed. I check to make sure he's breathing, but I don't wake him. I don't have any idea what to do. If I'm right about the curse, who's next on its list? My father? Hank? Starletta? Maybe Farrah or Paloma? I feel like everyone I love is in danger now.

I sit down on the bed and wait. That's all I can do. Wait.

Twenty-Six

"You really believe this curse is a thing, huh?"

I'm on the phone with Linda. It's the middle of the night on Saturday. Beside my bed, Millard Fillmore is asleep in his blanket bed. On the stereo, Roxy Music's *Avalon* is playing. I have it turned down low, and the music is sort of running underneath everything else, the guitars and keyboards throbbing while every so often Bryan Ferry's voice floats out of the darkness like some kind of ghost trying to get a message through.

"Of course I do," I tell Linda. "Look at what it's already done to our family. Now all of these things in a row? What else could it be?"

"Maybe just plain old bad luck?" she suggests.

"No," I argue. "It's got to be the curse. It got Lola, now it's after Millard Fillmore and Clodine."

"But Millard Fillmore and Clodine aren't dead."

"True. But I have a theory about that."

I wait for her to ask me what my theory is. When she doesn't, I tell her anyway. "Clodine has been doing magic for a long time.

And she and the curse are old enemies. Maybe she can't break it, but she can fight it. And Millard Fillmore is sort of magical himself. I can't even tell you how old he is. He's been living around the Grands' magic his whole life. Some of it's probably rubbed off on him. That's why I think he's not getting any worse. He's like Sleeping Beauty. He's in a holding pattern until something wakes him up."

"Have you tried kissing him?"

I know she's only joking about this because she's never experienced magic before, so I let it go. But I'm serious. I think Millard Fillmore and Clodine have been touched by the Weyward Curse and are fighting it.

"Hey, I wrote a song for you," Linda says.

"You did?"

"Remember the tarot card you drew?"

"The Eight of Swords," I say.

"After we talked, I was thinking a lot about what it means. I started writing some lyrics about it, and before I knew it, I had a song. I think it's pretty good. Here, listen."

"Let me turn off Roxy Music," I say. "Hang on."

I take the needle of the record, then get back on the phone. "Now I'm all yours."

Linda starts to play. The notes ripple out from her guitar. Then she sings.

8 of Swords
bind my hands

bind my heart
blind my eyes
blind my heart

i'm imprisoned by your swords
tangled thoughts and twisted words
hold me here afraid to move
afraid to speak afraid to love

mind my hands
mind my heart
find my eyes
find my heart

center, center, look inside
do not listen to the lies
that fill my mind like cawing birds
telling me i don't deserve

kind my hands
kind my heart
wind my eyes
wind my heart

undo the ropes, remove the mask
take the first step down the path
gather speed run toward the sun
war is over, battle won

"I love it," I tell her. "It sounds like the card, at least the way you described it."

"Thanks," she says. "It feels good to be writing again. Besides, there's not much else to do."

"Still foggy and wet there?"

"Yeah. Lots of rain. But that's okay. Writing is good for me. It gets stuff out. I'm not great at getting stuff out. Mostly, I hold it in. You know, let it all bottle up until I think I might choke on it. Then it all comes out at once, usually in some spectacularly inappropriate way."

"I can relate. Did I tell you I threw Tom Swift's dick in the creek?"

"How do you even do that?"

I explain to her about the Mr. Stiffy and the T. "But it came back," I say, and tell her about my dad's catch of the day.

"Another omen, I suppose," she says.

"Totally."

"Where is it now?"

"Still in the cooler in the back of the truck, I guess. I kind of forgot about it until now. I should probably get it out of there before my dad gets it into his head to mount it on the wall as a trophy or something."

"Trophies. Ugh," Linda says. "My father is a hunter. He loves to shoot things. I guess that's how he handles his anger."

"He's not mean to you, is he?" I ask, concerned.

"Not mean, no. He more or less ignores me and my mom. As my mother says, he shows he cares by bringing home deer meat and ducks filled with buckshot."

"Good thing you don't take after him. I think writing songs is probably a healthier way to deal with your feelings than killing things."

"Probably," she agrees. "But you can't eat a song. So, you were listening to Roxy Music before, right?"

"Yeah. Number thirteen on Ilona's list. It's not one of my favorites. I have to be in the mood for it."

"Why does she love it?"

"The note inside says that it's the perfect album to listen to when you want to go to another world."

"That makes sense. Avalon. Arthur. Camelot. Maybe she means fairyland. Maybe it reminds her of home."

Her talking about home reminds me of something else. "I've been thinking," I say. "Maybe if I survive this curse, we can actually meet up in person to celebrate."

"Yeah," Linda says. "Maybe."

"You still haven't told me where you are."

There's a long pause. Then she says, "Guess."

"Well, it always seems to be cold and rainy. Maybe Seattle?"

Linda makes a sound like a buzzer. "Strike one."

I think some more. "Iceland?" I know I'm not right, but it fits the description.

Another buzzer sound. "Strike two. Stick to North America. And I'll give you a clue. People leave their hearts here."

Her saying that triggers something in my brain, a memory of Starletta humming a song while dealing cards. "San Francisco."

"Ding, ding, ding," Linda says. "We have a winner. Your prize is a lifetime supply of Rice-A-Roni."

"I don't know what that is."

"Rice-A-Roni. The San Francisco treat? Don't you watch *The Price Is Right*? They're always giving it away. It's this instant rice stuff. Or pasta. I don't know. It's good, though."

"Clodine won't watch it since they replaced Bob Barker with Drew Carey. Besides, I don't think that's a prize anymore."

I have no idea what she's talking about, but I'm excited that now I know where she is. "I'd love to visit San Francisco," I say. "I think for gay guys that's like coming home to the motherland. Maybe at the end of the summer I'll use my tip money to fly out there."

I wait for her to say that that's a great idea. Instead, she says, "I can hear the foghorn tonight. It always sounds so sad, like some kind of lonely sea monster calling to the other monsters in the darkness. I picture him swimming around, trying to find another one like him, but never doing it. He just swims around and around, calling, and he thinks the other monsters are answering him, but really it's just big ships blowing their horns back to tell him to get out of their way."

"That's completely depressing," I say. "But also really beautiful."

"The best things are."

On the floor, Millard Fillmore talks in his sleep. "I should go," I tell Linda. "Millard Fillmore is having a nightmare."

"Go," Linda says. "Tell him everything will be okay. I'm going to listen to the monster for a while."

I hang up and get down on the floor with Millard Fillmore. I sit cross-legged and reach out to touch his ears. He makes a little whimpering sound and twitches. I rub his ears, and he calms down. I lie next to him. I'm tired, and somehow I fall asleep quickly despite everything that's on my mind.

Sometime later, something shakes me awake. I wake up, confused, and see Millard Fillmore has gotten up. He's turning around in circles next to me. Finally, he decides everything is the way he wants it, and lies down.

"I guess you're feeling better," I say.

He grunts softly. I put my arm around him. He licks my hand, as if to say, "I'm going to be fine. We're all going to be fine. You'll see."

Twenty-Seven

The next morning, I wake up to the sound of Foreigner blasting from the Airstream. My father only plays Foreigner when he's in a bad mood, so I know something is wrong. I get out of bed, leaving the still-sleeping Millard Fillmore there, and stumble downstairs. Hank and Starletta are in the yard, staring at the trailer. My father's voice, slurred and angry, dribbles from the windows as he tries to sing along with "Head Games."

"He's drunk," Hank informs me.

My father almost never drinks, and when he does, he only has one or two beers. I can't imagine what has happened to make him overdo it.

"It's always the same, and you know who's to blame," he wails.

"Oh, dear," Hank says. "He's relating to the lyrics."

"I'll go check on him," I tell her and Starletta.

I walk over to the Airstream. I don't bother knocking, since the music is so loud my father wouldn't hear me anyway. I just open the door and step inside.

My father is sitting in a chair, surrounded by a graveyard of empty and smashed Genesee Cream Ale cans. The trailer reeks of beer. My father, who is busy pretending to play a guitar solo on an invisible guitar, looks at me with half-closed eyes. He smiles. "Sammy!"

"Hey," I say, sitting down. "What's going on?"

My father stops playing the pretend guitar. He looks around for another beer, but apparently he's drunk all of them. He sighs unhappily, "No beer. No anything." Then he looks at me. "'Cept you and the Grands."

"And Millard Fillmore."

"Millard Fillmore," my father says. Then he begins to cry. "Poor Millard Fillmore. He's a good dog. I don't want him to die."

It's weird watching him cry. I don't know what to do. I start by going over and turning the music off.

"What happened?" my father says, looking around. "Is the show over?"

"For now," I tell him, sitting down again. "And if it makes you feel better, I think Millard Fillmore is going to be okay."

"Really?" my father says. "Good. He's a good dog." Then he looks sad again. "But what about Clodine?"

"I don't know about her," I admit.

He starts to cry again. "It's all my fault."

"What?" I say. "Why is any of this your fault?"

"Because," he says. "I should never have fallen for Ilona."

That's when I notice the photo in his lap. It's one of him and my mother. I've never seen it before. They're standing together, and my father has his arm around Ilona's shoulders. They're both smiling.

Now I get it.

"Don't ever fall in love, Sammy. Not ever, ever, ever."

"I'm trying not to," I tell him.

"Not even after your birthday," he says. "Promise me you won't ever fall in love."

"I don't know if I can promise that, Dad. I don't think it's something you can help."

He sighs again, then shakes his head. "You're right," he says. "You're right. Stupid hearts don't have on/off switches on 'em."

"They should," I agree.

I try to imagine what it's been like for my father. My mother left seventeen years ago, so technically he and I have been single for the same amount of time. But obviously I spent a lot of that time growing up and not even knowing what being in love meant. He's the one who's been alone. I don't think he's even been on a date since Ilona went away.

I always think of my dad as, well, a dad. Now I'm thinking about him as a person. A man. And not an old man whose life is mostly over and who has gotten to do all kinds of things. A man like me who would like to find somebody to love for as long as he can. All he ever got was the short amount of time he and Ilona had together, and for nine months of that, he had to share her with me.

My father tries to stand up, staggers, and sits down with a grunt. He tries again, and this time he manages to stay on his feet, although he's swaying a little. The photograph of him and Ilona has fallen to the floor.

"What are you doing?" I ask him.

"Gotta get to the Eezy-Freezy," he says. "Gotta make the burgers."

"First of all, it's only seven o'clock in the morning," I say. "Second, you're not going anywhere like this. You stay here. Becky and I can handle things today."

He shakes his head. "I don't wanna sit in here anymore. It makes me sad."

I think for a minute. "All right. Come with me."

He follows me out of the trailer and into the morning sun. He squints, holding his hand over his eyes. "Who turned the lights on?"

We go into the house, where Starletta is doing something at the counter and Hank is sitting at the kitchen table. I tell my father to sit down, then ask, "Do we have coffee?"

"Even better," Starletta says. "Tummy tamer." She sets a tall glass of milk and Coke on the table. Then she takes an egg and cracks it on the edge of the glass. She empties the egg into the glass and stirs it with a spoon, the yellow yolk swirling into the milky-sweet concoction. She hands the glass to my father. "Here you go."

My father takes a sip, his face wrinkling in disgust. "Ugh. It's like sucking the insides out of a dead possum."

"And how would you know that?" Starletta says. "Just drink it."

My father does as he's told, upending the glass into his mouth and downing it all in one long series of gulps. When he's done, he sets the glass down and rests his head on the table. "I'm going to be sick."

"You are not," Starletta says. "I added a little something for that."

"What?" my father asks, sounding suspicious.

"A dash of Tabasco," Starletta says. She glances at Hank and winks. "And a spider."

My father moans.

"Don't be such a baby," Hank says. "It was a small one. You didn't even know it was there, did you?"

"Leave me alone," my father says. "I want to die."

Hank pats his arm. "Go lie down in the guest room. You'll feel better by and by."

My father gets up and walks slowly out of the kitchen. We hear his heavy steps on the stairs as he goes to the second floor.

Hank looks at me. "You all right?"

"I guess."

"Two weeks," Hank says.

"Two weeks?"

"Until your birthday."

I'd almost forgotten about that. Now I glance at the calendar where the date is marked. Two weeks. Can I make it another two weeks?

"The curse is trying awfully hard," I say. "I think it might go all out before the seventeenth."

I wait for Hank and Starletta to contradict me. But they don't say anything, which means they agree with me. This scares me more than anything. If they think the curse is about to start working overtime, then it probably is.

"We're going to go in and see Clodine this morning," Hank says. "You mind taking over for your dad at the store?"

"I already told him I would," I say. "Is Clodine going to be all right?"

Starletta nods. "Right as rain," she says, although I can tell she's faking it.

"Don't you worry about Clodine," Hank tells me.

"Can I go see her tomorrow?"

Hank and Starletta look at one another.

"What?" I ask.

Hank says, "It might be better if you didn't. Not for a day or two, anyway."

"Why?"

"Just in case," Starletta says.

"In case what?" Then I get it. "You think I might take the curse with me. Is that it?"

Starletta shakes her head. "No one's saying that."

"But no one's *not* saying that." I stand up. "I'm going to work. I'll try not to kill anyone else if I can help it."

I leave before they can stop me. I'm not mad at them. Not really. I know they're doing what they think is best for Clodine. But it stings a little, especially on top of everything that's going on.

258

I get into the truck and drive over to the Eezy-Freezy. It's still early, and Becky won't be in until just before we open, so I have the place to myself. I go inside, turn the radio on, and spend the next two hours cleaning and prepping for the day. By the time Becky arrives there's nothing to do but wait for the first customers.

"Where's your dad?" Becky asks when she sees me standing at the grill wearing his apron.

"He's not feeling great today."

Becky looks surprised. My father hasn't missed a day of work the entire time she's been here. Actually, I can't remember him ever missing one. "Is he okay?" Becky asks.

Becky and I have never been best friends or anything. She was a couple of grades ahead of me in school, and is only working for us because she can't find anything better right now. But she's nice, and I want to talk. I tell her the story of my mother.

"Geez," she says when I'm finished. "That's rough, Sam. I'm really sorry."

"Thanks," I say. "I guess he was looking at that picture of the two of them and it made him sad."

"And on top of your great-great-grandmother being in the hospital. You're having a rough summer."

She only knows half of it. I don't tell her about Lola, or Millard Fillmore, or anything else.

"It's like somebody forgot to invite the bad fairy to your christening or something," Becky says as she pulls out a stack of waffle cones and sets them up. "Like you're cursed."

When I don't say anything, she turns around. "Oh, I'm sorry. That was a really stupid thing to say."

"No," I tell her. "It's okay. I know what you mean." *Believe me,* I think, *I know exactly what you mean.*

"In the fairy tales, they always get rid of the curse by finding the witch or bad fairy or whatever who cast it and making her take it back," Becky says. "Or killing her. Whichever."

She keeps on talking, but I ignore her and get to work making patties from the big box of hamburger in the pantry. It's nice to have something mindless to do. When Becky says she's going to take a bathroom break, I nod and keep going. A minute later, someone says, "Excuse me. Are you open?"

I turn around and see a woman peering in at me through the order window. She seems kind of familiar, but I can't place her. I think she must be one of the summer people who has come in once or twice before.

I take off the plastic gloves I'm wearing and walk over to her. "What can I get for you?"

She seems anxious, her eyes darting around and her forehead wrinkling up, as if she's not really sure what she's doing. She opens and closes her mouth several times. Then she starts crying. Her hand flies to her mouth.

"I'm sorry," she says. "My daughter was in an accident. We're on the way to the hospital to see her, and I want to bring her something she likes. But I can't even remember her favorite flavor."

"I'm sorry," I say. "I hope she'll be okay."

The woman wipes her eyes. "I think she'll be all right. Jennifer is a tough girl."

That's when I remember where I've seen the woman before. She's Mrs. McCracken. Tom Swift's mother. She doesn't seem to know who I am, though, and I don't know if I should remind her. But I want to know what's happened to Tom Swift.

"Our Roadkill Skunkcicle is really popular," I say, remembering what Tom Swift ordered on the day I met him. "That might make her feel better." I hate saying *her* about Tom Swift, but I don't have much choice.

Mrs. McCracken gives a little laugh. "What a terrible name," she says. "It sounds exactly like something Jennifer would think was funny."

"Coming right up," I say, and get to work making the ice cream. When I hand it to Mrs. McCracken, I say, "On the house. Tell Jennifer that Sam from the Eezy-Freezy hopes everything turns out all right."

Mrs. McCracken smiles. "I will," she says. "And thank you." As she leaves, I wonder what kind of accident Tom Swift has had. It sounds like he'll be okay, but who knows. I also can't help but think that the curse has tried to claim another person in my life. It needs to be stopped. But how?

"Anything exciting happen while I was gone?" Becky asks as she returns from the bathroom.

"What was that you said earlier about curses?" I say.

"Uh, I'm not sure. About how someone forgot to invite the evil fairy to your christening?"

"Later. About how you break them."

"Oh. Well, you either get the person who cursed you to take it back, or you kill them. Why?"

I'm thinking.

"Are you planning a murder?" Becky asks.

"Too late for that," I say. "I'm just wondering how you get a dead woman to take something back."

Twenty-Eight

When I walk up to the nurses' station at St. Anne's, the man behind it looks up and says, "Hello again."

It takes me a second to realize that he's one of the nurses who took care of Lola. "Hi," I say. "This time it's my great-great-grandmother. Clodine Weyward."

When he hears Clodine's name, he laughs. "Ah, yes," he says. "Miss Clodine. She's certainly a handful."

"Is she awake?"

"She was when I brought her lunch fifteen minutes ago," he says. "Apparently, she hates orange Jell-O. She's in room three-thirteen. Right down the hall."

"Thanks. I have a friend who's here too. Can you tell me what room she's in?"

"I can look her up. What's the name?"

"Jennifer McCracken." The name still feels weird when I say it, like I'm talking about a character on a TV show.

The nurse's fingers clatter on a keyboard. "She's on the fifth floor," he says. "Room five-forty-two. But it looks as if visitors are restricted to family."

"Oh," I say. A feeling of worry starts to rise up. "Does that mean she's really sick?"

"I don't know anything about that," he says. His voice is kind, which makes me worry even more, like he knows a lot more than he's allowed to tell me.

"Okay. Well, thanks for looking her up for me."

He nods, and I head for Clodine's room. As I do, I pass by the elevators. Next to the doors is a directory for the other floors. I glance at it, and see that next to the fifth floor are the words *Inpatient Psychiatric Unit*. I stop and stare at the sign for a moment. Why is Tom Swift in a psychiatric unit? His mother said he had an accident. The only kind of "accident" I can think of that would land somebody in a psych ward is suicide. Did Tom Swift try to kill himself?

I calm the rising panic in me, or try to. I know Tom Swift isn't dead. If he were, obviously he wouldn't be in the hospital. But something is wrong with him. Maybe something really bad. I feel helpless not knowing what, or whether he's going to be okay. Worse, I can't help feeling that it's somehow my fault.

I push these thoughts down as deep as I can, which isn't very far, and go to Clodine's room. The door is open, and I can see her sitting up in bed, frowning as she pokes at a tray of food. Before I go in, I check my pockets to make sure the things Hank and Starletta gave me are still in there: a Mercury dime from 1930 (the year Clodine was born), a fox tooth, and a small cloth bag containing iron nails, salt, and brick dust. Precautions, Starletta called them when she laid them out on the table this morning.

I try not to think about why these precautions are necessary. Because of me. I plaster a smile on my face and go inside. When Clodine sees me, she says, "'Bout time."

Her words are kind of slurred, a result of the stroke they say she had. And when she smiles, the right side of her mouth stays drooped a little. Otherwise, she looks pretty good.

"I hear you don't like the food," I say as I go over and kiss her on the cheek. "Good thing I brought you some Nehi."

I take a bottle out of the bag I'm carrying, open it, and set it on her tray. Clodine cackles happily. She reaches for it, and her hand trembles. She puts it back in her lap.

I don't say anything, but I take the bottle and pour some of the soda into the cup on her tray. There's a straw lying next to her plate, and I put that in the cup, then hold the cup toward her. She leans down and sips. When she's done, she smacks her lips.

"Better," she says.

I leave the cup on the tray, where she can reach down and drink from it when she wants to, and pull up a chair. I sit down.

"How's Millard Fillmore?" Clodine asks, although it comes out sounding like "Miller Fimore."

"He's good," I tell her. "Getting better. He barked at the chickens today."

She nods.

"The Wild Ruckus roses are blooming like crazy," I tell her. "I think he misses you."

She grins. "Be together soon enough."

I'm not sure what she means by this. Does she mean she's coming home? Or does she mean she's going to die? The doctors have said that her stroke wasn't a bad one. But they also warned us that she's old, and that things can happen. Complications again.

"The scent is something else," I say. "The whole house smelled like roses this morning."

Clodine sighs and closes her eyes. She seems tired. I wonder if she's thinking about home, Wild Ruckus, or something else. Maybe she just wants to sleep.

A nurse appears in the doorway. She comes over and says, "Are you finished with your lunch, Mrs. Weyward?" Then she looks at the bottle of Nehi and frowns.

"That's mine," I say quickly.

"You didn't eat much, Clodine," the nurse says, ignoring me.

"Ate enough," Clodine mumbles. She sounds far away.

The nurse picks up the tray. She leaves the Nehi. "She should sleep," she says to me.

I get her meaning. I've been there less than ten minutes, and there's a lot I want to talk to Clodine about, but I know she needs to rest. I stand up. "I'll be back later," I tell her.

She reaches out and takes my hand. Her eyes open. "Tell Ruckus I'll be home soon."

"I will," I promise.

Before I leave, I take the Mercury dime out of my pocket. Reaching down, I stick it under the mattress of Clodine's bed, pushing it as deep in as I can. I can just imagine what the person who changes the sheets will think when it falls out. Until then, though, it should work its magic and keep Clodine safe. Or at least safer.

I go into the hall and walk to the elevator. When I get inside, I start to hit the button to take me to the ground floor. At the last second, I reach over and press the 5. The doors shut, and the elevator goes up. When the doors open, I step out into a hallway that looks exactly like the one on the third floor.

I try to walk quickly by the nurses' station, as if I know exactly where I'm going and have every reason to be going there. But the nurse sitting there looks up as I pass and says, "Can I help you?"

I stop. I almost turn around and leave. I stick my hand in my pocket and wrap my fingers around the fox tooth. Then I say, "I'm here to see my sister, Jennifer McCracken. My mom said she's in room five-forty-two. Is that right?"

My heart pounds as the nurse looks at a clipboard. I expect her to tell me that I'm not on the list. Then she looks up and nods. "That's right."

I keep going, before she can change her mind. When I get to Tom Swift's room, the door is shut. But I can see through the narrow glass window set into it. Tom is in bed, sitting up and staring outside, looking unhappy. I don't knock before I open the door.

He looks over, and his face registers surprise, but not happiness. "How did you get in here?"

"Magic."

Now that I'm here, I don't know what to say or do. But Tom Swift doesn't tell me to leave, so I go over and sit down in the chair beside his bed. That's when I notice that his arms are covered in bandages. Three on each forearm.

"How did you know I was here?" he asks. "Did I make the newspapers?"

"Your mother stopped by the Eezy-Freezy."

He kind of laughs. "Right, the melted ice cream." He slips his arms under the sheet. "What did she tell you?"

"Nothing, really. I don't think she remembered me at all. Or probably she was just too upset to notice. She just said that her daughter had been in an accident."

"Accident," Tom Swift says, snorting. "Of course. She's already rewriting history so that she doesn't have to deal with anything real."

"So, no accident?"

Tom Swift shakes his head. "I regressed."

I'm not sure what he means, but the bandages give me a fairly good idea. "You tried to kill yourself?"

"What?" he says. "No. Just a little cutting. It's something I used to do to deal with things. I haven't done it in probably a year or more. Honestly, I didn't even really do it on purpose this time. It kind of happened before I even realized what I was doing. Otherwise, I never would have done it on my arms. Anyway, my grandmother walked in and saw me bleeding and freaked out. Now here I am."

I have a lot of things I want to ask him, but I don't want to make him more upset. So I say, "I'm really sorry. About everything."

Tom Swift shrugs. "It's not your fault."

"Some of it is," I say.

He doesn't tell me it's not.

"How long do you have to be here?"

"Until the shrink decides I'm not a danger to myself," he says. "So probably forever. I had to tell them about taking T. They thought the marks on my legs were from shooting drugs. I think my parents would actually prefer it if I'd been using heroin."

He sounds worn out. I wish I had something to say that would make him feel better, but I think his life is actually going to get harder once he's out of the hospital. I can't imagine his parents learning to understand what's going on with him, at least not any time soon.

"How's Millard Fillmore?" he asks me.

"I think he's going to be okay," I say. "We're more worried about Clodine right now." I tell him about her stroke.

"I hope she's all right," he says. Then he adds, "You're lucky. I wish I had your family. You get to be who you are, and they still love you."

I want to tell him that his parents love him too. And I'm sure they do. But I don't think they love who he really is, at least not right now. Maybe they never will. I think about Eulalie Householder setting the rag doll on Lola's grave. I know she loved him. But I don't think she ever said it. Now it's too late. I hope Tom

Swift's parents don't wait too long to figure out that he's always going to be their son.

I stand up and fish the fox tooth out of my pocket. I hold it out to Tom Swift. "Take this," I say. "It's a fox tooth. A good luck charm from the Grands."

He takes the tooth and holds in on his palm. "What does it do?"

"Outwits bad luck," I say.

He stares at it for a second. "Didn't work too well for the fox, did it?"

"Starletta says even good magic has a price. What's good luck for one person is bad for another."

"Hey, can you do me a favor?"

"Sure. I think. What is it?"

"Anna-Lynn doesn't know I'm in here. Would you tell her for me?"

"How much do you want her to know?"

Tom Swift thinks about the question for a little bit. "Tell her I'm okay and will explain everything when I get to talk to her."

"Okay. And when you get out, maybe we can go tubing again."

"I think my parents will probably assign armed guards to me," Tom Swift says.

I realize that I might never see him again. If his parents make him go home, he could be out of my life forever. This makes me incredibly sad, and for a moment I think I might cry. But I don't want to upset him, so I just say, "I'll see you later."

"Yeah," he says. "Thanks for the tooth."

I leave his room and go back to the elevator. When the doors close, I do start to cry. Everything I've been feeling comes out: my sadness about Clodine and Millard Fillmore and Lola, my anger at Ilona and now Tom Swift's parents, my guilt about Tom Swift, my fear of disappointing Farrah and Paloma. All of it. Tears stream down my face, and my body heaves as the elevator descends. I keep waiting for it to stop on a floor, for the doors to open and someone to see me making a mess of myself, but it doesn't. Not until we reach the lobby. By then I've sort of gotten it under control, but I'm still kind of shaking, and now my nose is running.

The thing about a hospital is that unless they're there to meet a new baby, almost everyone coming in and out is sad. So no one really notices someone who is upset. Or if they do notice, they don't judge, because it could just as easily be them. This makes it a little bit easier for me to walk through the lobby without feeling like a total idiot. But I'm still happy when I reach my truck and can finish working it out without an audience.

I sit there for a long time, letting it all out. And then a weird thing happens. Once everything I need to let go of is gone, it's like there's room inside of me, and that empty space fills up with a new feeling. Hope. Or something like hope, anyway. Whatever you want to call it, I realize that I'm tired of being afraid. I'm tired of waiting for bad things to happen. I'm tired of waiting for the curse I've worried about since I've been old enough to worry to come true.

And I decide to fight back.

Twenty-Nine

The public library of a small town on a sultry summer afternoon is not the happening place you might think it would be. When I push open the doors and walk inside, the only people in there besides myself are a bored-looking Penny Sudderline, my friend John's younger sister, staring at the Hot Summer Reading! shelf and Miss Endicott, the librarian. She's been the librarian here forever. In fact, I'm pretty sure they built the library around her, and then the town around *that*.

"Miss Sudderline, might I suggest you try Shirley Jackson's *We Have Always Lived in the Castle?*" she says to the girl looking at the books. "I think you'll find it quite to your liking. It involves a poisoning."

Penny picks up the book Miss Endicott has recommended and looks at it. I walk up to the long wooden counter behind which Miss Endicott is standing, surveying her domain.

"Mr. Weyward," she says. "It's been some time since you visited your friends in the stacks."

She's right. I haven't been to the library in a long time. I used to come in a couple of times a week, but I haven't been here since—

"The twenty-seventh of February," Miss Endicott says. "You returned Maggie Stiefvater's *The Dream Thieves*, which you professed to have enjoyed, but weren't able to check out the next book in that series because it was being read by another patron. However, that book, *Blue Lily, Lily Blue*, has since been returned and is available for you to check out. Would you like me to get it for you?"

"No, thank you," I say. "I'm not here for a book."

Miss Endicott removes her glasses and looks at me, her head tilted to the side. "Then whyever *are* you here, Mr. Weyward?"

"I'm looking for someone."

Miss Endicott looks around the room. "Unless that someone is myself or Miss Sudderline, then I don't know that I can help you." She sounds cranky, but I know that it's all an act. Miss Endicott is one of the nicest human beings on the planet.

"Actually, I don't think the person I'm looking for is even alive."

"That might be an easier thing to achieve, then," says Miss Endicott. "The dead generally aren't found wandering around, despite that popular television show that purports otherwise."

"*The Walking Dead* was actually a book first," I say. "Well, a comic book."

"Your familiarity with the zombie genre is duly noted," Miss Endicott says. "Since we're on the subject, can you tell me when zombies first made an appearance in popular literature?"

Miss Endicott is fond of these kinds of questions. I think about it for a minute, then say, "In *Frankenstein*?"

"That is an excellent guess," she says. "And you are correct that the monster in Mary Shelley's *Frankenstein* is a reanimated corpse. But he is not, strictly speaking, a zombie, as he possesses independent thought."

"I didn't know there was a technical definition of zombies."

"There is. Now that the rules have been clarified, would you like to make another guess?"

I shake my head.

"Then to answer my own question, the first notable appearance of zombies in popular fiction occurs in the work of H. P. Lovecraft, specifically in the serialized story 'Herbert West—Reanimator,' published in 1922."

"That was a long time ago."

"Indeed. Now, who is this probably dead person you seek?"

"Livvie Comstock," I say. "She used to live here around the same time as my great-great-great-grandmother, Vi—"

"—ola Weyward," Miss Endicott interrupts again. "Married name Viola Cattermole. I am familiar with your family tree, Mr. Weyward, and all of its peculiar branches."

When most people say your family is peculiar, it's not meant as a compliment. But the way Miss Endicott says it, I know she thinks that we're interesting. I wonder, though, exactly how much she knows about my family. Like, does she know about the curse?

We're interrupted as Penny Sudderline comes to check out her book. She's twelve or thirteen, and barely looks at me from under her long hair as she slides her books across the desk to Miss Endicott.

"Well-chosen, Miss Sudderline," the librarian says as she removes the cards from the little pockets at the back of each book. She holds up a copy of Flannery O'Connor's *A Good Man Is Hard to Find.* "I'll be very interested in hearing your thoughts on the title story of this collection."

Penny smiles as she takes the books back. She wraps her arms around them and holds them to her chest as she walks out of the library.

"Livvie Comstock was Viola's best friend," I tell Miss Endicott now that I have her attention again. "I've been wondering what happened to her."

If Miss Endicott knows about what went on between Livvie and my great-great-great-grandmother, she doesn't let on. Instead, she taps her fingers on the desk. I know from past experience that this means she's accessing the file cabinet in her brain.

Her fingers stop moving. "Livvie Comstock was an only child," she says, as if she's reading from a card. "But she had several cousins: Murgatroyd and Calliope Backspain and Johansen Lesk. Calliope married Nestor Carpenter and had five children."

Miss Endicott draws a figure in the air with her finger. I can tell it's a tree. She makes a line, forming a branch, and counts over four spaces. "One of those was Purity Carpenter, who married Wallace Sham and had one child, a girl named Christmas. Unfortunately for the girl, she married Peter Day and became Christmas Day."

She draws a new branch for each generation, and I can actually sort of see Livvie's family tree growing. Christmas and Peter Day now have their own limb.

"They had three boys and a girl, Holly."

"Holly Day?" I say. "That's so mean."

"People don't always think things through," Miss Endicott says. "Anyway, she's Holly Burling now, so that particular bit of regrettable whimsy is behind her. But I imagine she had a difficult time of it in school."

"Holly Burling," I say. "Anna-Lynn and Lynn-Anna's mom?"

"The very same."

"That makes Anna-Lynn and Lynn-Anna Livvie's . . ." I try to figure out the relationship in my head. "Fourth cousins?"

"A common assumption by those unversed in genealogical terminology. First cousins four times removed."

This is interesting. And weird. But it still doesn't tell me what happened to Livvie. "The Grands said Livvie moved away," I tell Miss Endicott.

"That she did," says Miss Endicott. "Which is where she exits the narrative of our town."

"Maybe Mrs. Burling knows what happened to her."

"Quite possibly, although few people these days even know who their relatives are beyond one or two generations. Still, it can't hurt to ask."

I nod. "Thanks," I say. "I'll let you know what I find out."

"Good luck, Mr. Weyward," says Miss Endicott. "I hope you find what you're looking for."

"Me too."

I leave the library and drive over to the Bi-Rite. Anna-Lynn and Lynn-Anna aren't the only ones who work there. Their father runs the produce department, and their mother is a butcher. I guess groceries are in their blood.

I haven't seen Anna-Lynn since Tom Swift asked me to tell her he was in the hospital, so I have a couple of reasons to be anxious as I drive to the store. Plus, the last time Anna-Lynn and I saw each other, things didn't go so well.

When I get to the Bi-Rite, I park the truck and go inside. The first thing I see is Anna-Lynn. She's ringing up old Mr. Pursell's groceries, tucking a bottle of milk into one paper sack and corralling half a dozen plums together into another bag along with a box of Corn Flakes. I wait until Mr. Pursell has left, then go up to the register.

"Hey," I say.

"Hey," says Anna-Lynn.

I'm not sure how to tell her that Tom Swift is in the hospital. I don't want to scare her, but I can't figure out how to say it in a way that isn't dramatic.

"Tom wants you to know that he's okay," I say.

Anna-Lynn snorts, so I guess my approach isn't the right one. "I don't hear from him for almost a week, and that's all he has to say?"

"It's not his fault," I say. "He's kind of in the hospital."

"What?" she says loudly, her tone doing a 180. "Why? What happened?"

I'm apparently not the best at delivering sensitive news to people. "It's nothing," I say, trying to calm her down. "I mean, it's something, but it's nothing huge."

This isn't really true, but I don't want to get into the interpersonal dynamics of the McCracken family in the middle of the Bi-Rite. Besides, I see Candy Ulsterberg heading toward us with her three little boys in tow and a basket filled with watermelons and corn on the cob.

"They think it's his appendix," I lie. It's the only non-life-threatening thing I can think of off the top of my head.

Anna-Lynn looks relieved. "But he's okay?"

I nod. "He said he'll call you as soon as he can. Hey, is your mom around? Starletta needs some, um, steaks."

Anna-Lynn points to the back of the store. "She should be back there hacking up a side," she says.

"Thanks."

I make a retreat from the checkout, sorry to have fibbed to Anna-Lynn but relieved to be getting away. I figure letting her believe that Tom Swift is in the hospital for his imaginary faulty appendix is better than letting her worry. Or maybe it's just better for *me*. Anyway, I check that item off my to-do list and move on to the next one.

When I reach the meat counter, I see Mrs. Burling through the window separating the customer area from the back. She's wielding a large knife, and her apron is spattered with blood. I tentatively tap the little bell sitting on the counter, and the sound causes her to turn and look at me. She holds up one finger, then disappears.

When she comes out, she's changed into a non-bloody apron. She comes up to the counter and says, "I scared the hoo out of a little kid today because I forgot to change out of my bloodies before I came out here." She chuckles. "So, what can I get for you today, Sam? Your grandmother doesn't want more cow eyeballs again, does she? I'm all out. What was she making with those?"

"Stock," I say. The cow eyes were actually for a tonic that was supposed to help Starletta with her rheumatism, but I don't mention that. "And no eyeballs today. No meat at all, actually. I was hoping you might be able to tell me something about an old relative of yours."

"I can try. Who is it?"

"Livvie Comstock."

Mrs. Burling laughs. "Crazy old Cousin Livvie, eh? What brought her name up?"

"Clodine mentioned her," I say. "I was just curious what happened to her."

"Not a lot," Mrs. Burling says. "Never married. Never had kids. Never had much of a life at all as far as I can tell."

"When did she die?"

"Oh, she's not dead. She's old, but she's not dead. Turned a hundred and four in May. My mother says she keeps on going because she never used up any of her life raising kids." She laughs. "Maybe my hair wouldn't be going gray if I didn't have the twins."

I'm shocked to find out that the source of the Weyward Curse is still alive. "Where does she live now?"

"Maine. Little town called Edgesea. She's in a place called

Kirkewood. It's an assisted-living facility. I think she's been there going on twenty years. The family tried to get her to come back a couple of times, as she's got nobody up there, but she wouldn't hear of it. I don't know why she wants to be all alone, but it seems to suit her."

Someone behind me makes a little noise, and I turn to see a woman standing there. I don't recognize her, so I peg her as a summer person. She seems impatient, so I turn back to Mrs. Burling and say, "Thanks. Clodine will be happy to hear that Livvie is still alive."

"Tell her I hope she's feeling better," Mrs. Burling says.

I leave her to deal with the waiting woman, and head back outside. As I drive home, I think about Livvie Comstock sitting all alone in a room in an old-folks home for twenty years. I can't help but think that the reason she doesn't want to come back here is because of the memories of what happened that day almost ninety years ago. Has she been thinking about it all that time? Every day, for almost a century? If she has, no wonder the curse seems to have gotten stronger.

Now the question is, can I get her to stop thinking about it and reverse the curse? I feel like I don't have a lot of time left to find out. I need to do something now.

When I get home, a quick internet search tells me that Edgesea, Maine, is a nine-hour drive from here. Another search locates the Kirkewood Home for the Aged. It's actually a former hotel, a sprawling old building that looks as if it probably houses as many ghosts as it does living people.

I input the address into an app on my phone, then look at my calendar for my work schedule. I work tonight and tomorrow, and won't be done until around midnight. But I have Sunday and Monday off.

Just enough time for a road trip.

Thirty

I pass the *Welcome to Edgesea* sign a little after ten o'clock on Sunday morning. I've been driving all night. It started raining about an hour outside of Portland, and the *whup-whup, whup-whup, whup-whup* of the windshield wipers has become background noise to my thoughts, which are all about Livvie Comstock and what I'm going to say to her.

Fifteen minutes later, I'm sitting in the parking lot of the Kirkewood Home for the Aged. It's even more imposing in person than it is in photographs, a hulking beast of a building crouched amid a cluster of tall pine trees, as if it's waiting to pounce. There are only a handful of cars in the lot besides mine, and I don't see anyone moving around behind the dozens of windows.

I smoke a cigarette, which, combined with the half a dozen cups of gas station coffee I've consumed on the drive through New York, Vermont, New Hampshire, and now Maine, makes me even more jittery. But it's a good kind of energy, nervous and electric and raw, even if I do wish I could brush my teeth. I wait until the cigarette is smoked out, then pop a handful of wintergreen breath mints I bought at the last mini-mart. They click against my teeth and burn away the stale aftertaste of nicotine and caffeine.

I get out of the truck and walk to the front doors, which I'm surprised to find aren't locked to keep the residents inside. Pushing them open, I step into what was obviously once a grand lobby, but which now looks a little threadbare. The flower-patterned carpet is worn, the chandelier that hangs from the ceiling is riddled with burned-out bulbs like missing teeth, and the furniture scattered around looks like it came from an estate sale. There's a faint smell of dust and something like mothballs.

A big desk is situated to one side of the room, and behind it is seated a man wearing a blue suit. I walk over to him and say, "Excuse me. I'm here to see one of the residents. Can you tell me where I can find Livvie Comstock?"

The man nods, grins, and says, "Good to see you again, Mr. Spatchcock! How's the feed-and-grain business? Have your regular room all ready for you. I'll have Winston bring your bags up lickety-split." He looks around, then leans in and whispers, "If you'll be needing company during your stay, there's a new girl in the housekeeping department who I can send up with a bottle of gin."

"That's enough of that, Gadwell," says a voice behind me. I turn to see a man in green scrubs standing there. "Gadwell is one of our residents," he tells me. "Used to be the concierge at a hotel. Thinks he still is. Did I hear you say that you're looking for Livvie Comstock?"

"Yes. Can I see her?"

"No one's been to see her in probably seven or eight years," the man says, looking me up and down. "You related to her?"

"Do I have to be?"

The man shakes his head. "Just wondering. Always been curious about Livvie's story."

"She and my great-great-great-grandmother were friends," I tell him.

"Huh. Hard to imagine Livvie with friends. Then again, she might have been a different kind of person a hundred years ago. Come on. I'll show you to her room."

As we walk, I ask, "How is she?"

The man snorts. "Same as always. She's Livvie. Doesn't talk much at all. Stays in her room. Like I said, no visitors."

"That's sad," I say.

"It's not unusual. People end up here because they have nowhere else to go. No one who really cares. Most of them only last a year or two. Livvie's the exception. She's our longest-staying resident by a mile. I don't think she'll ever die."

We reach a room with a closed door. The man raps on it, but doesn't wait for an answer before opening it. He looks inside. "Livvie? There's someone here wants to see you." He turns to me. "Go on in. You need anything, you just yell real loud." He laughs, then walks off down the hallway.

I step inside Livvie's room. It's small and closed-up, and it feels like walking into an attic or a garage. Someplace where used-up, unwanted things are kept. There's a bed and other assorted furniture, but at first I don't see Livvie. Then I notice a chair in one corner. Not an armchair or a rocker. A wheelchair. Livvie is sitting in it, slumped, her hands folded in her lap.

Livvie herself is short and thin. Her feet, which are encased in pink slippers, barely reach the footplates. She's wearing a nightgown, which is also pink. I think the color is supposed to be cheery, but there are some stains down the front of the nightgown, as if she's dribbled food and no one has bothered to wipe it away. Her pale skin is stretched over the bones of her face like tissue paper. Her white hair is cut short, as if nobody wants to be bothered to have to keep it looking nice.

"Hello," I say. "You don't know me, obviously, but my name is Sam Weyward."

I wait for her to respond to hearing my name. She doesn't. She continues to sit there, looking at me and saying nothing.

"I'm sorry to bother you," I continue. "I came to . . ." I stop. Although I've imagined this moment in my head a thousand times over the past two days, now that it's here, I don't know quite what to say.

I take a deep breath. "I came to ask you to take the curse back."

This time, she does respond.

"Curse?" she says in a voice that sounds like dust falling through a crack in a wall.

"The curse you put on Viola Weyward," I explain. "For marrying Otis Cattermole."

Livvie shakes her head very slowly, as if the muscles controlling it haven't been used in a long time. "I don't know any Viola."

"You do," I insist. "Viola Weyward. She was your best friend. But then you put a curse on her. On our whole family."

Livvie seems to think about this for a moment. "No," says. "I don't think I did."

I can't believe she doesn't know what I'm talking about. I go over and kneel down so that I'm looking into her face. "Viola," I say slowly, like maybe she just didn't hear me clearly. "Viola Weyward. Remember her?"

Livvie looks at me. Her eyes barely move, and now I see that they're clouded over, cataracts like clouds covering a blue sky. "Viola?" she says.

"Viola," I repeat. "Viola Weyward. Do you remember putting a curse on her?"

For some reason, I'm starting to panic. I need Livvie to say that she remembers. That she can take back what she started all those years ago. Instead, she shakes her head again. She coughs.

"No," is all she says.

I know she means she doesn't remember, but it feels like she's saying that she refuses to lift the curse.

"Just take it back," I say. "That's all I want."

I see that her hands are shaking. She's afraid. Of me.

I stand up and step back. Livvie Comstock is afraid of me. And then it hits me. Livvie is just an old woman. She's not a monster. She's an old, dying woman who doesn't even remember this story that is so important to me and to my family. And if she can't even remember it, if it hasn't been important enough to hang on to, maybe all these years there's never really been anything to be afraid of. Maybe there never was a curse. Not a real one, anyway. Maybe it's all just been a story that we tell each other to explain away things that are too hard to talk about in other ways.

Livvie's eyes are shut, as if she's having a bad dream and hoping that when she opens them, it will all be over and she'll be safe. As if I'm the one who's the monster.

"I'm sorry," I say, then turn and leave her room.

A minute later I'm back at my truck.

I drive away from Kirkewood. I'd expected to leave having gotten Livvie to remove the curse she put on my family. Instead, I'm leaving with nothing except more questions.

I drive back into Edgesea. I want to get out of there, but the thought of another nine hours on the road is exhausting. I decide to stop for something to eat first.

I get out on the main street of town and walk. As I pass the stores that line the block, something about them feels familiar. I pause and look in the windows of a hardware store, then an antique store. It seems as if I've looked into these places before. Then again, Edgesea looks like any one of a thousand quaint New England towns I've seen pictures of.

A few stores down, I come to a coffee shop that advertises breakfast. I decide it's as good a place as any to eat, and I go inside. There are a couple of other people in there already, two old men sitting at the counter and a mother and her little boy at one of the tables.

"Sit anywhere you like," a woman's voice says. "I'll be with you in a sec."

I sit down at a table and look at the menu. A minute later, a waitress comes over. "What can I get for you?"

I look up and see her name tag. *Rhonda*. Then I remember. My midsummer dream. I look down at the menu and see the name of the restaurant. The Perk Me Up.

"You okay, hon?" Rhonda asks. "You look like you've seen a ghost."

I look at her again. She's in her sixties. Red hair going gray. Exactly as she was in my dream. I sit there staring at her, not saying anything.

"Hon?" she says again. "You need more time?"

I shake my head, then say the first word that pops into my head. "Pancakes."

"Regular, buttermilk, or blueberry?"

"Blueberry."

"Bacon or sausage?"

"Bacon."

"Biscuit or muffin?"

"Muffin."

"Anything to drink?"

"Coffee."

The exchange is completely ordinary. She probably has it a hundred times a day. But for me, it's completely surreal. I'm sitting in a coffee shop I dreamed about, talking to a woman I've never met but who somehow turned up in my brain looking and sounding exactly as she does in real life.

"Be right up," Rhonda says. She takes the menu from me and walks away.

Now I look at the other customers again. Just as they were in my dream, the old men are reading newspapers. The woman sitting a few tables away takes a bite of pie. *One, two, three,* I think to myself, and the little boy dips his spoon into the bowl of ice cream in front of him.

This is where my dream ended, so I don't know what's supposed to happen next. What does happen is that Rhonda comes back ten minutes later with a plate of pancakes and bacon and sets it on the table, along with a little glass cup of syrup, another plate holding a muffin and a pat of butter, and a cup that she fills with coffee. I watch her do all of these things and don't say a word, but inside I want to scream, "Who are you? Why did I dream about you when I stuck a bunch of flowers under my pillow?"

"Can I get you anything else, hon?" she asks.

I shake my head. "I'm good," I say. "Thanks."

She leaves to attend to a table of customers who have just walked in, and I eat. I don't really taste anything, as I'm mostly watching her and hoping she doesn't notice me watching her. Why am I here? Why is she important? I know the Grands' magic well enough to know that this is no accident. I'm supposed to be here. But I don't know why, and I don't know how to figure it out.

I take my time eating breakfast, but even after I've finished the last bit of bacon and the last crumb of muffin, I'm no closer to any answers. When Rhonda comes over to my table to clear it, I know this is my last chance.

"Everything all right?" she asks as she picks up the plates.

"Actually," I say. "Not really."

She looks at me. "Didn't like the pancakes? Blueberries are in season, so they should have been good."

"The food was fine. I'm just kind of in a weird place." This sounds totally stupid, but I keep talking. "I came up here to see somebody and try to fix a situation, but it all went wrong, and now I don't know what to do."

Rhonda nods. "It'll be all right, hon," she says. "You probably just need to sleep on it. Morning is wiser than the evening."

"What did you say?"

She laughs. "Sorry. It's something my mother always said, and I picked it up. Morning is wiser than the evening. It's an old Russian saying."

"I have a friend who says that," I tell her, thinking about Linda. "Her mother says it to her all the time."

"Her mother is a smart woman," Rhonda jokes. "I used to say it to my daughter too."

A shadow crosses her face, a momentary sadness. Her use of the past tense registers, and I wonder if something happened to her daughter, or maybe between them. But she quickly recovers, and her smile returns. "Anyway, I'm sure things will work out," she tells me. "They always do."

She turns to go, and I start to panic. I know that she has something more for me. There's a reason I dreamed about her, a reason I've come to Edgesea. I thought it was to confront Livvie Comstock, but maybe I was wrong. Maybe Livvie was just the excuse I needed to get here, to find Rhonda. Now that I have, I can't let her go.

"Wait," I call after her.

She turns around.

"I, um," I stammer, my mind racing, searching for something to say.

She comes closer and leans down. "Honey, are you in trouble?" she says quietly. "You need someone to talk to?"

I nod.

She smiles. "It's all right," she tells me. "Tell you what. I get off here in an hour. You come back, we'll sit and talk. Okay?"

I nod again, afraid that if I say anything, she'll change her mind.

"Okay, then," Rhonda says. "I gotta get back to work now. But you be back here in an hour."

She carries the dishes away, passing through a door into the back of the restaurant. I pull out some bills, lay them on the table, and leave before she gets back. I walk back to my truck, get in, and sit there, listening to the rain tapping on the roof and wondering what I'm doing. I'm tempted to start the truck up and begin the drive home. What am I going to say to Rhonda? "Hey, you're going to think this is totally weird, but you came to me in a dream"? She's going to think I'm nuts.

Several times I put the key in the ignition. Each time, I pull it out again before starting the engine. Finally, I stick it in my pocket, lean against the door, and close my eyes. I'm so tired from the drive, and from my meeting with Livvie. I tell myself I'll just rest for a few minutes, but before I know it, I'm asleep.

In my dream, I'm back inside the Perk Me Up. I'm looking at the menu when someone comes up beside me. Thinking it's Rhonda, I look up to tell her why I'm here. But it's not Rhonda. It's Livvie Comstock. She's glaring at me with those black-button eyes. She opens her mouth, revealing hundreds of tiny, pointed teeth. Then her mouth keeps opening, growing wider and wider.

"The better to eat you with," she says.

I get up and run to the door of the coffee shop. I try to open it, but it's locked. I fumble with the door, trying to get it open, but nothing happens. Meanwhile, Livvie is walking toward me, her gigantic mouth stretching out hugely.

I bang on the glass of the door. "Let me out! Let me out!"

Livvie is almost upon me when someone jerks the door open. I fall, sprawling onto the sidewalk. Rain is falling in my face, and someone is asking me if I'm okay.

I open my eyes and look into Rhonda's face. I'm no longer dreaming. I'm awake. The door to my truck is open, and she's looking at me with a worried expression.

"Sorry," she said. "But you were screaming. Are you all right?"

I rub my eyes. "Yeah," I say. "Just a bad dream."

Rhonda walks around to the other side of the truck, opens the door, and gets in. "It must have been a doozy," she says as she pulls the door shut. "I heard you halfway down the block."

"Where are we going?" I ask her as I shut my own door.

"My house," she says. "You can tell me about your dream and why you drove here all the way from New York."

"How did you—"

"License plates," she says.

I start the truck and pull away from the curb. I still don't know why the midsummer magic showed me Rhonda, but I think I'm about to find out.

Thirty-One

Rhonda's house is small and run-down. Her car, an aging Plymouth Neon, sits in the driveway, looking like it's waiting for someone to put it out of its misery.

"Hasn't run for a couple of months," Rhonda tells me as I pull up behind it. "Can't afford to fix it right now. I take the bus to work, but it only runs once an hour, so if I miss it, I end up hitching. Good thing everybody in Edgesea knows me."

"I can take a look at it for you," I tell her as we get out and walk to the side door.

"Good at fixing things, are you?" Rhonda asks.

"Machines, anyway," I say as she opens the door.

We step into a kitchen. Like the outside, it's a little shabby, but neat and clean. I get the feeling that Rhonda works hard to maintain as much order in her life as she can.

"You want some coffee?" she asks. "Or did you get enough of it back at the diner? I think I have tea. Or how about a pop?"

"Don't you want me to look at the car?"

She shakes her head. "Talk first, car later. Sit."

I sit down at the table. It reminds me of being in our kitchen at home, and I wonder what the Grands are up to. I watch Rhonda bustle around, pulling mugs from the cupboards and spoons from a drawer.

"Since you didn't say, I'm assuming coffee," she says as she spoons coffee into a pot on the counter and adds water. "This is the good stuff. Not that crap we have at the restaurant."

As the coffee brews, she takes cream out of the refrigerator and sets it on the table along with a bowl of sugar. The sugar bowl is a ceramic clown head, and a small spoon sticks out of his mouth. Rhonda sees me looking at it and says, "I hate that thing, but it used to make my daughter laugh like crazy when she was little, so I keep it around for sentimental reasons."

Again I want to ask her about her daughter, and again I don't. A few minutes later, she brings two mugs of coffee over. She sets one in front of me, then takes a seat on the opposite side of the table.

"So," she says. "You want to tell me what you're running from?"

"What makes you think I'm running?"

A sad smile briefly creases her face. "Working at a place like the Perk Me Up, I see a lot of kids who are running. Edgesea is halfway between Somewhere and Somewhere Else. You get to know the look."

I pick up my mug and sip from it. When I set it back down I say, "I'm actually not running from anything. More like running to it."

295

Rhonda quirks an eyebrow. "Looking for answers?"

I sigh. "It's a long story."

"I've got time."

I look at her. "Do you believe in magic?"

I expect her to laugh, or to ask if I'm crazy. Instead, she says, "I've seen some things."

I tell her about the Weyward Curse, and about coming here to see Livvie Comstock and see if she would call it off. The whole time I'm talking, Rhonda doesn't say a word. But she also doesn't look like she's trying to figure out a way to secretly notify the cops that an insane person is sitting in her kitchen.

What I don't tell her about is my dream. I figure the curse is a hard enough story to swallow. Adding the fact that I dreamed about her, but that I had no idea she would be *here* in Edgesea, where I expected only to find Livvie, seems like too much. I'm hoping I can figure out what she has to do with things first. If I scare her off, I might never find out.

"Sounds like one of those fairy tales where the hero has to confront the wicked witch," she says when I'm done. "Or an ogre. Something bad, anyway."

"Yeah," I agree. "That's what my friend said too. Only I didn't win. Livvie did. So the curse is still out there."

"That's why they're called fairy tales," Rhonda says, "and not documentaries. Stories where the bad things win don't generally play as well to audiences. Think about it. What if the shark in *Jaws* had eaten everybody and swum off? Or if Darth Vader hadn't fallen down that whatever it was?"

"I'd actually be okay with that," I say. "It's more interesting than the good guys always winning."

"People tend to like happy endings," Rhonda says. "The thing is, real life doesn't usually have them. If you ask me, fairy tales were invented to distract people from how awful life can be."

"You remind me of my friend Linda," I say. "She said something like that too."

"Sounds like a smart girl. Look, I'm not trying to make you feel bad about this whole curse thing. All I'm saying is, life is hard, curse or no curse, and sometimes you just have to go on living it anyway, and be happy for the parts that are beautiful."

"You should totally put that on mugs," I say. "You'd make a fortune."

Rhonda snorts. "You and my daughter would get along great."

Since this is the third time she's mentioned her daughter, I decide to ask, "Does she live here too?"

"No," Rhonda says, shaking her head. "She's dead."

I immediately regret asking. "I'm sorry."

"It was a long time ago," she says. "Not that that makes any difference. Nineteen eighty-five. She was seventeen. She ran away from here." She looks at me. "Or maybe, like you say, she was running to something." There's nothing mean or angry in the way she says this; it's more like she never thought about it this way before.

"What was her name?"

"Persephone." She laughs. "I know. It's strange. I wanted her to have a unique name, though. Not be just another Rhonda or Jennifer or Linda."

"It's a pretty name," I say.

"I probably should have thought a little more about it," Rhonda says. "You know the story of Persephone, right? Hades, the god of the underworld, falls in love with her and kidnaps her. But her mother fights to get her back. Eventually, she ends up having to spend half the year underground and half the year up top. It's not ideal, but at least she's happy part of the time."

I wonder if she means that her daughter was kidnapped and killed, which would be horrible. But she says, "Percy—that's what we called her—fell for a guy who might as well have been the king of hell. Not that he was mean. Just sad. Doomed. Fancied himself a musician. Percy was the one with real talent, but she couldn't see it. Didn't believe in herself. She thought he was the genius. So when he told her shooting heroin helped him write better songs, she believed it."

I have a feeling I know where this story is headed, and it makes me sad. I almost want to tell Rhonda to stop. But I think it has something to do with why I'm here, so I sit quietly and let her continue.

"One day I came home from work and there was a note from her, saying she and the king of hell had taken off for San Francisco," Rhonda says. "She called me when she got there, to say she was okay. I tried to get her back. Even sent her a plane ticket. The day the flight came in, she wasn't on it. I called the police, and they found her in a crappy little motel by the beach. Dead. She'd overdosed."

"And the king of hell?"

"Never found him. He took off. I don't even know his real name, so he could be anywhere. Probably dead."

I don't know what to say to her. "I'm sorry," never feels like enough. It's just what you say because you have to say something. Instead, I say, "I wish that hadn't happened to you. Both of you."

Rhonda smiles at me. "Thank you, Sam. Of course, for a long time I thought it was my fault. I asked myself what I did wrong, or what else I could have done to convince Percy to come home. My husband told me to let it go and move on. Not that he didn't love her. He did. He just didn't see any point to asking 'What if?' Eventually, we couldn't live with how each other was dealing with it, and we divorced."

"Do you still ask yourself 'What if?'"

"Not as much. Sometimes. Mostly, I wonder what she might have become. The thing is, people choose what road they're going to take. You can try to tell them that this road is harder than that road, or that this one has prettier scenery and better rest areas than that one, which you know because maybe you've been down it yourself. You can even come along and help them out when they break down. But where they end up is ultimately up to them."

She's quiet for a minute as she sips her coffee.

"The night she died, Percy called me," Rhonda says. "I wasn't home, so she left a message. I still have it on the machine.

I know, nobody uses answering machines anymore. But I kept it. I couldn't bear to erase the last thing she ever said to me."

"What did she say?"

"Listen for yourself," Rhonda says. She gets up, goes to the counter, and returns to the table with a small box. She sets it down and presses a button. There's a beep, and then a girl talks.

"Hi. It's me. Are you there? I'll wait a little bit. Okay, I guess you're not. Well, I'll see you tomorrow anyway, right? I'm pretty much ready to go. I'm just sitting here listening to the foghorn. It sounds so sad. I had this crazy idea that maybe it's not really a foghorn. Maybe it's a lonely sea monster, calling to the other sea monsters out there." She stops talking, and there's a faint hiss. "That's weird, isn't it? Sorry. I'm a little tired. Okay, I'm going to go. I'll see you soon. Love you."

Rhonda pats the machine, as if it's a living thing. "I think that's how she saw herself," she says. "A lonely sea monster looking for another one like her."

In movies there's sometimes this moment where a character who has been trying to solve a mystery sees or hears something that suddenly makes all the bits and pieces make sense. As I sit in Rhonda's kitchen, holding a coffee mug in my hand and trying to keep my hands from shaking, this is what goes through my mind: Linda, San Francisco, Rice-A-Roni, foghorn, the midsummer dream, sea monsters, Janis Ian, *Scarecrow and Mrs. King*, songs.

Once my brain puts all the clues together and I see what they add up to—what I *think* they add up to—all I can do is sit there, trying to convince myself that I'm wrong. Rhonda, who has no idea that there's a tornado spinning through my head, looks out the window.

"So," she says. "It looks like it's stopped raining. Feel like taking a look at the car while I make some lunch?"

"Sure," I say, trying to sound normal.

Rhonda gives me the keys to the car, and I go outside and pop the hood of the Neon. I poke around, but I can't really focus. All I can think about is Linda and our conversations. Is it really possible that for the past couple of months I've been talking to Rhonda's daughter? Rhonda's *dead* daughter? Honestly, I'm used to weird things going on around me, but this is a little weird even for me. Not that I'm afraid that I might have talked to a ghost. That part is actually fine. What I can't figure out is why.

I thought I was coming to Edgesea to see Livvie. Now I get that my trip is about Rhonda and Linda. Persephone. Is there something I'm supposed to tell Rhonda? What? I don't know anything more than she does. And she doesn't seem like she's looking for closure, or needs to hear that her daughter is, what, still out there somewhere?

I work on the car for an hour or so. Pretty quickly, I figure out that it needs a new alternator. But I keep monkeying with it because I don't know what to say to Rhonda when I go back inside.

Finally, she comes out and tells me that lunch is ready. I go in, tell her about the alternator, and then sit down at the table.

Rhonda has made grilled cheese sandwiches and tomato soup. But there's something else sitting on the table. It's an old notebook.

"What's this?" I ask.

"Percy's songwriting notebook," Rhonda says. "One of them, anyway. She had a couple. She took most of them with her when she left, but this one was under her bed. I guess she didn't see it. I don't know why, but while I was getting lunch ready, I started thinking that maybe you would like to look at it."

I stare at the notebook, afraid to touch it. I don't know why. Assuming Linda really is Percy, I've already heard a bunch of her songs. But this is different. This is something physical that I can touch. Something *she* has touched. I feel like I'm looking at her diary.

"Maybe after we eat," I tell Rhonda. "I don't want to get it dirty."

All through lunch, I steal glances at the notebook. I talk to Rhonda about other things: her alternator, my mother, the Grands. I don't say anything about Persephone, but she's always there in the back of my mind. For some reason, I'm trying to convince myself that it's all a coincidence, that Linda is someone else who just sounds an awful lot like this girl who died more than thirty years ago and who also is obsessed with lonely sea monsters.

I've just finished the last of my soup when I realize Rhonda has asked me a question. "I'm sorry," I say. "What was that?"

"I said you look like you're about to fall asleep right in that chair," Rhonda says.

I yawn. I've been awake for a long time, and it's been a weird, rough day. "I guess it's catching up to me," I say.

"You need to lie down," Rhonda says. "Sleep for a bit. Then you can get on the road."

I start to protest, but she stands up. "I'm not having you get into an accident because you nod off at the wheel," she says. "Come on."

I stand up, pick up the notebook, and follow Rhonda as she leads me down a hallway and opens a door. I look inside, into what is obviously a teenage girl's room.

"I haven't changed it since she left," Rhonda says. "Don't worry, though. I clean it once a week."

I'm hesitant to step inside, but Rhonda is waiting. I go in and sit down on the bed. I look around the room. The walls are covered with posters of bands like the Cure and Siouxsie & the Banshees. A bookshelf beside the bed holds well-loved copies of books including *Watership Down, The Hobbit, The Bloody Chamber,* collections of fairy tales from various cultures, and pretty much every Stephen King novel ever written.

"Rest for as long as you need to," Rhonda says. "I'll be right out here if you need anything."

She shuts the door, leaving me alone. I get up and walk around, looking at things but touching nothing. On top of the dresser there's a framed photograph. I recognize Rhonda, or a younger version of her, anyway. She has her arm around a girl. Like Rhonda, the girl has red hair. She's smiling, but she looks sad at the same time. I touch my fingertip to her face for a moment.

I go back to the bed and pick up the notebook. Flipping it open, I look at the first page. It's covered in words, a lot of them crossed out. There are things circled, with arrows pointing to where they should be moved. At the top is written "Spacewalk." But it's crossed out, and in smaller letters underneath it says "Astronaut of Love."

I read the lyrics to the song that Linda sang me weeks ago. Now there's no doubt in my mind that Linda and Percy are the same person. I flip through the pages and see a couple of other songs I remember. But most are new to me, page after page of lyrics. I imagine Linda—Percy—sitting in this very room, scribbling the words onto the pages.

On the bedside table is a phone, an old rotary one like the one in my room. I pick it up, close my eyes, and dial. I don't know if the magic will work here, but I think it might. I listen as the phone on the other end rings.

"Hello?"

"Hey," I say to Percy. "It's me. We need to talk."

Thirty-Two

There's really no good way to tell someone she's dead.

"I think you might have overdosed," I say after running through the evidence that makes me believe Percy isn't currently among the living. She actually takes it pretty well.

She sighs. "I kind of suspected that might be it," she says. "That explains why it's always foggy outside the room, and why I never get anywhere when I try to leave. I just end up back at the door."

"It sounds as if you're trapped in the day you died," I say. I mention the foghorns, and how Rhonda played me her last message to her.

"So, she thinks that I think I'm a monster," Percy says. "I guess that's not too far off."

"She thinks that you're lonely. Are you?"

"I was," she says. "Until you called. How do you think that worked, anyway? Like, why you? Why me? Why at all?"

"Does magic always need an explanation?" I say. "Isn't that kind of why it's, you know, magic?"

"I don't like things that don't have explanations," Percy says. "It's too much like religion. 'We can't tell you exactly how this works, or why. You just have to believe that it does. Oh, and if you don't believe it, you're going to suffer forever.' Uh-uh."

"Yeah," I say. "I know. But this *is* working. We've talked a bunch of times."

"Maybe I'm dreaming you," she says. "Or you're dreaming me. Maybe one of us is crazy and this is all in our head."

"Do you really think that's what's happening?"

"No," she says. "So what happens now? If this is all happening for a reason, what is it? Are you supposed to help me cross to the other side or something? You know, 'Run to the light, Carol Anne!' and all that."

"Who's Carol Anne?"

"Sorry," Percy says. "Outdated cultural reference. I forget you're not in my year. Hey, what's it like now? Do we all have flying cars yet?"

"Not yet," I tell her. "But you can get famous for posting photos of yourself on the internet."

"What's the internet?"

I explain it to her as best I can. "Mostly people use it for arguing and looking at porn," I conclude.

"I think I might be glad I'm dead," Percy says. "It doesn't sound like things have gotten much better."

"Maybe a little better," I say. "I think the world takes baby steps. Gay people can get married, but you can also get shot going to school or to the movies. On the plus side, you missed 9/11 and Nickelback and a bunch of terrible Star Wars prequels."

She's missed a lot of things, both good and bad. I spend some time telling her about them. "Oh, and Madonna is still making records," I say. "But I have bad news about Michael Jackson and Whitney Houston."

"Maybe they're hanging out wherever I'm supposed to go next," Percy says.

Or maybe they're stuck in the places where they died, I think. I hope it isn't true.

A knock on the door interrupts us.

"Is that my mom?" Percy asks.

The door opens, and Rhonda sticks her head in. "Sorry," she says. "I thought I heard you talking."

I hold up the telephone receiver. "I was just calling home," I say. "To let them know I'm okay and coming home later. Sorry."

"It's fine," Rhonda says. "But that phone has been disconnected for years. I only use my cell now."

I stare at the receiver. I put it to my ear. "Hello?" I say.

There's no one there. I hang up.

"Want to use my cell?" Rhonda asks.

"That's okay," I say. "I left them a note when I took off. They won't worry."

"Okay," she says. "Well, do you want to get some rest now?"

I nod. "Just for a little while," I say.

She leaves the room. I immediately pick up the phone and call Percy back, but my fingers fumble on the numbers, and nothing happens. I give up and go back to her notebook, turning the pages and reading her words. One in particular jumps out at me.

Wrongskin

cut and stitch
not to wound
just some alterations
to a suit that doesn't fit

sleeves too short
legs too long
one size does not fit all
and no exchanges no returns

right heart in the wrong skin
wrong thoughts in the right head
changeling switch, just one wish
find some air that i can breath

mirror shows
stranger's face
speaking lines, missing cues
in a play i didn't write

ink in skin
pain reminds
opens doors that i keep closed
write my secrets in my blood

right heart in the wrong skin
wrong words in the right mouth
changeling switch, just one wish
find a song that i can sing

bruises bloom
fade to black
poisoned veins are running
with the sweetness of forget

fun-house mirror
sleight of hand
objects may be closer
what you see's not what you get

right heart in the wrong skin
wrong love in the right hands
changeling switch, just one wish
find a me that i can be

The lyrics make me think about Tom Swift and how he cuts himself to let out whatever's inside that he wants out. I've never done that. I also don't know what it's like for him to feel like he was born in the wrong body. But I definitely know what it's like to feel like your skin doesn't fit quite right. That's one of the things I love about drag. You can become anything you want to be, even if it's just for a little while.

Still, I relate to Percy's words. I think most people do at one time or another. Not to the extent that a trans person does, maybe, but we all (or at least most of us) sometimes wonder who we are and where we belong. I think if anyone says they've never felt that way, they're either lying or someone you probably don't want to spend a whole lot of time with. People who feel like they fit in all the time aren't people you can generally trust to understand very much.

I want to read more of Percy's lyrics, but the weight of everything that's been happening falls on me like a blanket. I tell myself I'll nap for half an hour, then get on the road. I close my eyes and fall asleep, my head resting on the pillow where Percy used to lay hers and dream.

I wake up when I feel someone sit on the edge of the bed. At first I think that I'm in my own room. Then the lingering sleep clears away, and I see Rhonda smiling at me. She's changed clothes.

"Good morning," she says.

"Morning?" I laugh, thinking she's making a joke.

"I was going to wake you up for dinner, but you seemed so tired that I thought I'd let you sleep."

I look at the light coming through the curtains. It really is morning. I yawn and stretch, and Percy's notebook slides off my chest. I catch it before it falls on the floor.

"Thanks," I say to Rhonda. "I guess I needed it."

"I have to get to the coffee shop, but you're welcome to stay here if you need to sleep some more."

"I should get on the road," I tell her. "I'll drive you to work first, then take off."

We drive back into town, where I plan on just dropping Rhonda off and leaving. But she makes me come inside and have some breakfast before I go. As I eat the eggs and bacon, I wrestle with whether or not to say anything to her about Percy. I know I was brought here to meet her, and if this were a movie or a book, I would say it was so I could bring some kind of closure to her. But I don't think that's it. She actually seems pretty okay with things, even though I can tell she misses Percy like crazy.

As I'm finishing my last bite of toast with strawberry jam, I decide not to say anything about ghost daughters or magic telephones. Rhonda comes over to the table carrying a menu, pulls out a chair, and sits down. "I wasn't going to say anything," she says, "but do you believe in fate? You know, that things happen for a reason?"

I hesitate a moment. "Um, maybe." I feel like the world's biggest liar, but I don't know where this is heading, and I'm not sure I'm ready for it.

Rhonda laughs. "I know it sounds hippy-dippy. But I do think things happen for reasons. Like there's a plan of some kind, even if we can't see what it is. Walter—my ex-husband— said I only wanted to believe there was a plan because accepting that horrible things happen to good people for no reason is too much to handle."

Her eyes get sad, and I can tell she's thinking about Percy. But then she smiles. "Maybe he was right. Maybe he wasn't. The point is, I think you and I met for a reason."

She takes the menu she was carrying, which has been on her lap, and sets in front of me. Only it's not a menu. It's Percy's notebook. "I want you to have this."

"I can't take that," I tell her. "It's the only one you have left."

"I've read this a thousand times," Rhonda says. "Maybe more. Looking for clues. Hearing her voice. It's time to let it go. And for some reason, I think you're meant to have it."

I put my hand on the notebook. "You're sure?"

Rhonda nods.

I take the notebook and stand up. Rhonda stands too, and opens her arms. I step into them, and she hugs me tight. "I think you and Percy would have been good friends," she says into my ear.

I feel a catch in my throat, and for a moment I think I might cry. Instead, I concentrate on how her arms feel around me. It feels good to be held like this, and part of me wants it to last forever.

Rhonda lets go, and I can see that she's holding back tears as well. "Thank you," I tell her.

"Don't be a stranger," she says. "Like I said, I don't know why, but something brought us together."

I nod, afraid that if I speak, I might cry. I walk out of the Perk Me Up, turn around, and see her watching me through the window. She waves. I wave back, then get into my truck and leave before I start bawling.

Percy's notebook sits beside me during the ride home. Every

so often, I put my hand on it, as if maybe I'll feel a heartbeat. It's weird to have been given something so personal, and I have no idea what I'm going to do with it. But I'm happy Rhonda trusts me enough to keep it safe.

The drive back seems to take forever, probably because I'm anxious to be home. I arrive at dusk, hot and tired and glad to be back. When I pull into the driveway, I see Hank and Starletta walking across the yard. They're barefoot and wearing white dresses. Both of them have crowns of roses and daises on their heads, and Starletta is carrying something in her hand.

I get out, and that's when the quiet hits me. The cicadas, which have been singing like crazy all summer, have stopped. Hank sees me and waves. I walk over to where she and Starletta are standing underneath the branches of the biggest elm tree in the yard. Hank is holding a small trowel in her hand.

"What are you doing?" I ask.

"Burying the queen," says Starletta. She holds up her hand, and I see that she's carrying a small white cardboard box tied with a pink ribbon.

"The queen?"

"Queen of the cicadas," Hank says as she kneels and pokes the trowel into the ground. She turns over a clump of earth. "Starletta found her this morning."

"How do you know she was the queen?"

"The singing stopped," Starletta says. "And of course the crown."

I look at the box. "You found a cicada wearing a crown?"

"She's the queen," Starletta says. "Queens get crowns."

Part of me wants to ask her to untie the ribbon and let me see what's in the box. Another part doesn't. I decide to believe that inside the box is a dead cicada with a tiny gold crown on its head.

"How was your trip?" Hank asks, still digging.

"Good," I say.

"Find what you were after?"

"I found something better," I say.

Hank finishes digging the hole. Starletta kneels beside her and places the box inside. She takes a handful of dirt and sprinkles it in. Hanks adds another, and they alternate handfuls until the hole is filled in again.

"There," Starletta says when they're done. "Now they can all sleep and dream for another seventeen years."

"All of them?" I ask.

"Of course," Hank says. "Once the queen dies, they all die."

I don't think this is scientifically accurate, but it doesn't matter. And the cicadas really have stopped singing, so maybe Starletta and Hank are right.

"Seventeen years," I say. "Just like the Weyward Curse. Maybe the queen fell in love."

"Help me up," Starletta says, holding out her hand.

I help her stand, and then the three of us walk toward the house. "How's Clodine?" I ask.

"Better," Hank says. "Still not talking right, but that'll come."

"Dad?"

Hank snorts. "You've only been gone two days, Sam," she says. "The world doesn't change that fast."

"Sometimes it does," I say. "Sometimes it changes in a second."

"John's fine," Starletta says. "Played that awful song about a nun for about six hours straight on Sunday night, and then he seemed over it."

"Which awful song?" I have no idea what she's talking about.

Starletta hums, off-key and not quite right, but I recognize the song immediately.

"'Sister Christian,'" I say. "She's not a nun. She's just a regular sister."

"Horrible song," Starletta says. "What's motoring, anyway?"

"I think it means driving," I tell her.

"Well, whatever it's about, it seems to have helped him get over things. He's been more himself."

I'm about to ask about Millard Fillmore when he comes walking into the kitchen and flings himself down on the floor with a groan.

"He's been sleeping on Clodine's bed," Hank tells me. "I think he likes the smell of the Wild Ruckus roses. So, you want to tell us where you went?"

I think for a little bit, then shake my head. "No," say.

Hank nods. "Fair enough."

"I'm going to go take a shower," I say.

As I walk by, I kiss first Hank and then Starletta on the cheek. Then I go upstairs to my room. I set Percy's notebook on my bedside table, then strip off my clothes and go into the bathroom. I turn on the water and step into the shower. It feels great on my skin and I stand there for a long time, until the water starts to run cold. Then I get out and dry off.

Still naked, I go into my room and walk over to the stereo. Instinctively, I reach for my mother's record collection and pull out record number 14, Nina Hagen's *Nunsexmonkrock*. I start to put it on the turntable, then stop. I slip the record back into its sleeve and put it away.

Instead, I pull out one of *my* favorite albums, Tegan and Sara's *If It Was You*. I put it on, drop the needle, and dance. I dance because I'm happy to be home with the Grands. I dance for Percy, and Rhonda, and Clodine. I dance for Millard Fillmore, my father, and the queen of the cicadas. I dance for Lola, and Tom Swift, and Farrah and Paloma. I dance for Ilona, and maybe even a little bit for Livvie Comstock, just to show her I'm not afraid of her and her curse.

Even if I still am.

Thirty-Three

I'm standing in the yard at dusk, tossing a ball of tinfoil into the air, when I see Tom Swift walking toward me.

"What the hell are you doing?" he asks as I throw the ball up and catch it again when it comes down.

"Playing with the bats," I say. "They like to dive-bomb the foil."

He looks dubious, so I show him. I launch the ball. A moment later, a shape flitters out from the open doorway of the barn and tumbles through the air. The bat swoops low, its wings flapping, then rises up and disappears into the shadows.

"So that's what you do out in the country for fun," Tom Swift says.

"Don't forget cow tipping," I say, pocketing the foil ball. "When did you get out?"

"This afternoon. Actually, they didn't let me out. My parents made them release me." He sighs. "They decided they didn't like what the shrink was telling them."

"Which is?"

"That there's nothing wrong with me. That they should

be supportive of my"—he makes finger quotes in the air—
"'exploration of my gender expression.'"

"But that sounds great," I say.

"Not to them. They wanted him to convince me that I'm not really a guy. That I'm just confused. When he basically said that they were the ones with the problem, my father went apeshit. Demanded they let me out so they can take me to a real doctor. It was sort of ugly."

"What did your mom say?"

"Nothing. As usual. She just wants everyone to pretend to be happy."

"So, what happens now?"

"We go home," Tom says. "First thing tomorrow. And I get to go see some doctor my father found who will fix me right up. Oh, and when school starts again, I'll be at an all-girls Catholic school. So that will be fun."

"Holy shit," I say.

Tom laughs. "Pretty much. I guess I'll have to learn how to rock a little plaid skirt."

He's laughing, but I can't imagine what he's really feeling. "Are you going to be okay?"

He shrugs. "Eventually. This is my last year of school. I think I can handle an asshole doctor, some mean girls, and a couple of repressed closet-case nuns for a few months. I've got the rest of my life to be me."

He's making it sound like it's nothing, but I know it's got to be scaring him. That's a hell of a lot of pressure to be under, even if you know there's eventually going to be an end to it.

"Anyway," he says, "I've got to get going. They don't know I snuck out. I wanted to say goodbye to you."

It means a lot to me that he's risked getting in trouble to see me. But I also feel guilty. "I'm sorry about throwing out your T," I say. "And, you know, everything else."

"It's okay," he says. "It's not like I'll be taking T for a while. And I'm sorry I was a dick to you."

"That reminds me," I say. "I have your dick if you want it."

Tom Swift laughs. "You know what?" he says. "I do."

"Come on," I say, and walk to the barn. I locate the cooler my father and I used the day of our fishing trip, and open it. "It might have a couple of little holes in it from the fishhook," I tell Tom as I take out the Mr. Stiffy and hand it to him.

"Do I want to know?" he asks.

I shake my head. "Probably not."

He shakes the Mr. Stiffy. It wiggles. We both laugh.

"Every time I wear it, I'll think of you," Tom Swift says.

Then he leans in and kisses me on the mouth. It's a good kiss, not rushed or like the kind you'd give a relative. A real kiss. I shut my eyes and enjoy the feeling of his lips against mine. Sooner than I like, he pulls back.

"I wish I was into boys," he says.

"Yeah," I say. "So do I."

He hugs me, holding me tight. "Thanks," he says, and I know exactly what he means without him saying anything else. This time when he lets go, it's hard not to cry.

"Call me," I tell him. "Text me. Email me. Whatever you can."

He nods, and I know he's having a hard time holding it together too. "I will."

He walks away. I stand in the doorway of the barn, watching him go. At the end of the driveway, he turns and waves. I wave back. Then he disappears into the shadows.

Normally, I love this time of the evening, when everything slows down to a twilight stillness and the daytime world and nighttime world hang out for a little bit. Now, though, it makes me almost unbearably sad. Without the cicadas singing, it's deathly quiet, and I'm acutely aware of how the summer is coming to a close. There are a few weeks left, of course, and it doesn't technically end until the autumn equinox in September, but already I can feel change coming.

My birthday is a week from today. Seven more days. But then what? Will Livvie's curse definitely be behind me? After seeing her at the nursing home, I'm mostly convinced that the curse was never even a thing, or if it was that it's worn itself out as she's gotten weaker herself. But there's still a small part of me that wonders.

I decide I need to be somewhere else, so I get in my truck and drive to Lola's house in town. Technically, I'm one of the owners of the house, so I don't feel like I'm trespassing or anything. Still, it feels a little weird to be going in there alone. I've only ever been there with Farrah and Paloma.

I hang around downstairs for a while, telling myself that I want to look at everything before I go upstairs, but really it's that I'm not quite ready to be alone in Lola's room. So for half an hour or so I go through the downstairs rooms, picking things up and putting things down, imagining Lola living here. I know the Lola I saw at the Shangri-La was one version of himself, the one he let people see. The one who lived here was a different Lola, one who apparently loved pickles (the refrigerator is filled with at least a dozen jars of them) and the *Mutts* comic strip (there are seven or eight of them stuck to the refrigerator with magnets shaped like fruits).

I wish I'd known this Lola, the private one who I'm guessing existed only in this house. I think this was the real Lola, and I think he was someone I would have liked even more than the Shangri-La Lola. The Lola from the club never would have drunk out of glasses with pictures of cartoon characters on them, but this Lola has a whole cabinet filled with them. Some of them I recognize, like the Pink Panther and Bugs Bunny, but a lot of them are from years ago, and I don't know their names. I assume they were Lola's favorites. I wonder if he drank mai tais out of them.

When I think I'm ready, I go upstairs and into Lola's bedroom. Without Paloma and Farrah here, it's as quiet as a museum, which is kind of what it is now. A museum to Lola's life.

For a few minutes I just stand in the room and breathe in the scent of it, a mixture of old house, powder, and some kind of perfume that reminds me of roses. I look at the things in the room, the furniture and pictures and knickknacks and clothes, and try to picture Lola in here. I find that it's already a little more difficult to remember exactly what he looked like, as if his memory is fading away a little bit at a time. This scares me, and I start to panic, thinking that I'm forgetting him. Then I look at the picture of him on the dressing table, and I remember.

I go over to the phonograph and put on a record, the cast album for *Sweet Charity*. As it plays, I walk to Lola's closet and open it. Inside there are dozens of outfits, and on a shelf there are several Styrofoam heads with wigs on them. I look through the clothes and take out what looks like a dressing gown. It's made of pink silk patterned with orange and yellow chrysanthemums.

I take off my clothes and put the robe on. It's too big for me, but I tie the belt around my waist and it's fine. Then I look at the wigs, selecting a blond one. I take it over to the dressing table and sit down. Inside the drawers of the table I find every kind of makeup and makeup tool I could possibly need.

Before I start, I look at the photo of Lola made up as the other Lola.

"Look," I say. "I need my fairy godmother back, at least for a little while. So if you're not too busy, could you help me out?"

I start to make up my face. I don't think about what I'm going for, or what kind of character I want to become. I just do it. As I work, I imagine Lola sitting in this same chair, in this same room, using these same brushes. I picture him listening to *Sweet Charity* and singing along. I picture him happy.

I finish my makeup, then put on the wig. I don't look like Lola. I don't look like me. I look like someone else. Someone beautiful. I don't know this person's name, but I like her. I like the way her eyes shine, and the way her lips pucker into a pout.

I like the way her hair falls around her face, and how she pushes it back behind her ear.

"Hi," I say. "I'm Sam. Who are you?"

I wait for her to answer me. At first, nothing comes to me. Then a name pops into my head, as if it's always been there, waiting for me to say it.

"Persephone."

"Persephone," I say, trying out the sound of it. It sounds right. I look at the woman in the mirror. Is that who she is? I think maybe so. She doesn't look like the other Persephone—like Percy—but I'm not trying to be her, or to imitate her. I'm trying to be me. And maybe this me shares a name with that one.

I make a few adjustments to my makeup. The record comes to the end of side 1, and I get up to turn it over. It's dark outside, and I hear the voices of some kids in the next yard. They're playing hide-and-seek.

"Ready or not, here I come!" a boy calls.

A moment later, there's a delighted shriek as he finds one of the hidden players. Then more laughter as the two of them hunt for the others. I listen to them for a while. Then I make a decision.

I turn off the record and put it away. I put away the makeup and brushes. I make sure Lola's room looks the way it did when I got there. But I leave on the dressing gown and wig, picking up my clothes and carrying them as I turn out the light and go downstairs.

I lock up the house and walk to my truck, not caring if

anyone sees me. I get in and start driving toward the Shan-gri-La. The bar has been closed since Lola's death as a sign of respect, but tonight it's reopening. I know Paloma and Farrah will be there, of course, and I have someone I want them to meet.

Thirty-Four

I'm sitting on the picnic table, Percy's notebook open next to me while I pick out a tune on my guitar, when the mail truck pulls up. The mail lady, Mrs. Wexler, waves at me out the open window. "Got a box for you."

I set the guitar down and walk over to her. She hands me a couple of envelopes, along with a small box.

"Sorry about the delay," Mrs. Weller says.

"Delay?" I say, not understanding.

"The package," she explains. "Don't know what happened, but that's been sitting around somewhere for a long time. Maybe because of the address. Good thing this is a small town and there's only one Sam Weyward."

I look at the box. My name is written on it, along with the town and state, but that's it. There's no return address. But the strangest thing is the date on the postmark.

"1985?" I say.

Mrs. Wexler laughs. "Must be some kind of misprint," she says. "You weren't even alive then. Anyway, it's here now."

"Thanks," I say as she drives off.

I carry the box back to the picnic table and sit down. I pull the paper off the box and open it. Inside is another box, along with a piece of paper folded in half. I unfold the paper and look at it. At the top is printed Surfside Motel. Underneath that, in the same handwriting that fills up the pages of Percy's notebook, is a message.

> I know you said your family doesn't celebrate birthdays until you turn 18, but I don't think I can stay around here another year. And since the sun is finally out and the fog is gone, I think I'm going to go for a swim. It's time to see if I can find the lonely sea monster.
>
> I don't think we can ever really know what the future has in store. Life is all about surprises, right? But maybe these cards will give you a glimpse every now and then. And when you use them, maybe you'll think of me.
> Linda

I put the note down and look at the cards. The box says *Aquarian Tarot* on the cover. I take the top off and tip the cards into my hand. They're well-worn, the edges slightly faded and the backs a little scuffed. I close my eyes and imagine Percy holding them, shuffling them before laying them out to read. I've never used tarot cards before, so I don't know what the different cards mean. But there's a little booklet in the box too, so that will be a good place to start.

I don't even question the fact that I'm holding something mailed to me by a dead girl from three decades in the past. It's probably not even the weirdest thing that will happen to me this week, maybe even not today. After seventeen years as a Weyward, nothing surprises me anymore.

As for turning seventeen, it's sort of anticlimactic. After worrying about the curse for so long, staring at the calendar in the kitchen every day and wondering if I'd make it, I kind of expected some last big push from Livvie. Not that I haven't been knocked around a lot in the past couple of months. She got some good hits in. But I'm still standing.

Since we've never celebrated birthdays, I'm not at all disappointed that the family isn't doing anything. Hank and Starletta are visiting Clodine in the hospital, and I'm going to work at the Eezy-Freezy later on. I've been spending the morning working on a song. Well, one of Percy's songs. I found it while leafing through the last pages of the notebook. She left it half-finished, so I've been playing around to see if I can do anything with it. It's been a long time since I've really played guitar, though, and I feel like my fingers are sticks of wood.

It feels really good to play. Making music, however bad I am at it at the moment, is fun. And I like that Percy and I are kind of doing it together. I wish she'd had the chance to give the world her music, but maybe she still does.

I play around for another hour, then head over to the Eezy-Freezy. When I walk in, my father is dancing around the kitchen to Mötley Crüe's "Kickstart My Heart," which is playing at ear-splitting volume. When he sees me, he turns the radio down.

"Happy Day-We-Don't-Talk-About," he says.

"Thanks," I say.

That's all we say about it. For now, anyway. Maybe we'll talk about it later. Maybe not. I think we're all tired of thinking about it, let alone talking about it. We probably need some time getting used to being uncursed. Then it hits me: Maybe the Weyward Curse really is over. Unless I have kids, there's no one to pass it along to. Which gets me to thinking about whether or not I do want kids. I don't know. Honestly, I've never thought about it. I think subconsciously I've been so afraid of the curse that I didn't let myself even consider it. But maybe I do. Since I've escaped the curse, I wonder if it's completely dead, or if any kids I have would be cursed too. I'll have to talk to the Grands about that.

The phone rings, and my father answers it while I straighten up the cones and ice cream scoops. When he hangs up, my dad says, "That was Hank. Clodine is coming home tomorrow."

This is the best birthday present I could ask for. "So she's going to be okay?"

"She's eighty-five, and she's had a stroke. But she'll be as okay as she can be. We'll make sure of that."

I get what he's saying. Our family isn't going to be together forever. Someday, there will be only two Grands, then one, then none. But hopefully that day is a long way off. And until it comes, we'll make as much magic as we can.

Things get busy, and before I know it, it's time for me to leave. Although my Weyward family isn't throwing me a party, my other family is. I drive over to the Shangri-La, where Paloma and Farrah are waiting for me.

They have to wait a little longer, since this isn't just a party for me, it's also a party for Persephone. But they do sit and watch as she comes to life. And of course they offer suggestions.

"Not that shade of purple, gurl," Farrah says as I start to do my eyes. "You'll look like a PSA for domestic violence. Go lighter."

"Don't listen to her," Paloma says. "Use *more* purple. And take it higher."

As they squabble, I do my makeup. Their arguing is actually kind of nice, like we're three sisters sharing a room and I'm the youngest. As I finish my eyes and move on to the rest of my face, I think about how I feel as at home here as much as I do in my actual house.

"I've made a decision," I say.

Because they're still debating the finer points of eye shadow, they don't hear me. So I say it again, louder. "I've made a DECISION."

Farrah turns to me, her hands on her hips. "About WHAT?" she snaps.

I turn in my chair, my wig in my hand. "About the Shangri-La. I know how I'm voting."

Farrah looks at Paloma, suddenly appearing a little anxious.

"That's great, Sammy," Paloma says. "But before you tell us, we have something for you."

"You don't want to know what I've decided?"

"Of course we do, honey," Farrah says. "But just in case somebody is going to be upset by what you've decided"—she points secretly at Paloma behind her hand—"let's do presents first."

"Presents?"

"You didn't think we'd let you have a birthday without presents, did you?" Farrah says. "Your sisters may be poor, but we ain't broke."

Paloma goes to one of the closets where we keep costumes, and comes back carrying something. "Actually," she says, "we didn't buy it."

Farrah gasps. "Secrets!"

"Queen, please," says Paloma. "Sammy knows where this comes from."

It's the framed *Damn Yankees* poster from Lola's bedroom. They've stuck a bow on the frame.

"Yes," Farrah argues. "But we *could* have sold it on eBay for a pile of cash, so it's sort of like we bought it."

"That's what I love about you," Paloma says. "You're so sentimental." To me she says, "I think Lola would love for you to have this."

She hugs me. So does Farrah. "I wasn't really going to sell it," she whispers in my ear. "Turns out, with shipping we wouldn't have made much from it anyway."

"I love it," I say. "And I love you two. Thank you."

"We got started on cleaning out the house," Paloma tells me. "We're going to put most of the stuff in storage until we can decide what to do with it."

"What's the hurry?" I ask.

Paloma looks at Farrah. Farrah says, "That's actually the second part of your present."

"What is?"

"The house," Farrah answers. "It sold."

"Sold! It's not even on the market."

"I know," Farrah says. "But the realtor put up a coming soon sign yesterday, and someone already called. I guess they're moving to the area and want to be settled before school starts."

"But that's in like two weeks."

"Exactly. Which is why we've got to get busy."

The news that Lola's house has already sold upsets me more than I expect it to. I don't know why. I knew we were going to sell it. I guess I just thought I would have more time to say goodbye to it.

"Anyway," Paloma says. "Farrah and I decided that—"

"Let me tell her," Farrah interrupts. "You got to give her the poster."

"Fine," Paloma says. "Go ahead."

"We decided," Farrah says, "that you're going to use the money from the house to go to college."

"What?"

"It might not pay for one of those fancy ones," Paloma says, "but it will get you through a state school."

"We don't have a check or anything," Farrah says. "Not until we close. But we're good for it."

I don't know what to say to them. Then I do. "You can't do that," I blurt out.

Farrah's eyes narrow. "And why not?"

"Because," I say, "I've decided I don't want to sell the Shangri-La. People here *need* this place. I know it's a lot of money to give up, but I don't want this turned into a stupid hardware store, or a coffee shop, or whatever it is those developers want to turn it into."

I look at Farrah and Paloma, my heart beating a thousand times a minute. I'm particularly worried about what Farrah is going to say. She's the one who wanted to sell.

"If you give me the money to go to college, then *you* can't go to film school," I say. "I can't do that to you. It's not fair."

Farrah doesn't say anything. She just keeps looking at me. Paloma is watching both of us, as if she thinks we might start grabbing at each other's wigs.

"Film school can wait," Farrah says. "I've got to make a couple of little films just to apply anyway."

"But—"

Farrah holds up her hand. "I don't want to hear any buts," she says. "So here's the deal. You want to keep this place going? Then you go to school and you major in business management, or running restaurants, or whatever. At least take some classes in that stuff. Then, when you graduate, you come back here and run this place while I take my turn in school. And if you decide you don't want to come back here, then we'll talk about selling. In the meantime, Paloma and I will do our best not to run the place into the ground."

I start to cry. I try to hold it in, but I can't.

"Don't you start," Farrah warns. "If you cry, I'll cry. And Lord knows this one over here will be wailing in three seconds."

Paloma is already dabbing at her face with a tissue. She looks so serious that I start to laugh. Then Farrah laughs. Then we're all laughing, and crying, and I'm hugging both of them.

"All right," Farrah says after a minute. "Enough of this. You know, now that there are three of us, we can do girl-group numbers. The Supremes—of course, I'll be Diana Ross. Destiny's Child—of course, I'll be Beyoncé."

"If you aren't too busy, Miss Ross, maybe you can help me sing 'Happy Birthday' to our sister," Paloma says.

She goes to the refrigerator and takes out a cake, which she brings over to us. She takes a single candle and sticks it in the middle. "Rule number one of being a lady," she says as she lights it. "Never tell anyone your age. From now on, you'll never be older than twenty-one. Well, once you *are* twenty-one."

"Besides," Farrah says. "It is your drag self's first birthday, so one candle is appropriate."

As I look at the cake, Farrah and Paloma sing.

Happy birthday to you.
Happy birthday to you.
Happy birthday, dear Persephone.
Happy birthday to you.

"Blow, gurl!" Farrah says. "And make a wish."

I blow. The candle goes out, and Farrah and Paloma clap.

"What did you wish for?" Paloma asks.

"Don't tell her," Farrah says. "It won't come true if you do."

What I wish is that nothing will ever change. I know this can't happen. And really, I wouldn't want to be stuck in one moment forever. It would get boring. But I'd like this feeling to last for a long time.

"Queen, what are you waiting for? Cut that damn cake."

Farrah's voice brings me back to the moment. I pick up the knife that Paloma hands me and cut into my birthday cake.

"Make sure Farrah gets a big piece," Paloma says. "You know what a size queen she is."

"Like you couldn't fit that whole cake in your mouth," Farrah teases back. "I've seen you swallow a Twinkie without chewing."

I plate up the cake, and we all start eating. It's fantastically good.

"Gurl, I will say this for you," Farrah says to Paloma in between bites. "You bake a mean cake. You should set one of these out on your front porch and catch all the men who show up to eat it."

"My *tres leches* brings all the boys to the yard," Paloma sings.

"I retract my compliment," Farrah says. "That cultural reference is at least a decade out of date."

"Says the bitch who wants us to be the Supremes and Destiny's Child," Paloma shoots back.

"Don't make me put down this cake," says Farrah. "Miss Ross and Miss Beyoncé Knowles-Carter are timeless."

"Mmm-hmm," says Paloma. "More like old. Like your look."

I sit back and listen to them while I eat my cake. I think about how much meeting these two—and Lola—has changed my life, and is going to keep changing it for a long time to come. Family shows up in all kinds of surprising forms, and I'm lucky to have such a large one.

I think too about the conversation I had with Lola about Shangri-La, and how it's a safe place for us. I understand that now. I also know the world is bigger than our little paradise, and that I'll have to venture outside of it to figure out exactly who I am. That scares me a little. But it helps knowing that I can always come back, and that Farrah and Paloma will be here, eating cake and insulting each other's wigs, just like the Grands will be at the kitchen table in our house, drinking Nehi and playing cards.

Not forever. Not for long enough. But for now.

Thirty-Five

Summer always seems to end before it's even really begun. One night you go to bed thinking about all the things you still haven't done, and all the time you have left to do them in, and the next morning you wake up and realize you're going to be late for the first day of school if you don't hurry up and get in the shower.

The weeks following my birthday go by in a rush. Clodine comes home. She still can't talk all that clearly, and maybe never will, but she manages to get her points across anyway. She and Millard Fillmore form a Weyward Curse Survivors club of two, and she spends a lot of time rubbing his ears and feeding him Oreos and other things he probably shouldn't eat. At first, Hank and my father try to get her to stop, but then Starletta says, "If Livvie Comstock's curse didn't kill them, nothing will," so now we let them eat whatever they want.

One night I'm in my room, listening to the Divinyls' *Desperate,* which is number 15 on Ilona's list, when I realize that although I love it (Chrissy Amphlett is hands down my favorite singer of all time, and every song on the album is pretty much perfect), I don't want to hear it. At least not right now, and maybe not for a long time.

That's when it hits me that Ilona's twenty-one albums have been the soundtrack to my life for so long that I've forgotten that these are *her* twenty-one perfect albums. I thought that I could understand her if I understood them, but that wasn't true. So, it's time to stop trying.

I still keep the albums in the box Ilona left them in. Now I put *Desperate* back into it, sandwiched between Nina Hagen's *Nunsexmonkrock* and Prince's *Purple Rain,* and I close the top. I take the box and put it in my closet. I'm not going to forget about it, and I'm not never going to listen to those albums again. There's a ton of good music on them. But it's time to make new music.

Over Labor Day weekend, the lake people leave. As I stand behind the window of the Eezy-Freezy for the last time this year, I watch car after car go by. A couple of people wave, but not as many as do when the summer visitors arrive in June. Mostly, they look sad to be going back to wherever they came from. Especially the kids.

I look for Tom Swift's grandparents' car, but I never see it. I know that they're gone, though, because when I drive by their cabin later, the windows are boarded up for the winter. I haven't heard anything from Tom since he left, and I hope he's okay. When I stop at the Bi-Rite to pick up some milk and Nehi, Anna-Lynn is working the register. She's had one text from Tom, saying that his parents were monitoring his phone and had cut off his social media accounts, so she doesn't think we'll hear much from him. But she's not worried. "He's tough," she reminds me.

We close the Eezy-Freezy the day after Labor Day, which for me is the official end to summer. As my father locks the door, I can tell he's a little depressed.

"This time next week, you'll be in school and I'll be in the garage," he says.

"We're looking for a new bartender at the Shangri-La," I say. "Toby's decided he'd rather be an X-ray technician."

He pretends to consider the offer. "Would I have to wear a tank top?"

"Farrah says you get more tips if you don't wear any shirt at all."

He shakes his head. "I want to be admired for my mind," he says, pretending to be offended. "Or at least my ability to fix a transmission."

Before when I thought about my senior year, I thought about it as an ending. Now it feels like a beginning. I have college visits to look forward to, and thinking about what I want to study.

When I walk through the doors for my last first day of high school, I see someone new. When there are fewer than a hundred people in your class, you tend to notice people you've never seen before. But I would notice this guy anyway because, well, he's really cute. Short. Stocky wrestler build. Dark hair. Wearing a T-shirt with the Hufflepuff crest. And he looks lost.

"Hey," I say. "Can I help you find something?"

He looks at the slip of paper in his hand. "English," he says. "With Mr. Bluh—Blus—Bluz —"

"Blaszczak. We just call him Mr. Blah."

"Is he that boring?"

"No, he's actually really great. It's just easier. And that's where I'm going, so you can come with me. I'm Sam, by the way. Sam Weyward."

"Hatch," he says. "Well, really it's Owen. But (a) that's kind of boring and (b) when I was little I thought I was hatched from an egg because I didn't have a mom, so my dads started calling me Hatch."

"Dads?" I say.

"Yeah. I have two dads. As in gay. Is that a problem?"

"Not for me," I say. "I'm gay too. Is *that* a problem?"

He shakes his head. "I'm just a little surprised. I thought in a place this small, I would be the only one. We moved here from Minneapolis, so I wasn't sure."

It takes me a second to realize what he's said. "Gay dads *and* you're gay?"

"I know," he says. "And one of my grandfathers is gay too, although it took him a while to figure it out. It's like a weird family tradition."

I laugh. "I know all about weird family traditions."

"I have to admit, when my dads told me we were moving here, I kind of freaked out. Not just because of changing schools and all, but because of it being such a small town."

"People here are pretty nice," I assure him. "And it's not

like they don't know anything about gay people. We have the internet, you know. There's even a gay bar."

"You're kidding. Out here in Nowheresville?" He laughs. "Sorry. I don't want to come off like the city boy looking down on the country people or anything. It's just different."

"I've never lived anyplace else, so I'm used to it," I say. "But look, you've already made a friend."

"Good point," says Hatch. He pumps the air with a fist. "Achievement unlocked."

"So, where do you live?"

"Just down the street," he says. "The blue house with the big porch."

He means Lola's house. I knew the buyers had closed and moved in, but Farrah handled everything, and I was sort of afraid to drive by and see someone else living in it, so I've avoided it. Now, hearing that a family of gay guys is living there, I'm unexpectedly overwhelmed by happiness.

"I know that house," I tell Hatch. "Which room is yours?"

"Second floor, overlooking the yard."

Lola's room.

"Do you know who used to live there?" he asks.

I nod. "Why?"

"This is going to sound weird," he says. "But every night since we moved in, around three in the morning I wake up because I think I hear someone singing. And there's always this faint smell of perfume. Something with roses. It's gone by morning."

I start humming "Whatever Lola Wants." Hatch stops and

stares at me, his mouth open, surprised. "How do you know that song? That's what I hear."

"It's a long story," I say. "A ghost story."

He grins. "My favorite kind. But seriously, what is that song?"

"How about you come over this weekend and I'll tell you all about it?"

"Okay," he says. "It's a date."

Now I grin. "Achievement unlocked." I'm surprised that I'm flirting with him, and I almost apologize. But he just smiles and walks into the classroom ahead of me.

It turns out we have a couple of classes together. And at the end of the day, when I see him at the lockers, I ask him if he'd like a ride home.

"Uh, it's like three blocks away," he reminds me.

"Yeah," I say. "But they're three long blocks. And you're new. You might get lost."

We walk to my truck, which Hatch proclaims the coolest thing he's ever seen, and I drive him home. It takes all of five minutes, and that's with me taking the long way. When we get there, I pull up to the curb and park.

"I'd invite you in," Hatch says. "But we haven't even really unpacked."

"Some other time," I say. I'm not ready to go inside Lola's house yet anyway. I think it needs time to get used to having new people in it. But I also think it's going to like Hatch and his dads.

"Well, thanks for the ride."

We look at each other for a long moment. I want to say a lot of things, but I don't say any of them, because they all sound crazy. Instead, I say, "See you tomorrow."

Hatch smiles and kind of blushes, which is completely adorable. "See you tomorrow," he says as he gets out.

He walks up to the porch, turns around, and waves. I wave back, and he goes inside. As the door shuts, I look up at the windows of what I now know is his bedroom. For just a second, I think I see someone looking down at me. I blink, and the window is empty.

I drive home, say hello to the Grands, who are playing cards and drinking Nehi as I think they'll be doing every day between now and the end of the world, and go up to my room. I pick up my guitar, sit on the bed, and get back to work on the song I've been trying to finish.

Song About a Girl

> there's a stranger in the mirror
> someone sleeping in my bed
> whispered voices in the darkness
> something playing with my head
>
> i'm possessed by the ghost, by the ghost, by the ghost
> of the girl that you wish i would be
> i need an exorcism, an excision, a division
> from the one i feel living inside me

holy water saints and jesus
save my soul and set me free
no more devils no more demons
cleanse my heart and let me be

i hear your prayers in the night, asking favors, making
*   bargains*
saying, "make her like she was before she changed"
i know i'm not the one you wanted, that you're troubled and
*   you're haunted*
by the girl who has replaced me in our game

wrestling with an angel
trying to win my soul
stitching two together
will not make me whole
deal with the devil
make another roll
meet him at the crossroads
can't afford the toll

two girls living in one body
at war, fighting to the death
one left standing, one victorious
one raised fist and one last breath

It's not quite there yet, but I know it will come. When it does, I'm going to record it as a surprise for Rhonda. Maybe

I'll do some of Percy's other songs too. I think the world should hear them. Maybe that's why we were brought together, so that I could help her finish what she started.

I set the guitar aside and pick up the deck of tarot cards that Percy sent me. I remember how she had me pick one card to signify what was happening in my life. I shuffle through the deck until I find the Eight of Swords. I look at the woman bound, blindfolded, and surrounded by swords. That really is who I was just a few weeks ago. But what am I now?

I put the Eight of Swords back and shuffle the cards. I'm not sure how it's supposed to work, exactly, but I remember what Percy did. I cut the cards and reshuffle a couple of times, thinking about my life and everything that's going on. Then I spread the cards out in a line on my bed.

I run my hands over the cards, waiting for something to happen. I don't know what, exactly. A feeling. A sign. A booming voice bellowing, "Pick that one!" in my ear. That doesn't happen, so I decide to just choose one.

I turn over the Eight of Rods. It shows what looks like eight branches flying through the air, each one tipped with a blossoming flower. I have no idea what the card means, so I look in the little book inside the box. "Momentum toward desired end," it says. "Great expectations, haste. May also denote the arrows of love."

The image of Hatch smiling at me as he got out of my truck pops into my head, and my stomach does this funny tingling thing. I also think about all the new plans I have for my future.

Does drawing the Eight of Rods mean things are happening for me? I hope so.

I decide to do a reading for Percy next. I don't know if tarot cards work for dead people, but I don't see why not. I shuffle again, this time thinking about her and picturing her in my mind. I lay the cards out and try the hovering thing again, waiting for a card to speak to me.

This time, I do feel as if I'm drawn to one in particular. I take it from the others and turn it over. An image of a sun with a face looks up at me. It's bright and colorful and radiates warmth. The sun isn't exactly smiling, but it looks happy.

I consult the booklet again for the card's meaning. "Contentment, liberation, attainment of personal or business goals." That's exactly what the card makes me think of. And I think it's a perfect ending to Percy's story. I like to think of the sun coming out and burning away the fog she'd been trapped in, turning the sea gold and lighting up the world for her as she swims into whatever's next.

I put the card back into the box, and set it on my bedside table. On the floor is the telephone. I pick it up, close my eyes, and dial. It rings.

"Hello?" says a voice. It sounds like a little boy.

I lean back against my pillow. "Tell me a story."

Author's Note

Although a work of fiction, this story was very much influenced by my own experiences and by the experiences of other people in my life. The character of Tom Swift in particular is a combination of many different trans people I have been privileged to know and love over more than thirty years. Everything that he experiences in this book has happened to someone I know.

This does not mean that all trans people experience all the things that happen to him. There is no such thing as "the" trans experience. The experience of each individual is different. Tom's story is a combination of stories, but ultimately it is his story. He does not represent an entire community, just one particular experience of it.

If you are a trans person without a support system and are looking for information or assistance, please consider contacting one of the following organizations:

Trans Lifeline
www.translifeline.org
877-565-8860 US
877-330-6366 Canada

Trans Student Educational Resources
www.transstudent.org

Trans Youth Equality Foundation
www.transyouthequality.org

KEEP READING FOR A SNEAK PEEK AT
MICHAEL THOMAS FORD's
CRITICALLY ACCLAIMED NOVEL, *SUICIDE NOTES*

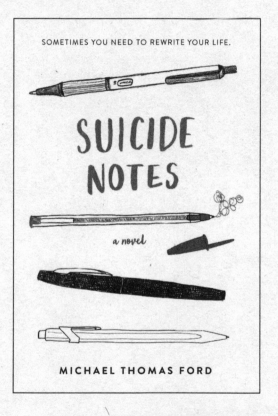

SOMETIMES YOU NEED TO REWRITE YOUR LIFE.

SUICIDE NOTES

a novel

MICHAEL THOMAS FORD

"Makes a powerful emotional impact."
—*Publishers Weekly* (starred review)

Day 01

I read somewhere that when astronauts come back to Earth after floating around in space they get sick to their stomachs because the air here smells like rotting meat to them. The rest of us don't notice the stink because we breathe it every day and to us it smells normal, but really the air is filled with all kinds of pollutants and chemicals and junk that we put into it. Then we spray other crap around to try and make it smell better, like the whole planet is someone's old car and we've hung this big pine-scented air freshener from the rearview mirror.

I feel like those astronauts right now. For a while I was floating around in space breathing crystal-pure oxygen and talking to the Man in the Moon. Then suddenly everything changed and I was falling through the stars. I used to wonder what it would be like to be a meteor. Now I know. You fall and fall and fall, and then you're surrounded by clouds and your whole body tingles as it starts to burn up from the entry into the atmosphere. But you're falling so fast that it burns only for a second, and then the ocean comes rushing up at you and you laugh and laugh, until the water closes over your head and you're sinking. Then you know you're safe—you've survived the fall—and as you come back to the surface you blow millions of bubbles into the blue-green water.

Only then your head breaks through the waves and you suck in great breaths of stinking air and you want to die, like babies when they come out of their mothers and find out that they should have stayed inside where they were safe. That's where I am now, floating in the ocean like a piece of space junk and trying not to throw up every time I breathe.

I'm not really in the ocean, though. I'm in the hospital. They say they brought me here last night, but I was totally out of it and don't remember anything. Actually, what I heard someone say was that I was kind of dead. Pretty close to dead, anyway.

I really do think I was flying around in space, though.

At least for a little while. I remember thinking that I'd finally find out whether anyone lives on Mars or not. Then it was like someone grabbed me by the foot and yanked me down, back toward Earth. I remember screaming that I didn't want to go, but since you can't make noise in space, my voice was just kind of eaten up.

Now that I know where I am, I'm not so sure I wouldn't be better off just being dead.

And maybe I *am* dead. I mean, it does kind of feel like Hell around here. I'm in this room with people checking in on me every five seconds. And by people I mean nurses, and in particular Nurse Goody. Can you believe that? Her name is actually Nurse Goody. And she is, too. Good, I mean. She's always smiling and asking me if she can get me anything. It's really annoying, because all I *want* is to be left alone, and that's the last thing they seem to do here. So many people run in and out of this room, I feel like a tourist attraction. I bet Nurse Goody is standing outside the door selling tickets, like those guys at carnivals who try to get people to pay to see the freak show. Barkers, I think they're called. That's what Nurse Goody is, a barker. She stands outside my door and barks.

But it's not like there's anything interesting in here. No television. No roommate (which actually, now that I think about it, is probably a good thing). Not even any magazines or books. Just me in bed looking out the window, which is the kind with wire running through the glass so you can't break it and jump out. The paint around the windows is all chipped, like maybe someone who was in here before me *tried* to break the window, then decided to claw their way out instead.

Now that I look at it, the whole room is kind of old-looking. The walls are this dirty white color, and there are some cracks in the plaster, and a weird brown spot on the ceiling that looks like a face. The Devil's face, maybe. Because, like I said, I think I might be in Hell. It would make sense that he would be watching me. Him and Nurse Goody are watching me. Good and Evil.

That's funny. Good and Evil. Maybe I'm not in Hell. Maybe I'm in that in-between place. What do they call it? Limbo. Where all the dead people go who don't have a "go directly to Heaven or Hell" card. Dead babies go there, too, I think. People no one knows what to do with, and dead babies. My kind of people.

Maybe I'm in Limbo, and the Devil and Goody are fighting over me. Or waiting for me to make up my mind where I want to go. What would I pick, Heaven or Hell? That's a good question. Seriously, I think I would pick Hell. The people there would probably be more interesting.

Come to think of it, it really is hot as Hell in here. There's a radiator under the window, the big old metal kind that shakes whenever water goes through it. I guess it's been working overtime. I swear, this place must be eleventy years old. It's like any minute now the whole building is going to fall apart. At least then I wouldn't be here.

It's raining, and the only thing I can see out the window is part of a forest. Since it's winter, though, it looks less like a forest and more like a bunch of skeletons holding their hands up to the sky. The rain is running down the glass, making it look like the skeletons are under water. Drowning. Although if they're skeletons, wouldn't they already be dead? So maybe they're just swimming. Anyway, the skeleton trees are kind of freaking me out. It's looking more and more like this really is Hell. Maybe I should tell Goody she's in the wrong place.

I'm really tired. The radiator is rattling, it's hot in here, and my head hurts. I keep looking up at the Devil's face, and I think he's laughing at me. I sort of wish Goody would come in and make him shut up. Maybe she's given up on me.

I know they're hoping I'll say something about why I did what I did. So for the record: I just felt like it.

Day 02

This just gets better and better.

It turns out I really *am* in the hospital. Not Limbo. I'm pretty sure that it *is* Hell. Because I'm not just in the hospital. I'm in the mental ward. You know, where they keep the people who have sixteen imaginary friends living in their heads and can't stop picking invisible bugs off their bodies. Whackos. Nut-jobs. Total losers.

I'm not crazy. I don't see what the big deal is about what happened. But apparently someone *does* think it's a big deal because here I am. I bet it was my mother. She always overreacts.

They weren't going to tell me—you know, about the

mental ward thing—but I found out when Goody left my chart next to the bed while she went to get something at the desk. Someone should tell her that you really shouldn't leave something like that lying around if you don't want someone to look at it.

Anyway, I just happened to pick up the chart, because that's what I do when someone leaves something around and I want to know what it is, and right there on the top of the first page it said PSYCHIATRIC WARD. At first I figured it was someone else's file, but then I saw my name. Let me tell you something, seeing your name and PSYCHIATRIC WARD on the same piece of paper isn't the best way to start your day.

When Goody came back she saw me looking at the file and the smile plastered to her face finally disappeared. "You're not supposed to be looking at that," she said, like I didn't know and would apologize.

"This is a psych ward?" I said, trying to read as much as I could before she grabbed the folder, which she did about two seconds later.

"It's time for your medication," she said.

"Uh-uh," I told her. "Not until someone tells me why I'm here."

"I think you know why you're here," she said, giving

me that look people give you when they know *you* know what they mean.

"I'm not crazy," I said.

"Nobody said you were crazy," said Goody, her smile returning. Suddenly she was all happy again, like there'd been a momentary blackout in her reception and now we'd returned to the regularly scheduled program.

"That file does," I shot back. "It says it in big letters."

"Take your pill," she said, ignoring me. "You'll feel better."

"No," I told her. "I don't even know what it is."

Goody smiled, which was starting to get on my nerves. "It's a sedative," she said.

"So you're drugging me?" I said. "Why? What the hell is going on here?"

Goody took the paper cup she was holding out to me and put it back on the tray by my bed. "I think maybe you should talk to Dr. Katzrupus."

"Catwhatsis?" I asked her. "Cat Poopus? What kind of name is that?"

"Katzrupus," she said again. "I'll get him."

She disappeared, taking my file with her, which she totally should have done the first time, because then we wouldn't have had this problem. At least not right now.

After she left, I stared at the cup with the pill in it. It was a small red pill, round like a ladybug. I almost took it, just to see what it would do, but I didn't want Goody to think I thought I needed it or anything, which I don't.

Goody came back a minute later with some guy. He was short, with really wild black hair that was about three weeks past needing to be cut, and he looked like he hadn't shaved in a couple of days either. He seemed way too young to be a doctor, and at first I thought he was some kind of student doctor or something, like I didn't even rate a real one.

"I'm Dr. Katzrupus," he said, holding out his hand.

"Why am I in the nuthouse?" I asked him, staring at his hand without shaking it.

"You're not in a nuthouse," he said, taking his hand back and pushing his glasses up his nose. "You're in a hospital."

"Right," I said. "The nut ward in a hospital."

"It's a *psychiatric* ward," he said. "And you're in it because we're concerned that something might be bothering you." He spoke in this really calm and casual way, as if he was telling you what he had for dinner. For some reason, that really bugged me.

"Something might be bothering me," I repeated, mimicking his voice. Then I laughed. "Why would something be bothering me?"

Cat Poop got this weird look on his face, like he didn't know what to say. I just kept staring at him.

"Are my parents around here somewhere?" I asked. "'Cause if they are, I'd really like to go home now."

"We need to run a few tests," he said. "And, no, your parents aren't here."

I thought it was kind of weird that my parents weren't there, and I wanted to ask where they were instead of being with their kid in the hospital, but I didn't. "I'm not so good at tests," I said instead. "Especially pop quizzes. Could I maybe have some study time first? I wouldn't want to bring the curve down for the whole class or anything."

He looked at me for a second. Then he said, "I'll see you later this afternoon."

After he left Goody came back with this other guy who I swear to God was a vampire. He took what seemed like three gallons of blood out of me, test tube after test tube of it. After the fourth one I started to feel really sick.

Finally, the Human Leech and Goody went away with his tray of tubes and a woman came in. "I'm Miss Pinch," she said. I swear. I'm not making it up. I don't know what it is with the names around here. I'm not sure this isn't all a dream, because in the real world people just aren't named things like Nurse Goody and Miss Pinch and Dr. Cat Poop.

"I need to ask you a few questions," Miss Pinch told me, pulling a chair up beside my bed.

Turns out that was the understatement of the year, unless to you "a few" means eight thousand and sixty-two.

"Have you ever taken Ecstasy?" Miss Pinch asked me, smiling and cocking her head like a bird. An irritating, nosy little bird.

"No," I told her, and she made a check mark on the folder she was holding.

"Methamphetamine?" she said. When I didn't answer right away she added, "Crystal? Ice? Tina?"

"I know what it is," I told her. "And no, I've never taken it."

She made another mark. And she kept making marks after every question and answer. Cocaine? No. Check. Alcohol? No. Check. Marijuana, GHB, snappers? No, no, no. Check, check, check.

I kept answering no to everything, because I really haven't ever done drugs, and she kept looking at me like maybe I was lying just to get her out of there. So finally I said that yes, okay, I'd smoked pot a few times, and that seemed to make her happy. Like it's not possible that there's a kid on this planet who hasn't smoked pot. Moron.

"How about glue?" she asked me.

I nodded, and she lit up like a Christmas tree. At least until I said, "I used to eat paste. In kindergarten. Bad habit. I totally gave it up, though. I swear. It didn't mix with the apple juice so well."

I have to say, I was a little disappointed that she wasn't madder than she was. Maybe talking to crazy people all the time makes you kind of immune to it. She just kept asking and checking. After we went through every drug known to science, Pinch said, "Now let's talk about sexual activity."

"Let's not," I said, giving her the same big smile she was giving me.

"Have you ever—" she started to say.

"Seriously," I said, interrupting her. "Let's not. It's none of your damn business."

"I'm only trying to help you," she said, still smiling.

"Well, you're not," I informed her. "You're just pissing me off. Now go away."

She stared at me.

"Seriously," I said. "Get out of here. There's nothing wrong with me. I answered your stupid questions about the drugs, and I'm not telling you anything else because there's nothing else you need to know. So either go away or else sit there while I take a nap, because this is the last thing I'm saying to you."

She snapped her file shut and stood up. "I'll just get the doctor," she said.

That seems to be what they do around here when you say no to them, like the doctors are the National Guard or something. So once again I got a visit from good old Cat Poop. This time he shut the door so that we were alone. I pictured Goody Two-shoes and Pinchface standing outside, pressing their ears to the door to try and hear what the doctor was saying.

"You're not making this very easy," he said.

"Sorry," I said. "I guess my kindergarten teacher was right when she said I don't play well with others."

"We want to help you."

"You know, everyone keeps saying that," I told him. "But I have to tell you, I'm starting to think you don't. Because if you did, you'd let me out of here. There's nothing wrong with me."